ONE PERFECT DAY IN LOVELY BAY

POLLY BABBINGTON

POLLYBABBINGTON

Want more from Polly's world?

authorpollybabbington.com

For sneak peeks into new settings, early chapters, downloadable Pretty Beach and Darling Island freebies and bits and bobs from Polly's writing days sign up for Babbington Letters.

1

As Cally de Pfeffer strolled up the driveway, she took her jumper off, tied it over her shoulders, and smiled at the magnificent sight of Lovely Manor perched on the landscape in front of her. Shaking her head as she took in the huge old house, she couldn't believe how long it had now been part of her life. She'd take it for the team, though. Not a bad place for your boyfriend to live, right? Had me at manor house. The day she'd first walked onto the property by way of its enormous old main gates, there'd been no way then that she'd had any idea what was coming. She wouldn't have thought that she would be in a serious relationship with one of the manor's residents. But here she was doing just that. Head over heels, loved up to the eyeballs, in very deep, all that stuff. The world moved in mysterious ways. Its recent movement was better than the ride it had taken her on in the past, that she knew for sure.

Looking over the perfectly manicured stripes in the luscious lawn, a bright blue sky greeted from above and a little cluster of butterflies fluttered over a long line of rose bushes to her far right. She could see the fountain in the ornamental garden to her left and just about make out the sound of its water trickling from the top. She nodded her head and thanked anyone who would listen that her luck had changed when she'd met Logan Henry-Hicks. Then she stopped mid-nod and tutted. Her luck *had not* changed. His had. Best she remembered that. It was her much-chanted narrative in her new life. He was the one who should be counting his lucky stars that he had her in his life. Henry-Hicks was one lucky man, indeed.

Continuing up the long drive, instead of her usual turn to the left past the stables and around the back of the main house, she veered in the direction of the rose garden. Weaving in and out of the willow trees set near the pond, she took a little path down past one of the huge old greenhouses and approached Logan's cottage from the back. Pushing open the gate, she loved what looked back at her; the little cottage garden was a picture. Tucked in the corner in a sunspot, a couple of vintage timber deck chairs with plump stripy cushions, sat on a terrace area with a table between them. On top of the table, a huge white wicker lantern was filled with candles, and in gigantic weathered terracotta pots, two large and well-established olive trees rustled in the breeze. Along the far side, the bricks of an old Victorian wall were covered in ivy, a weather vane turned on the top of a gorgeous old conservatory butted up to French doors, and a gravel-covered path led down to a small summer house. Cally de Pfeffer had undoubtedly come a long way. Not that she needed anyone or anything to reiterate that fact. She knew it well enough of her own accord. She welcomed it into her life every single day.

Logan, in a pair of jeans and a pale blue long-sleeved shirt with the sleeves rolled up and a pair of sunglasses on his head, strolled out of the house and stepped into the sunshine. Cally swallowed. Not bad, not bad at all. Very, very, *very* nice, in fact. She revelled in being in love with Logan. To her, it felt as if she'd bagged the best-ever prize. Like ever, ever ever. Staggeringly good-looking, the broad shoulders and long legs weren't bad, and he was nice to boot. Calvin Klein boxers. Say no more. *Really* good-looking and *really* nice. What the? Whatever... what more could a girl ask for? Sometimes, she had to pinch herself and hard. Sometimes, she felt as if she was living *the* dream, *a* dream, *any* dream. Her handsome and nice boyfriend, if that is what we are calling him, lived in an actual manor. Hello.

Logan leant on the architrave of the back door. The look on his face told her he felt the same way. 'Hey. How are you?'

Cally pretended he wasn't anywhere near as good-looking as he was and that she was nonchalant about rocking up to a manor house, even if it was one of its cottages, for the day. 'Good.'

'Looking good to me for sure.'

Cally giggled. 'It's such a lovely day.'

'Yeah. I wondered if you fancied walking up the hill or not. The weather couldn't be better, really.' Logan jerked his thumb to the right. 'I've packed up a bit of a picnic if you fancy it.'

Did she fancy it? Did she ever? 'Sounds good. You know me too well. Who wouldn't love a picnic on a day like this?'

'I wasn't sure whether or not you'd be up for a walk after walking here. We can just sit here...'

Cally shook her head. 'No, no, I'm fine. I like the stroll up here from Lovely.'

Logan pointed into the far distance. 'The view will be pretty special from the top there today.'

'You're right.' Cally nodded and wriggled her lips. 'We haven't been up there for ages.'

Logan stepped back inside. 'I'll just grab the stuff.'

'Did you get a picnic blanket?' Cally asked.

'Yeah.'

Cally chuckled to herself. *A boyfriend who packed up picnics, too? Keeper. I'll have two. Maybe forty-two.* She followed Logan through the door and into the kitchen, where a couple of baskets and a rolled-up rug were ready on the table. Cally smiled and inhaled. 'Ahh, a day of doing nothing. I need it. I might have to have a doze at the top of the hill there.'

Logan tilted his head in agreement. 'I reckon. Perfect place for it.'

A few minutes later, with a basket in her hands and the rug under her arm, Cally strolled along beside Logan. She smiled as they got further away from the manor and headed in the direction of Lovely. The sounds changed as they ambled alongside a small wooded area, followed a stream for a bit, and then turned to walk up the hill.

Logan stopped and pointed to a bench perched right at the top. 'Not too far. Once we get there, we'll just camp out there for the rest of the day and take in the view. Rest and recharge, I believe, is what it is called. Up for that?'

'Oh, yes. Works for me. Music to my ears, in fact.'

Ambling along in easy silence except for the sound of the stream in the distance, a few birds chirping away here and there, and the wind in the trees, Cally was thoroughly enjoying herself. She loved the perks that came with being part of Lovey Manor and walking around in its grounds was one of them. Once at the top of the hill and slightly out of breath, she stood with her hand shading her eyes and looked out at Lovely's view below. Under the bright blue sky, the sea shimmered in the far distance and the tall white Lovely lighthouse stood as if guarding everything below. Cally passed Logan the picnic blanket, waited for him to smooth it out on the grass beside the bench, and plonked herself down. She shook her head and leant back on her hands. 'It's so nice up here. Honestly, we need to come here more often. It's always so calming.' Cally inhaled a deep, long breath. 'The smell is something else and the view... I could sit here all day long and just stare out at the horizon. Free at half the price.'

'Yup. Totally agree.'

Cally looked in the direction of the lighthouse. 'That never fails to impress, does it? Always there, keeping everyone safe.'

'You always say that. It doesn't get old, no. It's like an old friend.'

Cally gestured around her. 'I need to do more of this. I've been charging around from one thing to the next these past few months.'

Logan pulled the wicker picnic basket over and began to unpack the food. He laid a small tea towel on top of the rug, added a cheese board, and whipped out two fabric napkins from inside the basket. 'I hope you're hungry,' he said, pulling out container after container. 'I might have gone a bit overboard with my order at the deli.'

Cally's eyes widened as she took in the spread. 'A bit? Logan, this looks like enough to feed an army!' She joked, 'You're useless. Who on earth did you think you were catering for? I'm glad I wasn't paying.'

Logan chuckled as he arranged the dishes between them. 'Well, you know how Alice gets when you mention a picnic. I think she packed half the shop. I collected it yesterday when you were at Eloise's.'

Logan unwrapped wax paper from a whole brie, popped it on the cheese board, and added a little cluster of red grapes and a small pot of what looked like chutney. Cally picked up the pot and unscrewed the lid. 'Ooh, this looks fancy. What is it?'

'Fig and something…' Logan flicked his eyes upwards. 'She did say. What was it? Fig and, oh, yeah, fennel. Someone local made it, but I can't remember who.'

'Nice. Oh, that brie looks divine, too,' Cally sighed. 'I love cheese. I think I could live on it. Give me *all* the cheese *all* the time.'

Logan gestured affirmatively, already opening another container. He pulled out a baguette, a dish of olives marinated in herbs and garlic, and a cherry tomato salad and started to unwrap a wide, shallow box. 'Spinach and goat's cheese quiche. Alice said it's the one you like. Is that right? I couldn't remember.'

'It is. Gosh, we'll be rolling down this hill by the time we're done.'

Laughing, Logan poured them each a glass of sparkling wine. 'Well, we've got all afternoon to work our way through it. No rush.' They clinked glasses. 'Cheers,' Logan held his glass up in the direction of the lighthouse.

Cally smiled. 'Nice idea to come up here. Cheers.'

'Yeah. Anyway, what's been happening with you? I missed you yesterday.'

'I have a bit of news. I was going to tell you last week, but I wanted to be sure before I said anything.'

'What?'

'I think I've got enough deposit saved up to start applying for a mortgage. Finally! It feels as if it's taken me my whole life to get to this point. If I'm honest, I'm over the moon about it. '

'Fantastic. I'm *so* proud of you. You've worked hard for it.'

Cally smiled. 'Thanks. It still doesn't feel quite real, to be honest. The idea that I might *actually* be able to buy my own place in Lovely Bay is a bit strange.'

'But exciting, right?'

Cally nodded, taking a bite of the quiche. 'Definitely exciting. But also a bit scary. It's a big step.'

Logan nodded as he spread some brie on a slice of baguette. 'It is.'

Cally thought back to her early days in Lovely when Birdie had saved her from what was more or less imminent homelessness. She remembered how vulnerable, lost, and unsure she'd felt and how she'd primarily operated on adrenaline and a gigantic bubble of underlying stress. Things had changed significantly. The stress bubble had burst and the adrenaline now worked in a good way. Now here she was, working three good jobs, she had a healthy savings account, and on top of that, she had the stability of someone like Logan in her life. Oh, how she was in a better place. 'It's a lot of responsibility. Owning a place, taking on a mortgage, but to be honest, I want it. I *need* to feel as if I have some roots. Do you know what I mean?'

Logan swigged his drink. 'You wouldn't be doing it alone, Blackcurrant.'

Cally looked at him quizzically. 'What do you mean by that?'

'Well, I've been thinking. About us, about the future. At some point, we'd be looking for a place together, wouldn't we?'

Cally felt as though all the air had been sucked out of her lungs. He'd pulled that out of the hat and surprised her. 'Together? What? Moving in together? What? Do you mean like properly? Would we? Like, officially?'

Logan shrugged. 'Yeah. I mean, we spend most of our time together anyway. You're either here or I'm at your flat. Makes sense, right?'

'True.'

'You could rent out the place then.'

Cally wrinkled her nose and frowned. 'Sorry. What?'

'The flat you buy. Just have it as an investment.' Logan gestured behind him in the direction of the manor. 'As I said, you're here a lot of the time anyway. No brainer. Am I right?'

Cally's mind whirled or perhaps twirled. What in the name of goodness? Logan seemed *very* casual about the fact that he'd just more or less asked her to officially move in with him. She wasn't really sure what to think. Buying a flat was a big, wild, gigantic deal for her. Absolutely massive. She'd worked towards getting her own place for years. Logan clearly wasn't quite as daunted by it.

Logan cocked his head to the side. 'It just seems like good timing to move in together, doesn't it? If you fancy it, that is?'

Cally couldn't quite believe what Logan was saying. Moving

in together, as far as she was concerned, was a significant step. Huge. 'I don't know what to say,' she managed finally.

'No pressure. It's just something to think about, yeah? We don't have to decide anything right now. I must say your flat is quite small. I'm still bumping my head daily…'

Cally took a long sip of her drink. She faltered for words. 'It's not that I don't want to. It's a big decision.'

Logan nodded. 'Of course. I get it. Like I said, no pressure. I just love you, Cal. Simple as that, really.'

'I love you, too.'

'Think about it. I'm not going anywhere.'

As Cally looked out over Lovely Bay, she wasn't quite sure what to think about what Logan had proposed. 'I've worked so hard to get to this point, to be able to buy my own place. Part of me feels like I need to do this on my own, you know? To prove to myself that I can. It's been my goal since, well, since you know when.'

'Totally. You've accomplished loads.'

'I've always been so independent, you know? Since I was very young.'

'I know. That's one of the things I love about you. It doesn't mean giving up your independence, but yeah, it's chill. Just do what you want to do. The offer's there. Whenever you're ready, *if* you're ever ready… I'm here.'

A little part of Cally was a bit put out. Or maybe a large part of her was. Logan was being *very* casual. It was hardly an earth-shattering proposal. He was so nonchalant about moving in together that she wasn't sure what to think. Almost as if she was a mate of his or something. She didn't like how it made her feel. There were no brass bands playing. Logan's words were so casual they almost did the opposite of their intention. Off-putting. She took a sip of her drink and attempted to change the subject. 'So much has changed since I first came to Lovely Bay. If someone had told me then that I'd be sitting here now, considering getting a mortgage and, well, everything else, I'd have thought they were absolutely bonkers.'

'I know. Life goes its own way, doesn't it?'

'It certainly does. It surprised me with you that's for sure.' Cally joked and nudged Logan on the elbow. 'I'm still trying to work out whether that's a good thing or a bad thing.'

Logan laughed. 'You are very lucky to have me.'

'Same.' Cally steered the subject further away as she held her head up to the sky and exhaled. She'd debrief the moving in together thing later. 'This was a perfect idea. I'd almost forgotten how beautiful it is up here.'

'We should do this more often. Get away from it all, just the two of us. Fresh air does wonders for the brain cells, or so they say.'

'It does. Maybe we should bottle it and sell it. Make our fortunes.'

Logan frowned. 'Why do we need to make our fortunes?'

Cally shook her head. She'd waited a long time to make her fortune and she'd certainly not come anywhere near yet. Of course, it wasn't the same for the person sitting beside her. He didn't have to worry about fortunes. He already had a nice, big, fat one under his belt. It wasn't even in his vocabulary. She made a noncommittal sound.

Logan shook his head and surprised her with what came next. 'I don't really need to make a fortune. I've got what I want right here beside me. I already feel like I won the lottery, Cal.'

Well played, Henry-Hicks.

You can stay.

For now.

2

The tinkle of the bell above the chemist's door signalled the departure of the last customer of the morning prescription rush. Cally watched Mrs Higgins, a very old and very established Lovely customer who was wearing one of the blue wax Lovely coats, stop and chat with Colin from the riverboat outside the shop's front window. A group of tourists, easily identifiable by their matching anoraks and confused expressions, huddled around a map on the opposite pavement. Cally smiled at the scene playing out before her on the street; she loved it. The small, seemingly insignificant moments in Lovely made her appreciate the quiet rhythm of life in the little town. She picked up a huge carton from underneath the counter, made her way past the dispensary, and plopped the box down in the back room.

Birdie poked her head around the corner. 'Have you got a minute? Fancy a cup of tea?'

'Of course. You're the boss. It's not our usual tea time. What's up?'

Birdie glanced towards the front of the shop and then

walked into the small kitchen. 'I'll pop the kettle on. Let's have a sit-down, shall we? I've been wanting a proper chat...'

Cally's heart rate picked up a notch. In all her time working at the chemist's, she'd never seen Birdie look quite as serious if that was even the right word. Maybe it wasn't serious. Determined or something? Scary, perhaps? Cally didn't know but she didn't like it that much. She internally fizzed as it ran through her mind that she was about to get the sack.

Here we go again, her inner voice taunted. 'Sure.'

Birdie smoothed down her always-impeccable white dispensary coat, picked up the kettle, and held it under the cold tap.

'Is everything alright?' Cally asked.

Birdie smiled as she plonked the kettle on its base and pulled two mugs out of the cupboard. 'Oh yes. Everything's fine. More than fine, actually. Things are very good. That's what I wanted to talk to you about.'

'I'm all ears.'

'So, you've been working here a while now.'

'I have.'

'How time flies, eh?' Birdie waggled her finger.

'It does. I mean, I've been in the flat for ages now. It seems as if, one minute, we were at Christmas, and now, before we know it, it will be here again. Yep, time has flown by.'

'I know. It's gone so fast. I remember taking you up there to the flat that day as if it were yesterday.'

'So, what did you want to talk about?'

'I'll get to the point. No point beating around the bush. To be quite honest, you've become indispensable to me.'

Cally felt her cheeks flush. She wrinkled her nose. 'Me? No, no. Don't be silly. Doing what exactly? Sorting out orders?'

Birdie held up a hand. 'Nope, let me finish. You really are good at what you do even though you think you aren't.'

'Am I?'

'Yes. You've got a way of organising everything, and since

I've taken on even more shops, I've just loaded stuff on you willy-nilly, and you've not even batted an eyelid. You've taken it in your stride. You really are *very* capable.'

Cally made a face. 'I hadn't really noticed. I mean, it has been quite busy when you say it like that.'

Birdie chuckled. 'See, that's *exactly* what I mean. Not a lot of people would have been able to deal with that quite as easily.'

'What?' Cally screwed her nose up. 'Not totally getting you…'

'You just get on with it and you've got a good head for everything. I've seen how you've streamlined our inventory system, how you've got ideas for expanding things, and you've made changes to the system to make things run like clockwork.'

Cally shifted in her seat. 'I just like things to run smoothly, that's all. Not being funny, but it's not really rocket science out the back here.'

Birdie's eyes widened. '*You* might not think so, but trust me, there are many people I have employed who have not worked as you do. You work off your own initiative, and you don't need me to hold your hand. Those two alone are worth their weight in gold.' Birdie poured hot water from the kettle into the two mugs that were sitting on the worktop.

Cally shook her head. Inside, it ran through her mind that she knew why she didn't need hand-holding, precisely because no one had ever done it for her. She just put her head down and got on with stuff. She always had done. She had a lot of experience in holding up the sky. Ever since she'd known what was what she'd juggled many different things in her life. She brushed off Birdie's words. 'It's fine.'

'I know it is, and that's exactly why I want to offer you a promotion,' Birdie words came out in a rush.

Cally frowned and blinked. Assuming she'd misheard, she repeated what Birdie had said back to her. 'Sorry, what? A promotion? Wait, what? You want to offer me a promotion? Why?'

Birdie nodded. 'Yes. I've been run off my feet since last year and I've been thinking about the future of the business. We've got the chain of pharmacies now, and it's growing quickly. The other shops' back ends are not in a good way. I know it, of course and it needs to change and fast.'

Cally nodded. She was more than familiar with the growth of Birdie's business. She'd watched it expand and seen with her own eyes the development of the ordering system along with the extra duties Birdie had taken on.

'It's getting to be a bit much to manage all the stores the way we're doing now. I need someone I can trust to help oversee it all. Someone with fresh ideas, someone who understands both the business side and, well, you know, the behind-the-scenes side of it.' Birdie gestured around the kitchen and in the direction of the shop.

'Right.'

'I would like it if that someone was you.'

Cally opened her mouth to speak, but no words came out. Birdie, seemingly understanding Cally's shock, pressed on. 'I know it's a lot to take in. You've got the skills, the drive, and you don't take fools gladly.'

Cally finally found her voice. 'I don't know the first thing about managing multiple shops. I just work out the back here.'

Birdie shook her head firmly. 'I'm not having that. You're far more than that. You always have been. And as for the rest, well, that's what training is for, isn't it? I wouldn't be throwing you in at the deep end, well, not totally. We'd work together and get you up to speed on everything. You already know most of it anyway.'

Cally's mind whirled. It was a good opportunity and one she hadn't seen coming. She thought about how she liked the familiar routine of the shop, how she loved working with Birdie, and how convenient it was.

'You'd still be a part of the day-to-day running of this shop. You'd just be taking on a broader role, overseeing operations across all the locations. Full-time and with all the benefits and a company van and computer etcetera.'

Cally tried to wrap her head around the idea. 'I didn't see this coming. It's a lot to take in, I err…'

'I know. I don't expect you to decide right this minute.' Birdie picked up her tea as she heard something from the shop. 'Have a think about it. We'll have another proper chat about pay and contracts and all that stuff, if you're interested. I'll send you a formal offer. If not, no dramas.'

As Birdie bustled out, Cally remained seated. She looked around at the familiar little kitchen. She loved the prospect of a new challenge. The possibility of a full-time role with someone she trusted and, more importantly, *liked*, was very attractive. She shook her head and took a sip of her tea. Lovely was the gift that kept on giving. Was this the start of a new chapter in her Lovely Bay story? She'd have a little think about it and wait and see. One thing she did know; she'd had worse offers in her life.

3

Cally was curled up on her favourite armchair, not that she had more than one armchair, so it had to be her favourite, in the corner of the sitting room, with a steaming mug of hot blackcurrant in her hands. She couldn't stop thinking about Birdie's offer. Her mind whizzed about the opportunity and whether or not it was something she wanted to do. She looked out over the rooftops of Lovely and watched the comings and goings down below as she thought about the job and what it entailed. There was one thing that she was more than aware of: Birdie's company was a great place to work *if* you pulled your weight. However, if you tried to get one over on Birdie, you'd know about it. Cally was also fairly certain that working for Birdie could, if she wanted it to, mean that she would have a secure job for life. Not a thing to be taken lightly.

She lost herself for a bit as she looked out the window to see Lovely Bay winding down for the day. A last few tourists made their way back in the direction of the train station, ice cream cones in hand, she could see someone outside the front of the chocolate shop pulling down the shutters, and a van was bumped up on the curb by the Co-op doing an end-of-the-day delivery.

Her mind mulled over Birdie's job offer. There was no doubt that it was an opportunity for our Cally. She was also well aware that it would certainly solve the headache of proving that she had a full-time income with the bank when applying for a mortgage. If she was really honest, though, working at the chemist full-time wasn't exactly her dream job. Were dream jobs really a thing, though? For most people, she assumed that working was a means to an end and quite far from anything even resembling a dream. A way to pay the bills every month. The more she thought about it and pondered back and forth, the more she realised that the job opportunity with Birdie had many positives and not many negatives. The main thing was that she trusted Birdie, and the business wasn't going anywhere soon—the stability of both those things suited Cally down to the ground. The actual buzz of the job, though? Not so much. She'd certainly not set out in life to work out the back of a chemist shop. There was quite a lack of pzazz in that career path as far as she was concerned.

Just as she was deciding whether or not to get up and make a cup of tea, she heard a thumping up the stairs and looked over towards the door at the sound of what she presumed was Logan's key turning in the lock. She heard his footsteps in the hall area, followed by the thud of his bag being put down.

'Cal? You home?' Logan shouted.

'Yep.' Cally called out as she straightened up in her chair.

Logan appeared in the sitting room with his tie loosened and sleeves rolled up after a day in the city. Handsome and then some. Broad privately educated shoulders and floppy hair. He smiled as he caught sight of Cally, crossed the room, and kissed her forehead. 'Everything alright with you?'

'Umm, yes. Good. You?' Cally made a funny, upside-down smile.

'What's happened?' Logan frowned. 'What's that look on your face?'

'Something's happened, for sure. Something big.' Cally chuckled.

'What?'

Cally took a deep breath. 'Birdie's offered me a new job!'

'Oh, right, has she? Doing what?' Logan narrowed his eyes and curled his lips upside down.

'I know it's a bit strange. I'm glad you're reacting like that, too.'

'Well, congratulations. Sorry, I didn't see that coming.'

'Me either. It's to run all the orders and deliveries across all the shops.'

Logan widened his eyes. 'That's good, then! Isn't it?'

Cally nodded. 'She wants me to oversee all the pharmacies, not just the one in Lovely Bay, including the online distribution side. At the moment, each store more or less does its own thing. This job would change that.'

Logan whistled. 'Wow. That's big. No wonder you look a bit shell-shocked.'

'Shell-shocked is right. I feel like I've been hit by a tidal wave.' She screwed her face up. 'I'm not sure if I'm the right person for the job. It's a lot to take on.'

'Birdie wouldn't have offered you the job if she didn't think you could handle it.'

'I know, I know,' Cally sighed. 'I'd just have to get on with it if I did take it.'

'What exactly would it involve?'

'Well, she didn't say much more. But it would be a full-time role with all the benefits. I'd be overseeing operations at all the pharmacies. Making sure they're all running smoothly, delivery logistics, and dealing with any issues that come up, I guess. What I do now but a lot bigger.'

'Sounds like a natural progression from what you're already

doing, just on a larger scale. Bye bye chatbot.' Logan waved his hand back and forth.

'I suppose. Then there's the online business, too. Since the pandemic, that has gone nuts.'

'Lots of opportunity then.'

Cally bit her lip. 'I don't know the first thing about running anything, Logan.'

'You're one of the most capable people I know. You've been practically running that chemist's back end for years. And as for the online stuff, I've seen you navigate that chatbot software like a pro.'

'Posting the odd thing on a retail chatbot is a far cry from running a whole online distribution solution for a company,' Cally protested.

'You'll be fine. How hard can it be?'

'Anyway, I don't know the full details yet, but yeah, that's my news for the day.'

'I reckon it's fate. You'd be great at it. If anything, it cements your place here even more.'

'I guess so, yeah.'

'You get to put all those brilliant ideas of yours for the chemist into action.'

'True. It's funny when I first moved to Lovely Bay, I never imagined I'd put down roots like this. I thought it was just a stopping point, somewhere to catch my breath before moving on.'

'And now?'

'Now I can't imagine being anywhere else. This place, these people, you. They're a part of me now. Almost as if Lovely has become like family. Weird, really, when you think about it.'

'Yep. Agree. So, is Birdie going to give you more details or what?'

'She's going to send me stuff.'

'Oh, right. Wait and see and decide then.'

Cally took a deep breath. 'Yeah. It feels like maybe it's the next step in my Lovely Bay story.'

'I reckon it is.'

4

A few days later, with a leather-handled market basket hooked over her shoulder, a rolled-up blue and white striped towel under her arm and one of Logan's hoodies over her swimming costume, Cally had just disembarked the riverboat after a long discussion with Clive. They had chatted away about this and that and Clive's loose plans to possibly go away to warmer climes for Christmas. Cally hadn't been sure what to think about that. Christmas dinner around a swimming pool, the weather hot and the smell of sunscreen in the air had never been part of her trajectory. Hmm. Perhaps, perhaps, perhaps. Or not. Cally wrinkled her nose as she walked in the direction of the beach and thought about it. She'd stick with hot mince pies, the notion of snow in the sky, and a Christmas movie after a way too big lunch.

Earlier in the day, Cally had been up early for a chatbot shift, Logan had gone off to work, and that afternoon, she was meeting Birdie in the deli for the discussion about the promotion. As she strolled along, she listed the pros and cons of the job in her head, went around in circles a bit and came to not much of a conclusion at all. Walking along the promenade, taking in the view of the sea and the sound of the waves, she decided that she'd have the chat with Birdie, look over the documents and make a decision then. To be quite honest, she was leaning heavily in the direction of taking the promotion and being done with it.

The part of her that felt as if taking the job was the easy route and that she should do something more exciting with her life was drowned out by the stability. Better the devil you know and all that. Did she really need excitement? Was a career path something she wanted? The more she thought about it, the more she didn't think it was. Who needed power suits and heels when she could have a nice, cosy little life in the third smallest town in the country without any worries? Who needed the aggro of offices, glass ceilings, profit and loss, and having to perform week in, week out? Not that she wouldn't need to perform working for Birdie but somehow it felt different; comfy, uncomplicated, and moreover, she knew precisely what she was doing. There was a lot to be said for that.

As she made her way down the steps to the beach alongside a breaker, she deliberated for a few moments on a good spot, laid out her towel and bag, and then sat with her back against the breaker and let the sun warm her face. Tucked up out of the wind, it wasn't long before the hoodie came off and her sunglasses went on. She watched a grandma with a little girl in a pink frilly swimming costume and matching sun hat potter along on the shore. They pootled by picking up shells and popping them in a red bucket. Just along from her, a dad with a couple of teenagers fussed with camping chairs and fishing rods. Cally exhaled and thanked her lucky stars for the nice day and living in Lovely Bay. The third smallest town in the country was on form, and she was milking it to the hilt.

After a little lunch for one and a carton of blackcurrant, she spent a long time just watching the sea and small soft waves crashing over and over again onto the beach. As the waves tumbled, her mind released, and she felt thoughts about the job drift away. With the sun-toasted timber from the breaker warming her back, she thought about going in the water and whether or not it would be too cold. In the end, deciding that it wasn't every day of the week, she was able to sit on the beach contemplating a dip in the sea, she got up, stripped off, and headed to the shore. As she tiptoed across the pebbles onto the sandy slope to the sea and walked by the water, she let waves tip over her ankles and wriggled sand in and out of her toes.

Wincing as the chilly water lapped at her calves, she grimaced at going for a swim. She'd known it would be cold; this was not the Mediterranean, but the reality made her catch her breath and shudder. Taking a deep breath, she waded in further, the sand under her feet giving way to stones and pebbles here and there. As the water reached her thighs, she steeled herself, plunged forward, kept her chin high and head out of the water, and submerged herself fully. Going for gold, she gasped as the shock of the cold water swallowed her. Flapping around a bit, she tried to think about minerals, vitamins, and good things in the water and pretended she wasn't cold. Somehow, despite the temperature, the sea against her skin, the salt on her lips, and the motion of the waves felt just right as she pondered further the job with Birdie.

After a few minutes of treading water and getting used to the temperature of the water, Cally turned away from the horizon and gazed up at the clear blue sky and the lighthouse, standing tall and proud. Lines of little white houses snaked away into the distance and she could just make out the harbour and boats to her far right. The whole scene was so quintessentially Lovely that it made her eyes prick at the place she now called home.

Attempting to swim for a few minutes, she then just stood

for a while watching a couple of children jumping off the breakers, and then, too cold to stay in, she waded out of the sea, shivered, and started an odd fast-walking-not-quite-jog in the direction of her stuff. With water streaming off her body, a breeze coming in off the sea raised goosebumps on her skin, and she hurried back in the direction of her towel and bag. Once the towel was wrapped around her shoulders, she waited for a minute and then rubbed vigorously to warm up, settled back against the breaker, reached for her bag, and pulled out her phone to see a message from Logan.

Logan: *Hey. Just having a tea with Mum. She told me to remind you that you need a cocktail dress for Scotland.*

Cally groaned inwardly and rolled her eyes at her and Logan's upcoming trip to Scotland. Like other social events she'd been to with Logan, she'd been invited to Scotland for a get-together that was a family tradition. It hadn't taken her long to work out that going to the estate in Scotland, just like the races had been before, was a non-negotiable part of the Henry-Hicks family's calendar. One she'd quite happily give a miss.

While the trip hadn't completely slipped her mind, she'd attempted to put it on the back burner and hadn't put too much thought into it at all. It wasn't that she wasn't looking forward to it; more that she couldn't be faffed with the weight of expectation that came with it. It wasn't just a casual weekend away, oh no, not at all. It was, rather, a Henry-Hicks family tradition, part of their social calendar that was fixed each and every year. Logan had explained that the family had been going to the Scottish estate for generations. It was a big deal, with a formal dinner, days of outdoor activities, and family outings.

No longer full of doubt around Logan's family, Cally was fine with the actual event itself, but the thought of spending days navigating their customs and traditions didn't fill her with utter joy. She shook her head and tried not to be mean. Logan's family had been nothing but welcoming to her; even if their world sometimes felt alien to hers, they hadn't put a foot wrong. There were definitely irritating members - entitled Alastair and his badly-timed comments sprang to mind, but overall, they were nice. She needed to suck it up and be more grateful.

Sighing as she looked out at the sea again, she thought about how far she'd come from when she'd arrived with nothing much other than the hope that Birdie extending her a lifeline would give her a fresh start. Now, here she was, rolling her eyes that she had to go on a trip to a Scottish estate with her boyfriend's family. She chuckled at the absurdity of it all as she rubbed her towel up and down her arms. If someone had told her a year before that this would be her life, she would have thought they were mad or drunk or both. Yet here she was, and despite her lack of enthusiasm, she was curious to see the estate that Logan had told her about.

Cally: *Thanks for the reminder. Really looking forward to it. Yes. I have a dress sorted. Xxx*

Sitting and pondering, Cally thought about the practicalities of the trip. From what Logan had said, she needed to pack for both warm and cold weather, lots of walking and outdoor clothes, and to be prepared for rain. Part of her wished they were jetting off to Spain. Sunbeds, cocktails, blue skies, and parasols or soggy walks in wet woods? Tricky one.

After popping Logan's hoodie back on, pulling off her swimming costume's straps and rolling it down, she hoisted her bag onto her shoulder and began to make her way back up the beach. As she walked along the promenade, her mind drifted back to the conversation she'd had with Logan when he'd first mentioned the Scotland trip. A few months before, they'd been enjoying a quiet evening at the cottage curled up on the sofa, half-watching a property show. Logan had casually dropped the trip to Scotland into the conversation as if it was nothing. He'd been nonchalant, but Cally had immediately registered that the Highlands was yet another non-negotiable part of family life.

She supposed if she and Logan were going to continue to be an item, she'd have to get used to popping a smile on her face and getting on with things she didn't always want to do. It was a tough life.

She nodded to herself and decided to open her mind. Maybe the Scottish trip would be good. She'd soon find out.

5

Cally was in the back room of the chemist, surrounded by towering piles of cardboard boxes in the middle of unsheathing a load of cough syrup from its outer carton. As she slid open an inner box and opened another carton, she checked off the contents against the delivery sheet and ticked off a stock list on the computer. Methodically going through the order, she thought about Birdie's job offer and wondered if she really wanted to be doing the job full-time for the rest of her life. Had she struggled to do her degree in the spare room of her grandma's house amidst her caring role to end up doing something she was mostly unqualified for? The honest answer was that she really wasn't sure. Where was the razzle-dazzle in unwrapping cough syrup for a living? The va va voom of unloading boxes of fish oil capsules wasn't exactly earth shattering.

She hadn't yet received the formal offer email offer from Birdie, anyway, so the decision was in limbo. They'd discussed the role further and Birdie had said that Cally should take some time to really think it over and that there was no real rush. Cally was more than happy with that.

Her phone pinged from its position on the side. She glanced at it expecting to see a message from either Logan or Eloise but instead saw a number she didn't know. Squinting at the screen, she tapped.

Hi Cally, Molly from Lovely Bay Coats here. Just a quick note to say you are at the top of the list. If you would like to go ahead with your Lovely coat, please click the attached link to book a slot for your first fitting. If you're no longer interested, if you wouldn't mind, please contact us so that we can offer your spot to the next one on our waiting list. Best, Lovely Bay Coats.

Cally gasped. She'd been on the waiting list for a much-coveted Lovely Bay coat for what felt like an eternity. The navy blue wax jackets were something of a Lovely Bay institution and locals wore them with a huge sense of pride. You did not mess with a Lovely coat or anyone wearing one. Lovelies had them for a lifetime and they were a much-cherished part of local life. To have one made for you was a big old deal. Cally shook her head as she reread the message. She couldn't quite believe that she'd finally made it to the top of the list. Nor could she get her head around the fact that she'd got on the list in the first place, but she wasn't going to tell anyone that. She let out a little whoop of joy.

'Everything alright?' Birdie's voice called from the dispensary area.

'Yes!' Cally called back, unable to keep the excitement from her voice. 'More than alright, actually. I've just had a text from the coat shop. They're ready for me to have my first fitting. At last!'

Birdie's head popped around the corner. 'You've been waiting for ages, haven't you?'

Cally nodded. 'Yes, I've been on the list forever. I'd almost given up hope. Ooh, exciting! I've wanted a coat to call my own since I started working for you. I'm always borrowing someone else's and they never fit me properly.'

Birdie chuckled, coming fully into the back room. 'Well, good things come to those who wait, as they say. And just in time for your trip to Scotland, too. That coat will come in handy up there, I'd wager. Always chilly in that part of the world, if you ask me. Not that I've ever been invited to go to the estate. Chance would be a fine thing.'

Cally winced a little bit at the mention of her upcoming trip. Even though she pretended on the outside she was fine, she was still getting used to the idea of being part of Logan's world and all that it entailed. A long weekend away with his family was a big step as far as she was concerned.

'You're right. It's perfect timing, really. How long does it take for the coat to be made? Do you know?'

'Once you're at the top of the list, not long. It's the waiting that takes the time. Those girls in there don't mess around.'

'Great. So, it might just be ready in time for Scotland.'

'Yep.'

'Woohoo.'

Birdie widened her eyes. 'Welcome to the club.'

6

Cally inhaled as she walked along the high street and made her way in the direction of Lovely Bay Coats. There was a slight crispness in the air but with the promise of a nice day on the horizon by way of a blue sky without a hint of a cloud. She inhaled the Lovely smell as she strolled; the scent of salt, seaweed, and the time of year in the air. Walking past the chocolate shop, she stopped to linger outside the front window for a bit, fantasised about a salted caramel truffle, said hello to Nancy, who was coming out of the pub, and then, as she got towards the war memorial, bumped straight into Colin from the riverboat. Colin was hustling along with a shopping bag in his arms coming the other way.

'Afternoon, our Cally! Long time no see. How are things with you? All good, I hope. You're looking well. Keeping well, are you?'

Cally beamed. 'Thanks. I'm feeling great as it happens.'

'Good to hear.'

'You?'

'Can't complain, as they say. Everything is good my end.'

'What have you been up to?'

Colin gestured in the direction of the lighthouse. 'Not a lot. We're off to Spain next week, so I'm trying to finish everything off. You know how it is before you go away. Up to my eyes in it, to be honest. I can't wait to get on the plane, sit back, have a drink and relax.'

'Ahh, yes, sounds like you're busy.'

Colin lifted his chin. 'Where are you off to?'

'Actually, I'm on my way to have my first fitting for my Lovely coat.'

'Ooh, congratulations are in order for you then,' Colin joked. 'You really are part of the furniture now. There's no going back. You've been locked in by way of a blue coat.'

'I've been on the waiting list for a long time.'

'Ahh, you're a real Lovely now. It's worth the wait, that's all I can say.'

'I suppose I am. It's been a long time coming.' Cally laughed.

Colin chuckled. 'Well, well. Our Cally, all grown up and getting her very own Lovely coat. I remember when you first arrived at the back of the chemist there. I bet you wondered where on earth you'd ended up, what with all our strange ways. I bet you thought we were all a bit bonkers. You would have been right.'

'It wasn't that bad, but yeah, there have been quite a few odd things to get used to. The three things beginning with C, don't they say? Coats, chocolate, and chowder.'

'You picked it up well enough.'

'Ha, I did.'

Colin winked. 'Now look at you now – a proper Lovely Bay local. Once you get that coat, you're not allowed to leave. You do know that, don't you?'

'It does feel like home now,' Cally admitted. 'I can't imagine being anywhere else.'

'And we wouldn't have it any other way.' Colin gave Cally a fond pat on the shoulder.

'Thanks, Colin.'

'So, what else has been happening? What have you been up to?'

'Actually, I'm going to Scotland soon. To Logan's family estate.'

Colin's eyebrows shot up. 'Blimey! Meeting more of the Henry-Hicks family, are we? That's a big step. It'll be wedding bells soon enough.'

'No, no, not for me anyway.'

'You're all going up there, are you?'

'I think so. They're all coming out of the woodwork for it. Apparently, it's a real old family tradition.'

'Right, you are. Well, with that Lovely coat, you'll look the part, too.'

'I will. If it's made up in time.'

'Oh, you should be okay. Once you're in our Molly doesn't mess around. Those girls know what they're doing. They've been schooled in making those coats since they first started to walk. I think they could make them with their eyes closed if they had to.'

Cally nodded. 'Hmm. Yes, I've heard that. Birdie said the same.'

'It'll be done in no time. I bet our Birdie is jealous that you got an invite to go to Scotland.'

'Ha, she did say that.'

'She's had an eye on going up there for years.'

'I'm getting in first.'

'I like it.'

'Right, you are. Well, thanks, Colin. I'd best push on or I'll be late. Nice to bump into you. I'll see you later.'

'See you. Next time I see you, you might be showing off your new coat.'

'Yes, hope so, see you later.'

As she got to the end of the road, Cally felt ridiculously excited about the coat and going into the shop for her fitting. She'd walked past the shop many times, but never actually gone in. She'd got on the waiting list itself by way of Molly, who owned the shop, coming in the chemist. The shop stood out at the end of a long row of similar buildings. Its exterior a bright white teamed with a deep navy blue that matched the famous coats it was known for. Cally stopped on the other side of the street and looked at the window displaying several of the coveted coats, and blue and white bunting strung along the top of the window. The bunting fluttered back and forth in the breeze next to an old-fashioned sign hanging just above the door.

After waiting for a few cars to pass, she crossed the road and peered in the window for a moment, then stepped up the little front step and pushed open a heavy wooden door. A small brass bell tinkled overhead, and she stopped in her tracks as her eyes adjusted to the light. A new to her but somehow familiar scent filled her nostrils. A gorgeous mix she'd smelt many times before as she'd gone about her business in Lovely; an amalgamation of waxed cotton, leather, and something indefinably old. The shop and its smell were something else, as if tradition, craftsmanship, and old-school Lovely had fused into one gorgeous hit and landed in a tiny little boutique at one end of Lovely Bay.

'Hello?' Cally's voice sounded muffled in the quiet, packed-to-the rafters shop.

'Just a moment!' came a cheerful reply from the back.

Cally looked around, drinking in every detail. Lovely Bay Coats was much smaller than she'd imagined, but somehow, that only added to it. Old timber floors, polished to a soft matte-like sheen, creaked under her feet as she stepped towards the back. The walls were lined with glass-fronted cabinets, their brass fittings tarnished with age, and floor-to-ceiling shelves stood in a row on a far wall. Inside the cabinets, neatly folded stacks of waxed cotton fabric in the Lovely navy blue looked as if someone had taken a lot of care to line them up perfectly. Spools of thread and old-fashioned cutting tools were neatly arranged on a side cabinet. To her right, a long timber counter stretched along the wall, its surface marked with the patina of years of use. Behind it, more shelves reached the ceiling, laden with more perfectly aligned bolts of fabric.

In the centre of the shop, a large wooden table dominated the space, its surface covered with a partly unrolled length of waxed cotton. Beside it, a half-finished coat was neatly folded with a label on its top. Nearby, a beautiful old sewing machine sat ready for use with a chair tucked underneath and a little sewing lamp beside it pooled light onto the table. Several dress forms were scattered around the shop each draped with a Lovely Bay coat in various stages of completion. A large bolt of the Lovely signature striped lining was laid out on another smaller table together with an old-fashioned timber utensils basket full of tools. Cally wanted to have a cup of tea and stay for the night.

A small seating area tucked in the corner with two worn leather armchairs was flanked by a low table and a leather-bound ledger of some sort took pride of place. In every nook and cranny, little lamps lit the tiny shop and every available surface seemed to hold some treasure – vintage buttons in glass jars, ancient-looking scissors, and well-worn measuring tapes neatly rolled up here and there. Cally couldn't quite get enough of it. Even the air itself appeared imbued with history. She whirled around, taking everything in as motes of dust danced in shafts of sunlight streaming through the front bay window.

'Ah, there you are!'

Cally turned to see Molly emerging from the back of the shop. In her thirties, with blonde hair pulled back in a neat bun and eyes that crinkled at the corners when she smiled. 'Hello.'

'Hey, our Cally. How are you?'

Cally clapped her hands together. 'I'm good, thanks. I can't tell you how excited I am to be here. A bit pathetic, but true.'

Molly's smile widened. 'Not at all! I can imagine. You've been on our waiting list for quite some time, haven't you?'

Cally nodded. 'I'd almost given up hope.'

'Ah, well, good things come to those who wait,' Molly said with a wink. 'Right, let's get you fitted. I hear we might have to do an express job for you.'

Cally laughed. 'Ha, who told you that?'

'Who do you think?'

Cally put her finger to her lips and pretended to think for a second. 'Hmm. Let me guess.'

'It might have been in a certain shop around here and we might have been accompanied by the dulcet tones of the Shipping Forecast.'

Cally shook her head. 'I can't get away with anything, can I?'

Molly chuckled. 'You most certainly can't if you work in there. I hear you're going to Scotland.'

'I am.'

Molly whistled as she led Cally to a small raised platform in front of a three-way mirror. 'Best we get on with it then.' As Cally stepped up onto the platform, Molly bustled around her, pulling out a measuring tape and tapping on a laptop.

'Now, let's see what we're working with,' Molly chatted away as she began to take measurements. 'Oh my. Well, this won't take us long. You're tiny.'

Cally laughed. 'I've been told that once or twice.'

Molly clucked her tongue. 'We'll make sure it fits you perfectly. These coats are meant to last a lifetime, as you know.'

'No room for me to pile on the pounds then,' Cally joked.

'There is that.'

As Molly worked, Cally again peered around the shop, taking in more details. It felt as if Lovely history was speaking directly to her from the beautiful old timber shelves lining the walls. 'So, how long have you been doing this?'

'Ahh, my whole life, and when I say whole, I mean since I was this high.' Molly held her hand out in front of her.

'Right, ages then.'

'Yep.'

'It seems like a badge of honour to have a Lovely coat. A sign that you're really part of the community.'

Molly nodded. 'That's about the long and the short of it. My family's been making these coats for generations. Each one is a little piece of Lovely Bay history.'

'I love that. I'm grateful to be part of it.'

'The coats all started with my great-grandfather's father, so what would that make him to me? Anyway, he was a fisherman, like most men in Lovely back then. He got tired of coming home soaked to the bone after every trip, so he started experimenting with waxing his own jackets and the lining and all that.' Molly continued her story, moving around Cally to measure her shoulders and back. 'Word spread, and soon, other fishermen asked him to wax their coats, too. Before long, he'd set up shop right here in this very building, though the pictures show that it was a bit different in those days, but not a lot.'

'That's amazing. So the shop has been here all this time?'

Molly nodded. 'Yep, generations of my family have worked within these walls. Sometimes, I think I could have done something a bit more exciting, but there are a lot worse ways to make a living, I reckon. Even though I have qualifications up to my eyeballs, I make coats for a living.'

Cally thought about how she'd had the same feelings regarding Birdie's offer. 'Yup. I hear you.'

Molly stepped back, consulted her laptop and squinted.

'Right then, I think I have all the measurements I need. I'll get you to try on a sample so I can have a look at the fit. Hang on a second. I'll go and get one.'

Molly disappeared out the back and Cally ran her hand along the smooth wood of the cutting table, wondering how many coats had been crafted on its surface over the years. A few moments later, Molly reappeared, a coat draped over her arm. 'Here we are. This is one of our smaller sizes; it's a short, but we'll still need to cut yours a bit differently. That's why it's made to measure, obviously. Though many places say that these days, it's actually not true, but it is here. Your coat will fit you like a glove and last you forever.'

Cally slid her arms into the sleeves of the sample coat and was enveloped in the scent of waxed cotton – earthy and slightly sweet. It felt solid, dependable, and oh-so Lovely as she shrugged it onto her shoulders. She couldn't wait to get her own.

Molly chuckled. 'Don't you look like a proper local? You want the coat before you go away?'

'Honestly, it doesn't matter if it's not ready. I've managed up to now.'

'It's cutting it a bit close, but I think we can manage it. You're off to the estate?'

'Yeah.'

'Gosh, we've made some coats for the Henry-Hicks lot over the years.'

'I know. I've seen them stashed all over the place.'

'There are probably a load of old heritage ones up in Scotland, too. You'll have to keep an eye open for them.'

'Oh, right, yes, of course. I might have to bring one home with me.'

'Well, if you do, I'll be able to tell you who it was made for and when.' Molly pointed to the ledger on the table. 'We keep a record of everything that goes out of this shop, even back to the old days.'

Cally sighed as she looked around. The coat was another component of her story with Lovely Bay. She was so very pleased to be part of it. It had ultimately changed the trajectory of her life. What she didn't quite know was that there was much more to come. Some of it not what she was expecting at all.

7

A few days or so later, as Cally approached Lovely Bay train station, she inhaled the familiar Lovely fresh sea air smell and drank in the prettiness of the old railway station right in front of her. With its traditional Victorian charm steeped in the history of the area, gorgeous fluttering bunting, and old faded advertising signage, the station itself had Lovely written all over it. Someone, she presumed Nancy, had done their utmost to make the station appealing. This was no dilapidated, shabby, old, in-need-of-love station complete with overfull litter bins, peeling paint and half-dead weeds flanking the front. Oh no, not in Lovely. Indeed, Lovely train station was the antithesis of that; everywhere possible overloaded hanging baskets swayed in the wind, the distinctive handmade Lovely bunting fluttered overhead, window boxes spilt with flowers and just outside the main entrance, an old train wagon doubling as a planter, showcased a lush array of greenery.

With a spring in her step, Cally pushed open the heavy door to the main ticket hall with its old-fashioned timber counters and gleaming glass partitioning. The station bustled with activity: a mix of locals going about their business, a group of mums with prams on a day out, and a gathering of eager-looking tourists clutching maps, cameras, and phones held overhead on long telescopic sticks. Just as Cally was idly watching the tourists, all with their necks craned along the train line, peering at the mechanics of the moveable platform, she spotted Nancy in the distinctive Lovely Bay coat coming down the stairs.

On seeing Cally, Nancy smiled and joked. 'Our Cally. What brings you to our bustling metropolis this morning? It's all happening here.'

Cally chuckled at Nancy's description of the small station. 'I'm here to meet Eloise. She's coming over for a coffee, and her car is in for a service. Her train should be arriving soon. What a nice day, eh? The station looks gorgeous. All your own work, is it?'

'Of course.'

'The flowers out the front there really are pretty.'

'We do our best.'

As they stood chatting, in Cally's peripheral vision, she could see the trainspotters on the far side. She pointed in their direction. 'Looks like you have quite a few visitors this morning.'

Nancy rolled her eyes good-naturedly. 'I've just been chatting with them. They're part of an Instagram trainspotting club. They're here for the moveable platform. I think we need to start charging for it. I'll make my millions yet.'

'I make you correct. You'd be rich.' Cally giggled.

'I even have a spiel after all these years of chatting with people who know the ins and outs of it. It's a piece of engineering marvel that. The spotters come from all over to see it in action. Honestly, I could write my own documentary series for Netflix on that thing.'

'Ha. You should start a vlog broadcasting live from the station every morning. You'd go viral.'

'Actually, now there's an idea.'

Cally shook her head. 'Only in Lovely Bay would a bit of railway equipment become a tourist attraction.'

Nancy laughed. 'That's us. We can make an event out of anything. Speaking of events, I hear you're off on quite the adventure soon.'

'News travels fast around here. I swear, local news travels faster in this town than the trains do.'

'You should know that by now.' Nancy chuckled. 'You can't do anything without the folk of Lovely knowing about it. So you're on your travels?'

'Yes, I'm going to Scotland with Logan. To his family's estate.'

Nancy's eyebrows shot up. 'Ooh, meeting the extended Henry-Hicks family, are we? That's a big step. Good luck with that one.'

Cally nodded. 'It is. I'm a bit nervous, to be honest. It's all so grand from what I've seen.'

'Nup, I'll have none of that nervous talking. You're past that part of the relationship. I reckon you'll love it. It's meant to be beautiful. I've heard loads about the estate up there over the years.'

'You think so?'

'I *know* so,' Nancy said firmly. 'What else has been happening with you? Just as busy as me?'

'Not a lot, actually.'

Nancy widened her eyes. 'Oh really. That's not what I heard.'

'What?'

'Apparently, you have a new acquisition coming your way.'

Cally wrinkled her nose and looked sideways. She hoped Birdie hadn't said anything about the job offer. Birdie had told her it was completely confidential and that Cally had plenty of time to make up her mind. She hadn't even received the formal in-writing offer yet. 'What's that?'

'A certain little something that means you're really a Lovely now.'

Cally clocked what Nancy was talking about. 'Oh, ha, the coat. Yes, I finally made it to the top of the waiting list.'

'I presume you'll be taking that on the Scottish trip for its first outing?'

'Hope so. If it's finished.'

As they continued to chat, the station got busier and the trainspotters on the far end of the platform began to buzz with excitement as a freight train approached. Nancy advised a couple of passengers, stepped into a side door for a bit, dealt with a train, and was back a few minutes later.

'So, this Scottish adventure. What will that entail?' Nancy asked.

'Not sure. Logan says it's beautiful – all rolling hills and lochs. There's even an old ruin of a castle.'

Nancy whistled. 'A castle, eh? Fancy that. You'll be the lady of the manor before we know it.'

Cally flushed. 'Don't even go there.'

'Don't worry. Us mere mortals down here will keep you grounded.'

As they stood there chatting away and putting the world to rights, the sound of another approaching train grew louder. The trainspotters at the end of the platform were practically vibrating with excitement, cameras poised and necks craned.

Nancy eyerolled. 'Oh, here we go. Brace yourself for the excitement of railway engineering at its finest. I swear I'll have to save a life one day when someone keels over or has a heart attack. Good job this station is equipped for any eventuality.'

As the platform began to move, the trainspotters erupted into a flurry of activity, snapping photos and scribbling notes. Cally watched the platform do its thing, fascinated despite herself. 'I have to admit, it *is* pretty impressive.'

Nancy smiled. 'That it is. Just another of Lovely Bay's hidden wonders. I include myself as one.'

As the train moved on, Cally looked up at the board over the platform. 'Oh, I think that might be Eloise's train coming in now.'

'Yep. Well, I'd better push off back to work. If I don't see you, have a wonderful time in Scotland.'

'Thanks, Nance. Yeah, I'll probably bump into you before I go.'

As Nancy headed off in the direction of the station master's house, Cally got lost in people-watching as she waited for Eloise's train. When it pulled into the station, Cally smiled and waved as Eloise arrived. 'Hiya! How was your journey?'

'All good. No delays, just a chatty person next to me who wanted to tell me his life story and had very questionable train snacks. But I'm here now.'

'It's so good to see you.'

'What have you been up to? Ready for your trip?'

'Ahh, loads, mostly working.' Cally filled Eloise in on the plans for the Scotland trip.

'I just can't help feeling a bit out of my depth. I mean, a castle ruin? I'm probably overthinking it all.'

'You'll be fine. Anyway, that's what I'm here for. To talk you down from your worried little ledges and remind you how amazing you are. You can tell me all about how you're planning to pack your entire wardrobe for the trip over coffee.'

Cally groaned. 'Don't even get me started on the packing. I have no idea what to take. Ballgowns to breakfast…'

Eloise laughed. 'I reckon your new Lovely Bay coat and wellies will do the trick. Come on, let's go. I need caffeine.'

Fifteen or so minutes later, they strolled along by Lovely Bay's harbour. Fishing boats bobbed up and down and the smell of fish and chips and the scent of salt, seaweed, and sunshine hung in the air. In other words: nice. Very nice, indeed.

Eloise linked her arm through Cally's as they navigated around an abandoned coil of fishing rope left on the harbour wall. 'So, are you going to tell me what else is going on, or do I have to guess?'

Cally smiled. Trust Eloise to see right through her. 'Am I that obvious?'

'Only to someone who knows you as well as I do. Come on, spill. You're up to something.'

'I wanted to wait until I saw you to tell you. Birdie offered me a promotion.'

Eloise stopped in her tracks. She made a funny face and widened her eyes. 'What? That's fantastic news!'

'Is it?'

'Err, you don't seem over the moon about it.'

'It's not that I'm not pleased.'

'What exactly did she offer you?'

As they reached the end of the harbour, Cally nodded at the coffee shop. 'I'll fill you in over coffee. It's a bit of a long story.'

Cally pushed open the door to the coffee shop. It was unusually quiet; a few Lovelies were scattered about at various tables here and there and a fabulous aroma of freshly ground coffee beans enveloped them as they walked in. They made their way to a small table tucked away in the corner by the window, where they had a view of the harbour and the sea beyond. As they settled into a couple of worn, comfortable wingback chairs, a local girl approached with a smile.

'Afternoon. Oh, hey, our Cally. How are you?'

'Good, thanks. You?'

'Keeping well.'

'What would you like? Coffees?'

'Yes, please. And maybe a couple of scones. Thanks.'

'Coming right up.'

Eloise sat down and leant forward, her elbows on the table,

chin resting on clasped hands. 'Right then. Tell me everything about this promotion. Bit of a turn-up for the books, eh?'

'Well, you know how Birdie's opened a load of new shops?'

Eloise nodded. 'Yup.'

'She wants me to oversee it all,' Cally continued, still hardly believing it herself. 'Managing the different locations, mostly the deliveries but also dealing with the odd staff issue, developing the online business – the whole lot.'

Eloise's eyebrows shot up. 'Wow, Cal. That's a big deal. She must really trust you.'

'That's just it.' Cally fidgeted with a sugar packet on the table. 'I mean, I'm just an out-the-back assistant. What do I know about running a whole chain of shops? Talk about in at the deep end.'

Before Eloise could respond, the girl returned with their order. She put down two steaming mugs of coffee along with a plate with warm scones. 'There you go. Enjoy.'

Cally smiled gratefully. 'Thanks.'

Eloise pulled one of the mugs of coffee towards herself. 'You're totally ready for it. Don't even let yourself think that.'

'Am I?'

'Yup. How hard can it be?'

'It's actually quite involved…'

'Right. So, what are you thinking about the offer?'

Cally wrapped her hands around her mug. 'I don't know. She's emailing me the formal offer. When it's in black and white, I'll make a decision. The thought of messing it up is a bit daunting.'

Eloise nodded. 'Yeah, think about it though – would Birdie have offered you this position if she didn't believe you could handle it?'

'I suppose not,' Cally admitted.

'Exactly. Birdie's no fool. She knows what she's doing. If she thinks you're ready for this, then you probably are.'

Cally took a sip of coffee. She stared out the window for a second, where a fisherman in bright yellow oilskin dungarees was loading a huge basket onto the harbour wall. 'Yeah. I don't know. If I take this job, I'll be spending more time in an office, dealing with paperwork and spreadsheets. It's not like my dream job, you know? What if I *hate* it?'

'You'll be out and about learning so many new skills.'

Cally blinked. 'True. There is that side of it.'

'What about the online business? That sounds exciting.'

'There's loads to do – improving the website; apparently, Birdie wants to offer online consultations and create educational content. From what she's told me, there's a long list of jobs.'

'Sounds like there's a lot of scope.'

Cally nodded. 'There is, I suppose.'

'Let's be honest, Cal – you've never been one to shy away from a challenge. You're the person who has been working three jobs for ages and doing it well.'

Cally frowned and turned her palms upwards. 'They're all easy jobs, though.'

'Pah! Said no one ever. Do you really think it's easy to juggle all that? Only you could say that! I've heard it all now. It's not easy to do three jobs, plus you get up at the crack of dawn for one of them.'

'Hmm. Depends which way you look at it.'

'Also, remember when you first came to Lovely? You didn't know a soul, had no idea what you were doing, and look at you now. When you try new opportunities, you open doors. Am I right, or am I right? I'm right. I mean, the Henry-Hicks thing alone.'

Cally laughed and batted her hand, but it was true – she *had* come a long way since her early days in Lovely Bay. She'd built a life, found a nice little community, and settled in in ways she couldn't have imagined. She straightened in her chair and wrinkled her nose. 'You're right. I did do that. I didn't know anyone when I came here to work that first shift, and now I live here, and not only that, but I love it.'

'You certainly did,' Eloise agreed.

'Hmm.'

'I reckon what you need to do is decide whether or not this is something you *want* to do. Not just something you think you should do or something you're considering because Birdie offered it. But something you *want*, if you see what I mean. You had enough of doing that in your old life and caring. Otherwise, you might as well continue what you're doing anyway...'

Cally paused. 'It might be really good for me in one way and in another way, it may stop me from going out in the world.'

'It will all sort itself out.'

'I guess so. I think I'll just ponder on it. Birdie said she's in no rush.'

'Good idea. The universe will give you a sign. I've no doubt about that.'

What Cally nor Eloise knew was that the universe was already cooking up a few little bumps for our Cally. Just to keep her on her toes.

8

Cally had spent the morning deep-cleaning the flat. It had been well overdue and had moved from something she had to do to whizzing up to the top of her list as a priority. Cleaning wasn't her most profound joy in life, however, needs must, and no one else was going to do it. Even though the flat was small, with Cally working three jobs and not having a whole lot of time on her hands, it had become fairly untidy and in need of a good top-to-bottom deep clean. Truth be told, she'd been procrastinating about it for far too long.

Once she'd knuckled down and got on with it, she had, in fact, quite enjoyed getting stuck in. The vacuuming, dusting, cleaning, bleaching, and polishing of the place to within an inch of its life and clearing out two bags for the charity shop had performed some sort of ritual cleansing that had been a long time coming. As she looked at the two sacks for the charity shop by the front door, it amazed her how, in not that long at all, and despite having a meagre budget for most things, she had managed to accumulate so much stuff. She'd still somehow acquired a multitude of this and that to clutter up her life. Easily done.

Just as she was putting the cleaning materials back under the sink and thinking about either walking up to the manor or popping to the library, her phone pinged with a text from Lovely Coats shop to say that her coat was ready. After a little whoop and more than pleased, with a spring in her step, she left the flat, took the steep stairs down to the ground floor, went through the deli onto the High Street, and made her way through Lovely.

On her way to the shop, every other person she passed wore a Lovely coat. Cally couldn't quite believe that she was going to have one of her own. Of course, she'd worn one of the much-coveted coats more than a few times before. Logan's mum had even given her one, but it was a bit big, and it wasn't quite the same as joining the crew of locals who had their own made-to-measure coat for life. Now, she was about to join the ranks.

She smiled as she got to the shop and peered in the window. As before, she was greeted with reams and reams of fabric, little glowing lamps everywhere, old-fashioned cubby holes neatly stacked with dressmaking tools, and the vintage shop counters. Stepping in, Molly, the owner, stood on the far side beside a mannequin, pinning a collar on a coat. She looked over her shoulder and smiled. 'Afternoon, our Cally. That was quick! How are you?'

'Good, thanks. I thought I'd come right away to collect it, seeing as I have a day off today. Thank you for doing my coat so quickly. I'm so excited!'

'You said you wanted to take it to Scotland with you, so we got our skates on.'

'Fab. It will be good to have it with me. Thanks for doing that. I appreciate it.'

Molly smiled and put down her pins and scissors on the cutting table. 'Well, let's not keep you waiting then. Your coat's just in the back. Won't be a minute.'

Molly disappeared into the back room and Cally stood a bit

mesmerised by the shop, just as she had the first time she'd been in. An aroma of waxed cotton filled the air, loads of bolts of fabric were stacked neatly on shelves, and everything appeared to be so well organised and in order that it made Cally feel as if she wanted to run home and reshuffle her whole life.

The sound of Molly's footsteps brought Cally's attention back to the present. Molly emerged from the back room, a garment bag draped carefully over her arm. 'Here we are. Come on over to the mirror. It should be just right, but we'll see.'

They moved to a large, ornate mirror tucked into one corner of the shop. Its gilt frame slightly tarnished with age, the glass spotless, reflecting the shop's lamps. Molly unzipped the bag with a flourish and Cally smiled. 'Ooh, I'm so happy to have this! It's beautiful.'

Molly beamed. 'I love this moment when someone gets one of these. Honestly, it never gets old.'

Cally nodded and shrugged off her cardigan as Molly lifted the coat from its hanger and held it out, helping Cally slip her arms into the sleeves. The moment the coat settled on her shoulders, Cally was happy. As a few people, including some at Lovely Manor, had said to her, there was nothing like getting your first Lovely coat. It just felt right. The weight was solid without being heavy, the fit impeccable without being too tight, and it felt as if it could and would take her through any and all weathers. Nice.

Molly stepped back, her head tilted critically as she examined the fit. 'How does it feel? All good over the shoulders there, or not?'

Cally turned from side to side and watched her reflection in the mirror. She stretched her arms out across her chest. 'It feels just right. Like it was made for me.'

'Well, that's the aim! It was. That's the beauty of a bespoke coat.' Molly patted the back of the coat over Cally's shoulders and narrowed her eyes. 'Yep, just how we like it. You can get a jumper on if you need to.'

Cally cocked her head to the side. 'Gosh. It really is nice to have my own one. The fit is perfect. Honestly, you're really good at this.'

'It's Lovely.' Molly joked. 'Let me check all the details at the side here.' Molly ran her hands along the seams and checked the fall of the fabric. 'The length is good,' she noted, more to herself than to Cally. 'And the shoulders sit just right. Yeah, nice.'

Cally watched in the mirror as Molly fussed with the coat, making minute adjustments here and there.

'Let me check the sleeves and storm cuffs. Hold out your arms. You want these to be right.'

Cally held out her hands and Molly nodded approvingly. 'Perfect. Long enough to protect your wrists from the wind, but not so long they'll get in the way. You don't want them too long.' She stepped back again, gesturing for Cally to move. 'Have a little walk around. Get a feel for how it moves with you. We can alter it if it's not right.'

Cally did as instructed, paced the length of the shop, put her hands in the pockets and flicked the hood up and down a few times. She stretched her arms out, twisted from side to side, and even did a little twirl that made Molly laugh.

'Well?' Molly asked. 'Happy with it? You need to be happy from the word go.'

'Yep. I've never had anything fit as well.'

Molly's smile widened. 'That's what we like to hear. Now, let me show you all the features.'

Molly pointed out a few details as she spoke. 'We've reinforced the elbows and shoulders for durability and the pockets are lined with flannel to keep your hands warm.' Molly flipped the coat open to the inside. 'There's a hidden pocket just inside. Perfect for keeping your keys safe and dry and this one on this side will perfectly fit a phone.' She pointed to another small pocket. 'This is for a battery pack. It'll stay dry if you're out getting wet on a boat...'

'Oh, wow, I haven't seen that before on any of the coats I've borrowed.'

Molly shook her head. 'No, you wouldn't have. The battery pack thing is only on our newest coats.'

As Molly continued to point out the coat's features – a storm flap at the back, adjustable cuffs, and a two-way zipper hidden beneath the button placket, Cally marvelled at the thought and care that had gone into every detail.

'It's fully waterproof. You could stand in a downpour and stay dry as a bone underneath.'

Cally grinned. 'Knowing Lovely Bay's weather, I'm sure I'll be putting that to the test soon enough.'

Molly laughed. 'I've no doubt.' She reached into her apron pocket and pulled out a small brass tag. 'This is for you to engrave if you'd like. Most folks put their initials or the date they got their coat. It's a bit of a tradition.'

Cally took the tag and turned it over. It was a simple rectangle with a hole at one end for attaching to the coat. 'Where would it go?'

'Usually just inside, near the label,' Molly explained. 'But it's up to you. Some people like to keep it in that hidden pocket I showed you as a sort of secret talisman.'

Cally nodded. 'Nice.'

'You don't have to decide now. Take it home, think about it. You can bring it back any time to have it engraved and attached.'

'Thank you,' Cally said, slipping the tag into her pocket. 'I'll give it some thought.'

'Good. A Lovely coat is for life, after all. You want to make sure it's just right.'

Cally turned back to the mirror. She felt a bit bonkers, but the coat had seemed to transform her somehow. Made her feel as if she belonged. 'It does.'

'Happy with it?'

Cally nodded emphatically. 'More than happy. Thank you *so* much.'

Molly beamed. 'My pleasure. Right, the care instructions will arrive via a PDF to your email. Honestly, it's best if you follow them.' Molly touched the cuff of Cally's coat. 'People joke about it, but a Lovely coat really can last a lifetime if you treat it right. Do you want to wear it out, or shall I pack it up for you?'

Cally hesitated for a moment. 'I think I'll wear it,' she decided. 'If that's alright?'

Molly chuckled. 'Of course it is.'

As Molly tapped on her phone to complete the sale, the shop door chimed. Both women looked up to see Nina coming in.

Nina smiled. 'I thought I saw you through the window. Hey, our Molly, how are you?'

'Good. Just getting Cally sorted.'

'Ahh, I thought so. Congratulations on your coat!' Nina laughed.

Cally nodded. 'What do you think?'

Nina looked Cally up and down. 'It's gorgeous. The fit! Molly, you've outdone yourself as usual. Ooh, I loved it when I got my first coat. Such a good feeling! I think I stroked it for weeks,' Nina joked.

Molly waved off the compliment, but Cally could see she was pleased. 'Cally made it easy, being such a good model.'

Cally smiled and looked down at the front of the coat. 'I feel like I've joined a club.'

'I know the feeling. It's a beautiful coat, and you look lovely in it.' Nina agreed. 'I remember when I got my coat. It feels like joining a secret society or something, doesn't it? I thought I was losing the plot having feelings for a coat, but there you are.'

Cally nodded, relieved that someone else understood. 'Exactly!'

'You'll keep noticing other people's coats now. It's like a weird shared experience.'

Molly chuckled. 'You're one of us now—a proper Lovely Bay resident. Plus, you have a new model with the updated pocket situation. Not many have that one yet, so keep an eye on it.'

Cally nodded. Molly may well have laughed, but she didn't know just how good the coat made her feel. She very much liked being in the club.

9

Cally had just come in from a long day doing a decluttering job with Nina in a hoarder's house in the next town. Suffice to say, it hadn't been pleasant. As she walked into the deli building, Alice poked her head around the door and wiggled a couple of letters that had arrived that morning. Tucking them under her arm, Cally smiled and nodded as she walked up the stairs at the thought of what the two letters contained. She'd been paperless forever, but now that she was completely and utterly debt-free and in possession of a very nice healthy bank balance, she wanted it in black and white in front of her. Therefore, she'd ordered paper statements to come in the post.

Chuckling to herself about the power of the little things, she thought that perhaps she'd frame both balances and put them on the wall. Slipping her shoes off, she plonked her bag down, did a wee, washed her hands and face and popped the kettle on. Ten minutes later, she was sitting with a hot blackcurrant and the crinkly credit card envelope in front of her. Splitting open the top, she read down to the bottom. A big fat load of zeros all in a nice neat row. Sighing, she felt a huge wave of relief. The credit card *had* and still *did* embody horrible things to her. Like a noose around her neck, it had always denoted her lack of control. It wasn't as if she'd ever used it for nice holidays, designer bags, fancy shoes or the like, either. It had been for emergency use only and had saved her bacon a few times. The zeros winked happily at her from the bottom of the page.

The information in the other envelope was all the better. She read down the deposit column over and over again. Little bits of money here and there that added up to what was in front of her now. Long hours, three jobs, early mornings, bleary eyes. Sacrifice. All of it looked back at her. Oh, how fabulous did those numbers look? Freedom, security. Time to exhale.

Finishing her blackcurrant, she sat at her desk and thought about packing for her upcoming trip to Scotland, but instead added up her sums for a mortgage application for the hundredth time and then checked her emails. She was pleased to see that here was an email from Birdie's company with the formal job offer, just as Birdie had promised.

After getting up and making herself another blackcurrant, she sat back down at her desk, opened the email, scanned down its content and felt her chin drop to the floor. Surprise whacked her around the chops a bit. This was no rubbish little add-on job to what she was already doing. Benefits, a very good salary, and bonuses swam in front of her eyes. What she hadn't realised was that the chemist was part of a co-op type affair in the industry and that a full-time job included all the good things that came with that. Subsidised healthcare, all sorts of discounts on all sorts of things, gym membership, sick pay, a company vehicle, paid leave. Ding blimming dong.

Cally stared at the screen, her eyes wide and unblinking as she tried to process the information before her. The job offer from Birdie's wasn't just a step up as Birdie had intimated; it was a giant leap, as far as Cally was concerned, into a whole other world. She blinked and shook her head repeatedly as she scrolled through the details again, not quite sure it was real. She thought that if she looked away for a minute, she'd realise that she'd imagined the whole thing or that it might all disappear.

As the enormity of what the offer represented began to sink in, Cally felt a lump in her throat. The emotion she felt wasn't entirely because of the offer, the salary, the benefits, the car, or any of it. It was the fact that the job represented the end of holding up the sky. Like the real end. No more having it teetering there on her circumference waving at her from the side.

Tears pricked as she thought about the scrimping and saving she'd done over the years. The nights she'd lain awake in the vile house on the estate worrying about how to make ends meet. The putting up and shutting up. The memory of standing in the supermarket carefully calculating. Deciding on whether or not to choose the blackcurrant with the gold top. All of it dropped on her head like a dead weight.

She swallowed, felt another prickle in her eyes and then a tear. It slipped down her cheek, followed by another. The sky falling down by way of the offer from Birdie was so intense, it almost made our Cally want to be sick. She laughed a strange macabre sound and wiped her eyes with the back of her hand.

Pull yourself together, she muttered in her head. Security and stability floated in front of her eyes. How long had she been chasing that elusive concept? It didn't take a rocket scientist to work it out; her entire life. A constant struggle to stay afloat, to keep her head above water, to do all the things. Now, here in front of her, by way of an email in her inbox, it felt as if someone was offering her something on a silver platter. The realisation that Birdie had seen her potential and believed in her enough to put her money where her mouth was blew Cally away. After years of trudging along feeling invisible, another cog in the machine of life, Birdie valued her. Boy, oh boy, did that feel good.

All of a sudden, her mind was back to when she'd been waiting for her grandma to go when money had got really tight. She'd hated that time wrapped up in sadness and worry. She remembered all the invitations she'd turned down over the years, when she'd not been able to afford to go out, the lack of holidays, the fear about taking time off because of the worry about how she'd pay her rent.

Glancing at the balances on the sheets of paper next to her laptop, she again took in the numbers. They embodied the struggles in the front of her mind and how she'd put her head down and got on with it. Now, the job offer represented something else, too: that her future was going to go down a different road altogether.

Cally reached for her phone and scrolled down to Eloise's name. If anyone would understand the magnitude of the moment, it would be Eloise. As she pressed the call button, she felt a really strange, odd sense of coming full circle. From struggling to make ends meet to being offered a position that could change her life, it all seemed almost too much to comprehend.

'Hey, Els. You'll never guess what's just happened...'

'Are you alright? You sound weird. Very weird. What's that voice?'

Cally let out a watery chuckle. 'I'm fine. More than fine, actually. I just received the formal job offer email from Birdie. We've had a few meetings but I now have the nuts and bolts details.'

There was a pause on the other end. 'Oh? Right?' Eloise's tone was carefully neutral.

Cally's voice caught. 'They're offering me a full-time position with so many benefits and everything. I can hardly believe it. I didn't think she meant like, well... I thought it was, you know, what I already get but full-time with a few things chucked in here and there.'

'So what's the offer? Like what?'

'Like a company vehicle, an amazing salary, like holiday pay, gym membership. It's overwhelming.'

'You deserve every bit of it. You've worked hard for this, Cally. I've seen it firsthand. Sorry, I'm going to have to say it, but *why* are you surprised? I'm not.'

'I don't know. It doesn't feel as if someone like me should get things like this, you know?'

'Nope. Birdie wants to scoop you up. You can't see it, Cal. I've been telling you this for years.'

'I can't believe I've been offered it.'

'Why not? You've juggled multiple jobs, learned new skills, and faced challenges that would have broken others. You just don't see those as worthy things because you just get on with it. Honestly, there are some real muppets out there.'

'I suppose so.'

'Think of all the doors this will open for you. This isn't just a promotion, Cal; this gives you a choice.'

'Right.'

'I'm serious. This is a turning point.'

Cally thought about all the dreams she'd put on hold, all the things she'd told herself she couldn't have or do. The narration in her head that she wasn't going anywhere anytime soon.

'You think so?'

'Yep. I *know* so. You know what? I'm proud of you. Really proud. You need to give yourself a pat on the back. You put in the work, you showed up every day, and *you* never gave up. This is all *you*.' Eloise swore. 'Suck it up, girlfriend and feel how good this is.'

Cally nodded. Perhaps Eloise was right—she usually was. Maybe it was time to just sit back and do just that.

Hello, proper job offer in a good company, hello prospects. It's Cally. Nice to meet you.

10

It was the end of the week and Cally and Logan were on a train on their way to Scotland for the family weekend at the Scottish estate. Cally had decided to think about the job offer for a bit. In fact, Birdie had insisted on it until she came back from Scotland. It was a nice piece of news to travel with.

Similar to the races event Cally had attended with Logan, going to Scotland was a non-negotiable part of the Henry-Hicks family calendar. If Cally was being totally honest, which she wasn't, she wasn't that keen on the whole idea of the weekend at all. As her relationship with Logan had grown and settled, she had become more used to his family's extensive social calendar and all that it entailed, but she still wasn't all that enamoured with it. She kept that very quietly to herself.

However, there was now one major difference from when she'd first been going out with Logan; she no longer withered away with self-doubt about herself when she had to smooch with his family. She was now mostly okay with it *and* them. That wasn't to say she liked it. A lot of the time, the social high jinks were just not her cup of tea in the slightest, but she put up and shut up. The Henry-Hicks family had been more than generous and accommodating to her, so she was prepared to play the game. Apart from the irritating Alastair and his badly timed comments, and even he wasn't that bad, she had no reason not to feel fine about being part of the Henry-Hicks contingent. All the doubting, if there was, indeed, any left, was purely and simply her own.

The weekend away in Scotland, though, was a whole different kettle of fish, and it hadn't taken her long to ascertain that being part of it was a *big* deal. As the preparations for the weekend and talk about it had started to circulate as it had got closer, she'd realised that being invited meant that her feet were now well and truly under the family table. She'd sat at worse tables in her life. She liked the nice gilded one she was at now.

The weekend involved various arms of the Henry-Hicks family decamping to their summer holiday estate to indulge in some good old rest and relaxation. As you do. Cally had heard all sorts about what the weekend entailed and wasn't quite sure what to think. After doing a bit of secret investigating by way of her laptop, she had, though, decided that some parts of the Scottish estate were right up her street.

She'd been determined that she would not focus too much on hobnobbing with family members, but instead, she intended to revel in the wonderful scenery and nature and would do her darndest to enjoy a whole long weekend in the country. She'd always loved being out and about in nature and was going to jolly well make the most of it. She'd packed hiking trousers, was the proud new owner of a highfalutin suitcase, and she had a very nice and, to be quite frank, extremely fancy pair of wellies packed in the boot of Logan's Aunt Cecilia's car.

Sitting back in the first-class compartment of the train, Cally watched out the window as it trundled through the countryside. It then slowed to a snail's pace, lowered down into a loch area and almost came to a stop as it waited at a signal. Since crossing into Scotland, the majority of the scenery had been beautiful as the train had snaked in and out of towns. But as it slowed on its approach to the town outside the estate, the view slowly morphed from beautiful to absolutely breathtaking. Logan put his hand on Cally's leg as she sat glued to the window, looking out at the jaw-dropping scenery filtering past outside. Her eyes widened as the train wound its way through the increasingly dramatic Scottish landscape, and she became more and more pleased that she'd said yes to the weekend away. She exhaled as the rolling hills they'd first encountered became more rugged, and heather-covered moorland stretched as far as the eye could see. Laid out in front of her, a beautiful muted patchwork of purples and greens seemed to shimmer in the light. It was almost as if colours Cally had never seen before had decided they might like to get to know her and hug the side of the train. She couldn't quite get enough.

With her nose practically pressed against the glass, she exclaimed. 'You totally undersold this! It's absolutely stunning. The scenery! What the heck, Logan? Why didn't you say?'

Logan squeezed her leg. 'I *knew* you'd love it. Just wait until we get closer to the estate. You are *not* going to be disappointed.'

As if on cue, the train rounded a bend, and Cally gasped as the track ran alongside a pristine loch. Its surface was so still it looked like a mirror reflecting the hills around it. Cally blinked and shook her head. 'I don't know what to say. I've never seen anything like it. It's like we're in a book.'

Logan chuckled. 'It has that effect on people up here. I'd forgotten that. I remember feeling the same way the first time I came up here as a boy. You haven't seen the half of it yet.'

Cally frowned. 'How old were you when you first came up here?'

'Tiny, I guess. But I first remember what you're feeling when I was about seven or eight, I think. I remember being absolutely gobsmacked by it all. I spent the entire weekend running about like a wild thing. Alastair and I went nuts up here. I never get tired of this place, which is why I wanted you to come. I know you'll like it.'

'I can just picture it. Logan gone feral.'

Logan laughed as the train passed a patch of dense forest. 'Yeah, something like that.'

'Oh, wow,' Cally breathed at tall ancient Scots pines. 'Look at those trees. They must be hundreds of years old. This is *stunning*.'

Logan nodded. 'The estate has been working on a project to protect and expand the forest. It's one of the things Uncle Reg is most proud of. Honestly, though, fair warning: don't even think about mentioning it to him because once he starts, he will chew your ear off about it. I'm surprised he hasn't already.'

'Actually, I'd quite like to hear about it.'

'I'm sure he'd be thrilled to enlighten you.'

Cally laughed. 'I'm going to be in my element here. I'm glad my coat was ready.'

'You're going to absolutely love this weekend. There's so much to explore on the estate.'

All Cally's doubts flew out the window. 'I'm looking forward to it now we're here.'

'There are miles of walking trails and some easy strolls around the loch, others go up into the hills for some spectacular views. There's one trail that winds up through the pine forest and then opens out onto a highland clearing. The view from up there is breathtaking. You can see for miles in every direction.'

Cally rubbed her hands together. 'Ooh, this is going to be such a good weekend. I can't wait to see it all.'

'Have you done fly fishing before?'

Cally raised an eyebrow. Of course she hadn't. There hadn't been many opportunities for Cally to do fly fishing. Funny that. Sometimes she did wonder if Logan had *any* clue at all what her childhood had encompassed. 'Fly fishing? No, I haven't. I'm not sure I'm posh enough for it,' Cally joked.

Logan laughed, shaking his head. 'Trust me, it's not about being posh. It's about patience and a lot of luck. There are some rare species of eagles, too.'

Cally's jaw dropped. 'Wow, eagles?'

Logan nodded. 'If we're lucky, we might spot one.'

As Logan continued to describe the estate, Cally got excited about the weekend. Leading up to leaving for Scotland, she'd thought about the whole affair simply as a family obligation that she'd have to suffer through with gritted teeth. Now, though, as the train weaved its way through the countryside, she felt herself start to relax. From the train window, it was pretty clear that she was about to have the opportunity to immerse herself in some of the most beautiful wilderness she'd ever seen. Bring that right on.

'There's a sunken garden on the estate. It's been there for centuries, and it's absolutely gorgeous at this time of year. The poppies will be out soon, too. Honestly, Blackcurrant, they'll take your breath away.'

'Nice. I think I'm going to have a weekend to remember if that is anything to go by.' Cally jerked her thumb at the scenery going past the window. The train passed through a glen and steep hills rose up on either side of the track. A small stream tumbled down a hillside and a little series of miniature water-falls glinted in the sun. 'It's like every few metres it gets more beautiful.'

Logan nodded. 'I forget how nice it is. It was a good idea of Cecilia's that we come on the train so that you would get to see this. It *is* pretty special up here.'

'Mmm, you're not wrong.'

'There's a local legend that says the glen we're passing through now is home to fairies.'

Cally turned to him, eyebrows raised. 'Fairies?'

'The old folks in the town swear by it. They say if you leave a dish of milk out on a full moon night, you might catch a glimpse of them dancing.'

Cally laughed, shaking her head. 'Now you're pulling my leg.'

Logan held up his hands. 'It's a legend. Whether or not it's true is another matter.'

'I suppose we'll just have to keep our eyes peeled for any mischievous fairies this weekend,' Cally said, playing along.

Logan joked, 'They're said to be fond of playing tricks on unsuspecting visitors.'

As they continued to chat and laugh, the train began to slow even further. Logan gestured out the window. 'We're nearly there now. You can just see the edge of the estate.'

Cally peered out. In the distance, she could make out a collection of buildings. A large, sprawling main house – if you could call such a grand structure a 'house' – built of grey stone that seemed to grow organically from the landscape. Turrets and chimneys rose against the sky, giving the whole place an air of old-money grandeur. 'It's enormous.'

Logan nodded. 'We won't be staying in the main house. I didn't want to bother with all that. I thought we'd be better off on our own. We'll be in one of the cottages on the estate.'

'Much more me, I think.'

'I just prefer it in one of the cottages.'

Cally gathered her phone and tucked it into the inside pocket of her Lovely coat, picked up her water bottle and put her handbag in the front pocket of her suitcase. As they rounded a final bend, an old white timber-clad Victorian station came into view. A platform stretched out before them, covered by a long, sloping roof supported by intricately detailed iron columns painted white. Cally squinted at the deep shade of green on the roof, its delicate wooden fretwork butted up to a central station building of grey stone and white-painted wood. Large, arched windows gleamed in the afternoon sun, an ornate clock tower rose from the centre of the building and little details here and there were painted in the same green as the roof.

Cally raised her eyebrows. 'And I thought the station at Lovely was nice. Wow, it's like stepping back in time looking at that. I can see I am going to love it here. It's beautiful. Is this really where we're getting off?'

'Yep. It used to be the royal station back in the day.'

'As in, for the *actual* royal family?'

'The very same.'

As the train came to a stop alongside the platform, Cally looked at hanging baskets overflowing with flowers, an immaculately kept waiting area with smooth stone flagstones, and a row of benches painted the same crisp white as the iron columns, their backs featuring an intricate design. She heaved her tote bag over her shoulder and clicked the handle up on her cabin bag. Logan grabbed the rest of their stuff and they prepared to disembark. Cally peered out the door where an old-fashioned luggage cart stood at the end of the platform, its wooden slats weathered but well-maintained, a vintage weighing machine with brass fittings gleamed in the sunlight and a huge old sign for the waiting room swung back and forth in a strong, cool breeze.

'We've travelled through time,' Cally said as they stepped off the train onto the platform. She inhaled crisp, clean air full of the scent of pine.

'Welcome to Scotland,' Logan chuckled. 'Let's pray to the weather gods because we will surely need prayers. It gets cold up here any time of the year.'

As they made their way along the platform, Cally looked up at lovely old iron rafters, the timber roof, and a series of information boards mounted on the wall. Each one detailed a different aspect of the station's history, complete with black-and-white photographs showing royal visits of years gone by.

She whipped her phone out and took a photo. 'I'll send this to Nancy. It'll make her laugh.'

'They certainly knew how to build things to last back then. This station must have weathered a lot of Scottish winters.'

Cally nodded at the thought of the Scottish winters. She loved winter, Christmas, and everything snow. She tried to imagine the whole scene sparkling in a dusting of white. From what she'd seen so far, she'd most definitely be coming back to see it in the flesh. She nodded to herself. This was going to be good. Really, really good. At least, that's what she thought.

11

After trundling through the station with their bags, Cally and Logan made their way outside. Just as Logan was pulling his phone out of his pocket, an old Land Rover more or less flew around the corner, bumped up onto the pavement, and a man with a bushy beard, green overalls, and a flat cap jumped out.

'Ah, young Logan!' the man called out, his Scottish accent thick and welcoming. 'Good to see you, lad. And this must be the lovely Cally we've heard so much about.'

Logan grinned, stepping forward to shake the man's hand. 'Cally, this is Angus. He's been the estate's gamekeeper for, well, forever, really. Is that right?'

'Aye, not quite forever.' Angus chuckled. 'Just the last wee fifty years or so. Lots more left in me yet.'

Cally smiled, held out her hand, and bantered, 'It's lovely to meet you, Angus. I hope people haven't been telling too many tales about me.'

Angus caught on immediately. His eyes twinkled. 'Only good things, lass. Only good things. Now, let's get you two up to the house. I'm sure you're ready for a wee rest after that long journey. Welcome to the Highlands. Where the wildlife is as breath-taking as the scenery and the weather keeps you on your toes...'

Cally beamed. 'I'm enchanted already, just by the train journey and the station.'

Angus's smile widened. 'Aye, it's a special place right enough. Has young Logan here told you about its royal connections?'

'He has,' Cally nodded. 'It's fascinating. I can't wait to learn more about it.'

Cally climbed into the back seat of the Land Rover as Logan and Angus popped their bags in the back. As the Land Rover pulled out of the station road, she gazed out the window while Logan and Angus chatted. In between chatting, Angus pointed out various landmarks and shared snippets of the little town's history as they made their way through the main street.

'And over there,' Angus gestured to a hill, 'that's where the old clan battles used to take place. They say on a quiet night, you can still hear the echo of the bagpipes carried on the wind.'

Cally leaned forward. 'Really? It's hard to imagine battles taking place in such a peaceful setting.'

Angus nodded. 'Aye, but that's the thing about this land. It's seen its share of troubles, but it endures.'

As they drove through a small town, Cally's eyes darted from one quaint shop front to another. Stone cottages with colourful gardens lined the streets, and everywhere she looked, there were reminders of the deep-rooted Scottish heritage. 'This is so nice.'

Logan smiled. 'It's a great place for a wander. There are some excellent little cafés and shops.'

As they left the town behind and the road began to wind its way into the countryside, the scenery got more and more majestic. Rounding a tight bend in the road, the main house came into full view. Cally swallowed. She really had moved up in the world. It was even more impressive in real life than what she'd seen via her laptop. A magnificent grey stone building with turrets reaching skywards sat on vast grounds. 'Wow, it's much bigger than I thought it was going to be.'

Logan chuckled. 'Wait till you see the inside. Thank goodness we're staying in one of the cottages.'

'Aye, a good thing too. The big house can be a bit draughty even at this time of year. The cottages are much cosier, in my humble opinion, but don't tell anyone I told you that. I saw you'd bagged the wee cottage, Logan. Well played.'

Cally tried to take it all in, not quite believing it was real. 'It's beautiful.'

Angus chuckled from the driver's seat. 'Aye, it's not a bad view, is it? When you see it at dawn, though. That's when the Highlands really show their true colours.'

As Angus brought the old Land Rover to a stop in front of a stone cottage, Cally snapped her seatbelt off and hopped out. Standing with her hands on her hips she took in a huge deep breath of crisp Highland air. The scent of pine and heather filled her lungs and she shook her head in disbelief. The air was incredible, the scenery mind-blowing, and the house in front of her was not what she would have called a "wee cottage". It was a substantial stone building with weathered grey walls speaking of centuries of history. Large windows reflected the lush greenery surrounding them, a dark slate weathered roof sloped overhead, and a door in the centre held a huge wreath woven with blue tartan and heather.

'This is what you call a cottage?' Cally laughed.

Logan chuckled. 'Welcome to the Highlands. They do everything differently up here.'

Gravel crunched under Cally's feet as she made her way to the front door. She put her hand on the stone wall and took in the patchwork of greys and soft browns. Little patches of lichen here and there added muted pops of pale green and yellow, and ivy climbed one corner of the building. Wide sash windows, painted a brilliant white, stood out against the rugged stonework. Gabled porches covered each of the doors, little fences lined a lush sloping lawn, and two gigantic potted plants sat on either side of the front steps. To the far left of the cottage, a white picket fence guarded a glass conservatory greenhouse which was nearly as big as the cottage itself. Beds lining either side of the conservatory door showcased flowers nodding their heads in the breeze, a plethora of lavender and rosemary bushes rustled to themselves, and in the far distance, ancient trees towered over the whole scene. Cally was a long, long, *long* way from the horrid '70s housing estate she'd once called home. She was never, ever, *ever* going back.

Leaving Angus and Logan chatting, Cally followed a path to the side of the house where she came to a small cottage garden with shrubs, beds and hedges on land gently sloping away in the direction of the main house. A small loch glimmered in the distance and a smaller conservatory sat just to the right. Taking a few stone steps down to a terrace surrounded by old walls where despite the cool air, the sun warmed Cally's face. She'd be having a glass of wine and taking in the view from the little spot, that she knew for a fact. The air in the garden seemed even fresher than when she'd first stepped off the train. She could taste it on her tongue, clean and pure. She took another deep breath, feeling as though she would never get enough of the Highland air. Her weekend away was looking up.

For a bit, she just stood very still, listened, and vacuumed up the view. A few birds sang here and there, leaves on the huge old trees rustled, there was a faint bubble of a stream somewhere and a hoot of an owl came from the direction of the forest. Unless she was imagining it, the scenery, sounds, and smells had already softened her edges.

She continued her circuit of the cottage, stopping here and there until she was back at the front where Logan was just finishing unloading their luggage from the Land Rover. He slammed the car door shut and smiled.

Angus came out of the cottage. 'Everything to your liking?'

Cally nodded enthusiastically. 'Oh yes. Absolutely. Thank you. It's exceptional.'

'It's a special wee place, right enough. Wait till you see it in the morning light. That's when it really shines. Sit out the back there with a nice tea and watch the whole place come to life before your eyes.'

Cally smiled. She would be doing that with Scottish bells on. She picked up her bag and nodded. She could get used to the Highland life.

12

C ally stepped into the front entrance, slipped her shoes off on the mat, and popped them in a panelled closet-cum-boot area directly to her right. Walking over the hallway, she pushed the door open to a sitting room and didn't quite know where to look first. She did know she wanted to hibernate under a tartan rug with a book and not come up for air for a very, very, very long time. Maybe for her whole life. A rich, earthy scent of wood and smoke mingled with beeswax, lavender, polish, and pine circled her. The smell seemed to whisper history and care and made her feel instantly at home. *Come to Mumma.* A beautiful old fireplace with an ornate wooden mantelpiece intricately carved with Scottish motifs dominated the far wall. A slightly wonky model sailboat with delicate fabric sails sat on top next to a carving of a deer's head. Beautiful old navy-blue tartan wallpaper lined the walls on either side of the fireplace and framed sketches of local scenes were dotted all over the place. A little Tiffany lamp to the left of the mantelpiece glowed, an ancient, slightly drunk-looking chandelier hung from the ceiling, and somewhat worn velvet cushions appeared to have been plonked on top of anything and everything that didn't move. Cally was in decorating and for that matter, life, heaven.

Moving further into the room, she stepped over a beautiful old rug and stood for a minute, taking in all the bits and bobs on the shelves beside the fireplace. Neatly stacked piles of leather-bound books, an old clock ticking away to itself, a variety of glass cloches displaying finds, an old bamboo birdcage, and depression-era glass scattered here and there. Overstuffed leather armchairs were perched on either side of the fireplace, and a deep peacock blue, slightly faded velvet sofa adorned with muted colour cushions beckoned for guests to sit and relax. She looked around with her chin dropped and counted five neatly folded tartan rugs in various blues and reds on the backs of chairs. The room spoke of heritage, Scotland, and comfiness all at the same time.

'Oh, my,' she whispered to herself. 'I could get used to this.'

She ran her fingers along the mantelpiece and looked up at an imposing stag portrait hanging above. Its antlers reached towards the ceiling, and she wondered who had painted it. Oh, to be able to paint.

Logan came in and stood beside her. 'All good? What do you think? Do you think you'll be okay here? I thought you'd prefer it to being at the house.'

'Will I be okay? Oh, wait, I'll just think about that. I love it, duh.'

Logan looked relieved. 'I thought you might like it.'

Cally turned, plonked herself down, and sank into one of the overstuffed armchairs. 'It's so cosy and, I don't know, rich and warm at the same time. Like being wrapped in a hug or something. It's just so… what is the word? Comfy. Quiet too.' She pointed to the bookshelves lining the walls, the stacks of magazines, and neat rows of old encyclopaedias. 'I could just stay right here all weekend and read. I don't even need to go out.'

Logan nodded. 'I think some of those have been in the family for generations.'

'I bet.'

Logan moved towards the door. 'Tea? I'll put the kettle on.'

'I'd love one. I need a cup of tea after that long journey. I don't want to move from this chair, though. It's so cosy in here.'

As Logan disappeared into the kitchen, Cally took in every inch around her – the gorgeous tartan wallpaper, the little details here and there, and the lovely throws neatly folded on the backs of the chairs. The sound, or lack thereof of the place, as if somehow the room was insulated from the real world. The old clock on the mantelpiece ticked away to itself, about the only sound she could hear.

A few minutes later, Logan returned with a tray with two mugs, a steaming teapot, and a plate piled with what looked like homemade shortbread. He popped the tray down on the coffee table, and Cally leant forward and raised her eyebrows. 'Just what I need.'

'A proper Scottish welcome for you.'

Cally inhaled the buttery scent of the shortbread. Her mouth watered. 'Ooh, I love shortbread. Homemade?'

Logan poured the tea. 'Mrs MacPherson, the housekeeper, made it according to the note out there. It's her speciality – an old family recipe, apparently.'

Cally took a sip of tea. 'Ahh. Tea, shortbread, and feet up. We'll just stay put here for the whole weekend, eh? You can serve me shortbread for breakfast, lunch and dinner.'

Logan eyerolled. 'No such luck. We have the family dinner tomorrow night and various other things to go to. A family trip to the pub is always on the cards. What else do you fancy doing?'

'Ha, not much. I could sit right here and do nothing but stuff my face with shortbread, get cosy under a tartan rug and read all day long.'

'Works for me.'

'Joking. I'd love to explore. It looks absolutely stunning out there. What's the weather forecast for tomorrow?'

'Good, I think. We could pack a picnic and make a day of it if you like.'

'I don't mind, really. Up to you.' Cally smiled, reached for a piece of shortbread, took a bite and widened her eyes in surprise. 'Oh my goodness, this is amazing. I might need Mrs MacPherson's recipe before we leave.'

Logan laughed. 'Good luck with that. Her recipes are guarded as if they're state secrets.'

Cally sat back in the chair and sipped her tea. 'So, what sort of wildlife might we see?'

'There are deer in the hills, and as I said, if we're lucky, we might see some eagles. They nest in the crags up there. Otters, red squirrels in the woods.'

'It all sounds so magical. It's *much* better than I thought it was going to be. You really undersold this "cottage" as you call it. Logan, it's just *so* nice.'

Logan took another piece of shortbread. 'I was a bit worried you might find it all a bit, well, remote and boring. It's quite different from Lovely Bay.'

Cally shook her head emphatically. 'It's like stepping into another world. A quieter, wilder world.'

'You wait until we go walking.'

'It feels restorative already, or am I just imagining it? Do I sound odd? It's just much, much better than I thought it was going to be.'

Logan nodded. 'Yup. That's why I love coming up here.'

Cally tucked her feet under her, leant forward, and took another slice of shortbread. 'Hello to a weekend of relaxing. No work and no blasted chatbot customers. Hooray.'

'There is one thing we should probably discuss, though. The family dinner tomorrow night.'

'What should I expect?'

'It's a bit of a tradition when any of us come up to the estate. Nothing too fancy, but put it this way – there won't be any chowder.'

'Right. Who will be there that I don't know?'

'My cousin James and his wife Sarah will be there. They might bring their kids. Let's see, who else? Ah, Aunt Agatha will probably be there. Just nod and smile, and you'll be fine. I'm not sure who else but there'll be quite a few of us.'

'Right.'

'It's usually just family when we're up here. Though fair warning – Aunt Agatha will go on about her stamp collection. It's her pride and joy.'

'Noted.'

'And then of course we have the delightful Alastair. Mum, Cecilia, and Reg.'

'Is Alastair bringing Octavia?'

Logan nodded. 'Yep. They're practically inseparable these days. It's all happened quickly.'

'It has.'

Logan took a sip of his tea. 'Alastair's already talking about rings.'

Cally nearly choked on her shortbread. 'Rings? As in engagement rings? But they've only been dating for a while.'

'You know Alastair. When he sets his mind on something, he doesn't hang about. I guess he's no spring chicken these days. Doesn't want to hang around getting shrivelled is what he said.'

Cally shook her head in disbelief. 'Wow. That's quite something. And Octavia? How does she feel about all this?'

Logan shrugged. 'From what I can tell, she's just as keen. They seem to be very much on the same page. Remember when I had dinner with them the other week when you were feeling poorly? He mentioned it then. Sorry, I completely forgot to tell you.'

Cally sat back, processing this information. She'd met Alastair's partner Octavia a few times at various events in London and at the manor, and while she'd found her pleasant enough, she hadn't warmed to her much. 'Octavia's from quite an old family, isn't she?' Cally asked, trying to keep her tone casual.

Logan nodded. 'The Fitzwilliams. They've got estates all over England. Octavia's father is an Earl.'

Cally felt the familiar flutter of insecurity in her stomach. 'Right. Of course. Because everyone has an Earl for a father.'

Logan raised his eyebrows. 'Ouch.'

Cally sighed. 'Sorry. I forget how different your world is from mine. Earls and estates and whirlwind romances. Honestly, it really is very different. I'm still getting used to it…'

'We've had this conversation. Don't even go there. Your world, my world – whatever.'

Cally internally rolled her eyes. It was alright for *him* to say that. 'I know. I don't want to go down that road again, but yeah…'

'I get it.'

Cally nodded. *You really don't*, she said in her head.

Logan continued. 'I'm pretty sure Octavia feels the same way sometimes. She might come from an old family, but she's still finding her feet, just like you.'

'Really? She always seems so composed and…' Cally wanted to add "full of herself" but didn't. There wasn't any point. She'd keep Octavia at arm's length and leave it at that. She searched for a word. 'Calm.'

Logan chuckled. 'I reckon it's all an act. The story goes that she's been head over heels for Alastair for years and now she's got her chance. She hates the stuffiness of her upbringing, apparently. I think that's part of why she and Alastair get on so well. I think he enjoys shocking the Fitzwilliams with his casual approach to, well, everything.'

Cally raised an eyebrow. 'And Octavia's okay with that?'

'From what Alastair's told me, he's giving her permission to be herself, in a way.'

Cally nodded slowly. 'Right.'

'So don't worry too much about Octavia being some sort of aristocratic ice queen. Maybe you can form a secret society for partners trying to navigate the madness of the Henry-Hicks family gatherings.'

Cally laughed. There was no way she was going to be even thinking about doing something like that. Maybe at some point she'd be friends with Octavia but really she couldn't see it. She'd keep her distance, be civil and friendly but not get too close. 'Ha. Yeah.'

'So, that's it really. The dinner is the least interesting bit of this weekend, but it is what it is. Has to be done.'

'I'm sure it'll be fine.' Cally answered as she leant forward and helped herself to more shortbread. She hoped the dinner would be fine, but mostly, she was just happy that these days she was actually not *absolutely terrified* of the social gatherings of those with the surname Henry-Hicks. She was sure that she could survive a formal dinner. Couldn't she?

13

Cally opened her eyes, realised she wasn't in her flat, heard nothing much but the sound of silence, and remained dead still for a minute or two. She looked around at her unfamiliar surroundings and glanced at an antique clock on the bedside table. Its hands showed it was just past five in the morning. As usual, because of her regular early morning shifts on the chatbot, her internal body clock had woken her much earlier than she would have preferred. Beside her, she could hear Logan's breathing and feel his chest rising and falling in a steady rhythm. Careful not to wake him, she slipped out of bed, pulled the cable out of the bottom of her phone, winced as ancient floorboards creaked under her feet, and tiptoed to the door. Pausing with her hand on an old enamel door handle she glanced back at Logan, as deep in sleep, he shifted and turned over.

On the stairs, a lovely, thick tartan runner felt cosy under her bare feet, and the air on the landing was cool as she held onto the handrail and made her way as quietly as she could down the stairs. Rubbing the side of her arms as goosebumps appeared, she grabbed Logan's hoodie that was draped over the banister, pulled it on, yanked down the sleeves over her hands, and breathed in the Logan smell. Yes please.

As she made her way down the stairs, each step made a funny little groan as if the actual boards themselves were calling out in protest at the early hour. Cally imagined the wood underneath the tartan runner worn smooth by generations of feet on their way down to the first floor. As she got to the bottom in the dark, the cottage was veering dangerously close to the spooky side. The whole place was eerily quiet, the only sound the soft ticking of the grandfather clock in the hall, the distant call of an early-rising bird, and the hum of the fridge freezer coming from the open kitchen door.

Once in the kitchen, she clicked the door closed behind her, fumbled for the lamp switches on a stripped pine dresser and blinked as the little wicker lamps filled the room with a glow. Just like the rest of the cottage the kitchen held an amalgamation of bits and bobs that resulted in a cosy, homely, chucked-together feel. A charming mix of old and new sat together quite happily resulting in Cally feeling instantly at home. Whoever had added the new touches had got it right. A lovely old Aga in the corner, a gleaming modern fridge sitting comfortably alongside well-worn wooden countertops, vintage crockery next to a brand spanking new coffee machine and a deep original Belfast sink. She filled the kettle and put it on to boil and stood looking out the window not really focusing on anything at all. As the kettle bubbled the sound of it getting to boiling point interrupted the pre-dawn silence. As she waited, she continued to gaze out at the garden where the estate was shrouded in a thick, low to the ground swirling mist which appeared to be resting on top of the grass. The huge foggy cloud was doing a very good job of muting all colour and sound and adding to the slightly spooky feel. The kettle clicked off, she made a mug of tea, popped milk in the top, gave it a slow stir, and then stood with her hands wrapped around the mug and leant against the back door. Deciding she wanted to go out and stand in the mist, she winced as a loud click filled the quiet kitchen as she turned an old iron key in the lock. Swinging the door open with a creak, a rush of cool, damp air carried an earthy scent of wet grass, heather, fog and pine. Divine.

Cally stepped out onto a small stone patio area. The rough texture of flagstones beneath her bare feet felt cold compared to the wooden floors inside. She stood for a bit by the edge of the lawn, blowing on her tea, and taking in the ethereal landscape around her. The thick heavy mist hung in the air, an outline of ancient trees loomed in the distance, and closer to the house, tended flowerbeds were barely visible under their shroud of fog. Flowers appeared as muted smudges of colour in the dawn light and she could see a couple of lights on over at the main house. Tiny little droplets of mist appeared to cling to her skin and hair. She could taste the mist on her tongue as she stood there, wrapped in Logan's hoodie lost in contemplation.

About ten minutes later, nearly at the end of her tea, she squinted as a movement in the trees caught her eye. Suddenly realising she was not alone, she didn't move or take her eyes off a beautiful deer as it got closer. Deciding it might like a better look at Cally, the deer then stood perfectly still at the edge of the garden, so motionless that for a moment Cally wondered if she was imagining it. Then, as if sensing her gaze and thoughts, the deer turned its head, regarded Cally as if she had no right to be there, turned and melted back into the mist as silently as it had appeared. Cally sighed, blinked and shook her head. It felt so unreal she hardly believed what her own eyes had just told her she'd seen. Unreal and so very nice.

After making another cup of tea, pulling a tartan rug from the back of the sofa in the sitting room, then grabbing a tin of shortbread and sitting out on the terrace, she was so engrossed in the view and the sounds of the estate that she didn't hear Logan until he appeared around the corner of the back door.

Logan smiled and raised his eyebrows. 'Morning.'

'Oh, morning. How did you sleep?'

'Like a log. You?'

'Same.'

'You were up early.'

'I know.' Cally gestured to the scenery. 'I've been sitting out here thinking and putting the world to rights.'

'Enjoying the view?'

'I've never seen anything like it. Angus said it's amazing in the morning and he wasn't joking.'

'Yup. I used to love getting up early when I was a kid, just to watch the mist clear. Never gets old.'

Cally nodded. 'I saw a deer. It was right there at the edge of the garden. I'm still not sure if I was seeing things or not.'

'Legend has it that seeing a deer at dawn is lucky.'

Cally giggled. 'Would this legend happen to be one you've just made up? Like the fairy thing?'

Logan's eyes twinkled. 'I would never. It's an ancient Highland tradition. Passed down through generations of Henry-Hicks.'

'Ancient tradition, my left foot. Next you'll be telling me that the Loch Ness Monster is real and she takes her tea with two sugars.'

Logan grinned. 'Well, now that you mention it...'

'Tea?' Cally asked.

'I'll do it. Do you want another one?'

'A third tea for me? Oh, go on then. You twisted my arm.'

'You just sit there and soak up the magic of the place. This weekend you're doing nothing.'

Cally nodded. She liked the idea of that indeed. It had been a long time since she'd spent her time doing nothing. So long that she didn't even know what it felt like to just sit back and not worry. She tutted to herself as she thought about how she hadn't really been that bothered about the trip to Scotland. In fact, she'd dismissed it a little bit. How utterly wrong she'd been. Her perspective so far told her that trying new stuff, going new places and experiencing other ways of the world was a positive. What she didn't know; that thing called life had a few other things waiting for her just around the corner.

14

Cally had traded her usual uniform of short skirt and ballet flats for jeans and wellies. She also had one of Logan's cashmere jumpers over her shoulders and a green estate travel mug with hot blackcurrant in her hand. The weather in Scotland performed. A clear blue sky with a scattering of puffy white clouds topped the beauty of the landscape. Her funny stick-y out-y fine baby blonde hair was scrunched up on top of her head in a clip and she had not a scrap of make-up on her face, just how she liked it. As she stomped along a path lined with heather, it was an understatement to say that our Cally loved the Scottish version of Lovely Manor. She didn't just love it. An odd little part of her felt as if she was at home. Strange, but true.

As she walked along, lost in the spectacular scenery, it hit Cally how little she'd travelled. Like just about everything in her adolescent and young adult life, her care role had put paid to travelling around the world or anywhere at all, really. She'd not travelled for many reasons but mostly because there hadn't been anyone else to take over the responsibility of her caring job, not enough money and even less time. Now, with hindsight, it felt worse.

To somehow try and make herself feel better about her sheltered life, she'd always half-heartedly told herself that she'd not really wanted to travel anyway, so what did it matter? To negate the premise that she might be missing out, she'd staunchly maintained that she liked staying put right where she was. She'd reiterated until she was blue in the face and had actually perceived it to be true that travelling was for other people; those who weren't like her. She'd made herself believe that she probably wouldn't like exploring anyway. That other places wouldn't be nice and she'd be out of her comfort zone. She'd fed herself the same old, tired narrative so many times that she'd actually come to believe it in the end. She'd managed to make it through most of her life not going anywhere much because the story she'd told herself had clipped her wings. Now, her wings were spreading. By way of a Scottish estate, Cally de Pfeffer could feel herself flying high. Could she, in fact, give an eagle a run for its money? She'd have a damn good try.

As she walked along, blown away by the breathtaking scenery and loving the different far-reaching views, the change of outlook did her the world of good. She felt as if someone had picked her up by the top of her head, swiftly zoomed her up to the other end of the country and put her down again in a completely different environment altogether. Somewhere outstandingly beautiful that was making her reassess her life and existence. Our gorgeous Cally was experiencing that wonderful, almost discombobulating feeling of clarity when away from day-to-day life. It was breathing new energy into her left, right and centre.

As she pounded along, things floated and percolated through her brain. Her relationship with Logan and what she wanted from it, her job in the chemist and the promotion opportunity and whether or not she was going to accept it, applying for a mortgage, deciding whether or not to move in with Logan, looking for a flat. All of it whirred through her head as she walked along, taking in more beautiful scenery every which way she turned. She stopped for a minute and looked up at the ancient trees above and watched their tops swaying gently in the breeze. The whole area seemed to be slowly undulating and moving to its own little beat and somehow whispering to her at the same time. She blinked and shook her head as it went through her mind that the trees were having a conversation with her. Saying hello. She smiled and said hello back.

Half an hour later, making her way back in the direction of the cottage, she stopped outside the large conservatory greenhouse situated just along from the house and peered in. The beautiful old glass building with its old-fashioned panes, tall doors, and roof with gorgeous old fretwork appeared from the outside so perfect that it looked almost unreal. However, on peering in, it was more than obvious that the conservatory was very much a working part of the estate. Long lines of timber benches held various pots with plants at different stages of growth. An old copper watering system ran along the top of the roof, and on the left hand side, rows of luscious plants in hanging baskets stretched from front to back. Masses of terracotta seedling pots lined up by the windows held plant babies leaning towards the light, and line upon line of seed trays filled with soil were labelled with little wooden sticks.

As Cally peered into the conservatory, she squinted against the glare of the sun on the glass and made out a woman in green dungarees, with her hair pulled back in a ponytail under a green estate baseball cap. The woman looked up, catching Cally's eye through the window.

'Hi,' the woman called out, her voice muffled through the glass. She made her way to the door, its old hinges creaked, and the bottom scraped along the floor as she pulled it open. 'You must be Logan's Cally. I'm Morag; head gardener is my official title here at the estate. Or HOG for Head of Gardening. Really, it's a fancy title for the fact that I get to mess around with plants all day.'

Cally smiled, extending her hand. 'Lovely to meet you. Yes, I'm Cally. I hope I'm not interrupting anything.'

Morag waved away Cally's concern with a soil-stained hand. 'Not at all, lass. I was just tending to the seedlings up the back there. Would you like to come in and have a look around?'

'Oh, I'd love to. It's so nice.'

As Cally followed Morag into the conservatory, she was hit by warm, humid air, totally in contrast to the crisp, fresh Scottish day outside. The scent of damp earth, greenery, and growing things enveloped her as she followed Morag down a narrow path between benches overloaded with plants on the far side. The masses of plants reminded her of the few pots of herbs she'd bought from B & Q and tended on her windowsill back in Lovely Bay. And she'd thought she was a gardener. Hilarious.

Cally didn't know where to look first. From the outside, the conservatory had looked *fairly* impressive. From the inside, it was much bigger than it appeared and a whole different ball game altogether. 'This is incredible.' Cally said almost to herself as she took in the rows of plants in various stages of growth. Everywhere she looked plants, cuttings, hanging baskets and shrubs jostled for space. 'I've never seen anything like it.'

Morag beamed. 'Aye, it's a special place, this. It's been part of the estate for generations. The original structure was built in the 1850s, though we've made a few upgrades since then. Every time I come in here, I just get lost and enter a whole other world.'

Cally ran her hand along one of the timber benches, feeling the smooth surface worn by years of use. She peered up above at an extensive pulley system engineering the opening of the windows in the roof. 'It's amazing that it's still standing after all this time.'

'Oh, these old buildings are tougher than they look,' Morag chuckled. 'But you're right; it takes a fair bit of upkeep. We had to replace most of the glass about a decade ago, but we kept as much of the original structure as we could. The elements up here make things work for their keep. This old place just keeps on going. Even in the winter, it's gorgeous in here what with its own heating system and all. Can't complain.'

As they turned at the end and walked along the central aisle, Morag pointed out various cuttings. She gestured to a row of small, leafy plants. 'These are herbs for the kitchen. Rosemary, thyme, basil – all grown right here on the estate. We dry them now too and they're sold in a shop in town. We have another lot of greenhouses on the far side, too. This one here is good because of its position. They knew what they were doing when they built this. Someone had their head screwed on the right way around.'

Cally inhaled the scent of the herbs, closed her eyes for a second and felt a bit pathetic about the few straggly pots on her balcony. 'I bet they taste amazing fresh from the garden. I have a few at home. I snip them into things, and it's been an eye-opener. Nothing like this, though, obviously.'

'That they do,' Morag agreed. 'The cook swears by them. Says they're what makes her cooking so special.'

They moved on to another section, where long lines of larger plants were growing in thick old terracotta pots marked with time and age. Morag pointed to another long bench. 'These are some of our medicinal plants. We've been growing them here for centuries. Some of these plants have literally passed down through the generations.'

'Medicinal plants? Like what?'

'Oh, all sorts. Chamomile for sleeplessness, peppermint for digestion, and echinacea for all sorts. Lavender, stevia, borage, and suchlike. Anything and everything. You name it, we've tried to grow it.'

Cally nodded, impressed. 'It's like having your own little pharmacy right here in the garden.'

Morag smiled. 'That's exactly what it is. In the old days places like this were essential, apparently. Some of the people of the house would often act as the local healers, using plants grown right here in the conservatory.' Morag nodded. 'Yeah, I read all about it in one of the books in the library there.'

As they continued the little impromptu tour, Cally couldn't quite get enough. Fascinated by the history and knowledge embedded in the glass structure, she could feel her wings spreading just that little bit more. Fly high, our Cally, fly. 'Amazing how plants are medicinal when you think about it.'

Morag nodded. 'Aye, that's it exactly. Medicine's come a long way, but there's still wisdom in these old ways, I reckon.'

'For sure.'

Pointing to a large plant tucked in the corner, Morag smiled. 'This is my fave. A cutting from a plant that's been in the family for over two hundred years. Legend has it that it was a gift from a visiting member of royalty from faraway lands.'

Cally's eyes widened. 'What kind of plant is it?'

'A type of rose,' Morag explained. 'Doesn't look like much now, but when it blooms... Well, you've never seen anything like it. The flowers are a deep, deep red, almost black in some lights. And the scent is like nothing else on earth.'

'Ooh, how interesting. I'd love to see it in bloom.'

'Well, if you're lucky, you might just catch it. Keep your eyes peeled.'

As they made their way back towards the entrance, Cally loved it. The conservatory had caught her eye when they'd arrived, but now she'd been inside and chatted to Morag, it felt so much more than just a pretty glass building, almost as if it was breathing goodness, history and tradition. Helping her to spread her wings.

'Nice job you have.' Cally smiled.

'I've had worse jobs in my life.' Morag chuckled.

'Oh really. So, you've not always worked here?' Cally asked.

'No, no. Gosh, no, I've done some dead-end jobs in my time.'

'Oh right.'

'I moved up here about twenty years ago. Best thing I ever did.'

'Ahh. Where did you move from? I thought I heard a twang of a different accent.'

Morag sucked air in through her teeth. 'No one can ever place me by my accent. I was born in London, then raised in Suffolk, then we moved to Cheshire, then Somerset and then via an ad in a magazine, I found myself here. And I've never looked back and I won't be going back anytime soon. Not ever.'

'Aww. Nice story.'

'You?'

Cally chuckled. 'Nothing quite as exciting as that. I've lived, worked and mostly stayed in the same county my whole life.'

Morag clucked. 'Right you are. So the trip up here is a good place to start your travelling bug, eh?'

'Indeed. I loved it from the moment the train crossed the border.'

'It happens.'

'Thank you so much for showing me around. It's been fascinating.'

'My pleasure. Just pop in whenever. We'll have a nice wee cup of tea, Scottish Breakfast, of course.' Morag pointed in the direction of the far corner. 'That's a little suntrap down there. Lovely to bring in a cup of tea and look out over the gardens while you toast your skin. Let me tell you, sometimes if you sit there it's so warm you might as well be in Marbella, or so I kid myself.'

'Ha, I might have to take you up on that.'

Morag chuckled. 'Be my guest.'

As Cally stepped back out into the crisp air, she looked up at the glass panes glinting in the sunlight and felt her wings spread. She'd be taking a nice cup of tea back to the conservatory to enjoy the little spot in greenhouse Marbella that she knew for sure.

15

Cally and Logan had been out for another long walk
around the estate. In fact, since the moment they'd
stepped out of the Land Rover when they'd arrived, they hadn't
left the grounds. Cally had seen little point in going anywhere
when there was so much on her doorstep. As far as she was
concerned, she was more than happy to stay put and spend her
long weekend in Scotland doing nothing but taking in the beautiful scenery and drinking in the fresh, restorative air. Easy to
please and all that. Cheap at half the price, too.

They were on their way to the main house, where Logan's
aunt Cecilia was having tea in the kitchen. Unlike the day
before, which had been bright and sunny, the weather was over-
cast but not cold. Cally and Logan's tramp across the estate,
around the loch and through the forest on the far side, had left
both of them with their jumpers off and enjoying the beauty of
the outdoors.

After going through the estate's very impressive sunken
garden, they walked past the front portico with its wide steps
up to a huge oak door and strolled past the windows to the

main hall. Cally peered in as they went past to see a large fire-place with an ornately carved dark wood mantel and a framed picture of some family member or another, which was nearly as big as her whole flat. Going around the back and stopping to have a look at what was growing, Logan then opened a green side door to a long, narrow utility room packed to the rafters with picnic baskets, outdoor weather gear, cool boxes, old oars, and lanterns. Stuff to facilitate a life outdoors was crammed into every nook and cranny. Amongst green Barbour gear, a fair few of the navy-blue Lovely coats were hung by their hoods, fishing rods were stacked up in the corner, rubber waders were lined up by another door, and waterproofs of all shapes and sizes were jammed onto brass hooks here, there and everywhere.

Squeezing past a rack of fishing rods and a battered old gun cabinet, Cally followed Logan through a tall, narrow door into an inner utility room clearly more for household use. Warm, indoor air scented with lavender, a clean floor smell, and centuries of tradition filled her nose. Using her right foot to lever her welly boot from her left foot, Cally yanked it off, did the same with the other one and then handed her boots to Logan who placed them neatly on a worn double-width mat by the door next to his own. The room was dominated by a large Belfast sink in the centre, its white porcelain surface marked with signs of years of use. Above it, a Sheila's Maid clothes airer hung from the ceiling laden with damp tea towels and dish-cloths. The faint hum of a washing machine provided a back-ground noise punctuated by the occasional gurgle of pipes and a radio somewhere in the distance played happily away to itself.

Cally loved how it felt like a second home and looked around the cramped space where any and every outdoor gear item possible was crammed onto shelves, hooks, and hanging from the high ceilings. Three of the walls were lined with wooden pegs, each one weighed down with tweed jackets, waterproofs, and the occasional kilt. In one corner, a stack of welly boots, their rubber surfaces caked with dried mud, lined up on a long, wide coir mat printed with the estate emblem. In little timber cubby holes, leather Chelsea boots were stacked neatly and along a row of brass hooks, printed baseball caps, tweed flat caps, and wide-brimmed felt hats jockeyed for position.

'Quite the collection,' Cally remarked, running her hand along the sleeve of a Lovely wax jacket. 'I know where to come if it starts to rain. Oh, wait, no, I have my own coat now, ha!'

Logan chuckled. 'You should see it during the winter. You can barely move in here for all the tweed.'

Cally imagined how pretty it would be at the estate in the winter. 'Hopefully, I'll be coming back. I love the cold months. It must be beautiful up here.'

As they stepped through into a large kitchen, a rush of warmth hit Cally square in the face. The kitchen was enormous, easily the size of her entire flat back in Lovely Bay, and like the kitchen in the cottage, a lovely blend of old and new. A massive old Aga range with a dark green enamel surface gleamed in light streaming in through tall, heavily curtained windows. All manner of pots and pans hung from a rack above a square scrubbed pine table, its surface scarred and stained from years of use. A jumble of mismatched chairs surrounded the table, and a gigantic enamel pitcher full of heather was plonked in the centre. The kitchen and the table spoke of cosy family meals and gatherings in the warmth after a long day outdoors. On the far wall, a few modern appliances under a commercial stainless steel surface juxtaposed an aged exposed brick wall. A very fancy-looking shiny Italian coffee machine sat next to a white KitchenAid mixer beside a jumble of what looked to Cally like homemade preserves. Somehow, it all worked together; it was functional, cosy, and oh-so-homey all at the same time. Cally loved it.

Cecilia, wearing green wax trousers, a cream Aran jumper, and a navy tartan scarf, smiled.

Logan greeted. 'Aunt Cici. We're back. You're rugged up!'

'Ah, there you are! I've been sitting still getting chilly. I was beginning to think you'd got lost out there. I wasn't sure whether my message had come through or not, seeing as there's no reception in that part of the estate.'

Logan whipped out his phone and frowned. 'Oh, sorry, I didn't see that.'

Cecilia shook her head. 'Maybe it arrived as you got a signal.'

'Yep.'

'Have a seat. You must be parched after your walk. I've just put the kettle on.'

As they settled around the table, Cally got lost in the kitchen. Like the kitchen at Lovely Manor and Logan's cottage, it screamed old money, oozed good taste, and something no amount of cash could buy. Old, well-worn wooden worktops scarred with life sat on top of handmade cupboards, and a collection of mismatched mugs hung from hooks beneath painted cream-white cabinets. Above the Aga, a massive copper hood dominated the wall, its surface patinated with age, and hanging from a rack beneath it, an impressive array of pots and pans, sizes ranging from tiny milk pans and small saucepans to enormous stock pots, which looked as if they'd been there forever. Perhaps they had. Deep window sills housed pot after pot of herbs, pump dispensers of hand cream, jugs stuffed full of dried heather, and everything and anything else in between. A gorgeous, jumbly curation of family and holidays and happy mess. A conglomeration of things Cally had sorely missed.

At the far end of the kitchen, a massive fireplace took up nearly an entire wall. Cally imagined it at Christmas, crackling with a fire and a real fir garland from the trees outside draped across its top. From heavy beams over her head, huge bunches of drying herbs and strings of onions and garlic added to the homely feel and smell. Tucked to the left of the table, a large dresser housed an eclectic collection of crockery. Chunky pottery mugs, delicate china teacups, and terracotta pots shared space with sturdy earthenware bowls.

As Logan chatted to Cecilia about the family gathering later that evening, Cally sat with her chin on her hand, taking in the little details of the kitchen. Every surface, nook, cranny and space seemed to hold some interesting object or tool. It was as if various people had used the kitchen at various times and left a little bit of themselves behind. Ancient biscuit cutters hung from a wire rack, a collection of wooden spoons their handles smoothed by years of use stood in a ceramic jug next to the Aga, and a huge stack of old-fashioned mixing bowls looked as if it might topple and smash on the floor at any given time.

Cally shook her head. 'This is such a beautiful kitchen. It feels so lived-in and cosy. I could curl up on that rug there and have a nap.'

Cecilia laughed. 'Oh, it is. That and the air outside does it to you. Let me tell you, though, this kitchen's seen more drama than a soap opera. Meals cooked, arguments had, celebrations enjoyed, tears, laughter – it's all happened right here. I don't think we've had a death yet, so... not in my time, anyway.' The kettle whistled from the Aga. Cecilia lifted it off and poured boiling water into a large Brown Betty teapot. 'Milk, no sugar, isn't it?' She said to Cally.

'Just a splash of milk, please.'

'So, Cally,' Cecilia said as she put a steaming mug of tea in front of her. 'How are you finding it up here in this neck of the woods?'

Cally wrapped her hands around the mug. 'Much better than

I thought it was going to be. No wonder you all love it so much. It's absolutely beautiful. I've never seen anywhere quite like it.'

Cecilia beamed. 'It *is* rather special, isn't it? Been in the family for generations, this place. Originally, like a long, long time ago, it started out as just a small hunting lodge, if you can believe it.'

'Really? How did it end up like this?'

Cecilia sat down. 'It all started back in the day. You'll have to go to the library and have a look at some of the old photos.'

As Cecilia launched into the tale of the estate, Cally's tiny spare box room study at her grandma's house flashed in front of her eyes. She realised that the room she'd sat in where she'd logged her uni assignments was not much bigger than the fireplace at the end of the table. She remembered how bitterly cold it had been in the early hours as she'd tried to focus. She was so far from her little life in that tiny room it didn't even feel possible. Cecilia got up to refill the teapot and Cally squinted at a collection of photographs on the wall near the Aga; a mishmash of old and new, some in faded sepia tones, others in colour. 'I love all the old photos.'

'They're a family timeline. That one is Logan's distant relative...'

'Not the story about the bagpipes again, Aunt Cici.'

Cecilia laughed. 'I'll save that for later, then. When we've all had a few whiskies.'

For a moment, Cally felt a pang of something – envy, jealousy, bitterness, or all of the above. She wasn't quite sure what it was, but it didn't feel that nice. A wistful sort of longing. These people lived a life that seemed gilded. Nothing bad ever seemed to happen. Nothing went wrong, or at least that's how it felt to her. Her own family history was so different. Apart from the actual class differences, which were so very far apart, her daily life had been much more fragmented and, to be frank, not that pleasant at all. No cosy, rosy, posy chats around a beautiful kitchen fireside in our Cally's world. Bed hoists, mental health issues, and liquid diets more like. She sucked it up just as she always did and pushed her horrid thoughts aside. There was nothing she could do about the past. Nothing she could change. Onwards and upwards was really the only path she could take. At least the path nowadays was on its way to somewhere nice. She really hoped it stayed on track.

16

The next day, Cally had spent a few dreamy hours tucked up on the sofa with a book she'd found on a shelf next to the dresser in the kitchen. Logan had popped down to the local pub with Alastair for some much-needed catch-up time. Cally had been more than happy not to go and had not required much persuasion to snuggle up in the sitting room and do her own thing. With her companion being a hot chocolate with marsh-mallows on top and rather too many shortbread biscuits she had cocooned herself in not doing anything apart from switching her body into recharge mode. After a long time working three jobs, it had been a long time coming. The rest and relaxation by way of the gorgeous estate air and under-stated luxury of the cottage suited her well. She could get used to the life.

After lazing on the sofa and getting lost in the book, she proceeded to wallow in the bath with Scottish bath salts hand-made in the local town, no less. Now, she was standing in front of a long mirror in the bedroom in her underwear, trying to decide between the two outfits she'd brought for the family dinner. From what she'd gathered, the dinner was not quite a spaghetti bolognese on a tray in front of the telly kind of affair. Oh no. It was an occasion where one dressed up in a nice frock and shiny shoes. To give her a choice on the night, she'd brought a simple little black dress in a soft crepe with a slash neck and half sleeves and a pair of heavy satin trousers with a plain velvet jacket with a nipped-in waist and beautiful cut. She put the dress on, looked out at the mist rolling in from the hills, felt as if she was going to be too chilly, took the dress off, and pulled on the trousers. Topping them with a pretty high-neck blouse with a ruffle, she shoved the jacket over the top and critically analysed the result. Standing back from the mirror, she tilted her head as she assessed her reflection. She would probably only ever admit it to herself, but she wasn't half bad. The trousers were classy and a nice change from her usual tights and skirt scenario, and the velvet jacket added a touch of luxury that felt appropriate for a family dinner at a Scottish estate. She'd done well.

Not bad, de Pfeffer, she said in her head, as she smoothed down the front of the jacket. *Cinderella will go to the ball.*

Dabbing a few blobs of foundation on her skin, she patted it in with a foundation brush, swiped a chunky black eyeshadow across her top lid, and added a load of mascara, some high-lighter, and a nice pale pink lipstick. As she blended, she could hear the sound of Logan, returning from the pub, downstairs. Just as she was finishing up with another layer of mascara, Logan came through the bedroom door. His eyes widened as he took in Cally's appearance.

'Wow, you look incredible, Blackcurrant. I like it very much.' Logan laughed and joked.

Cally blushed. Inside, she was delighted by his reaction. 'Thanks. It's not too much?'

Logan shook his head. 'Not at all. Just right. It's perfect.

However, I might have to keep a close eye on you. You can't trust this lot.'

Cally laughed at the same time remembering when Logan's ex-wife had relished in informing her how the Henry-Hicks men were known to wander. 'Behave, you. Now go on, get ready. We don't want to be late. How was your catch-up with Alastair?'

'Yeah, good. He's up to something, I can tell.'

'Like what? What do you think he's up to?'

'I've no idea.'

'How can you tell?'

Logan held his hand out in front of him. 'Because I've grown up with him. We've been together since we were very young, and I know what he's like. I can read him like a book.'

'Ooh, I wonder what it is?'

'I assume we'll soon find out.' Logan rolled his eyes. 'He likes drama and an announcement. No doubt he's got something up his sleeve for tonight.'

As Logan disappeared into the en-suite for a shower, Cally took the jacket off and pottered around tidying up the bedroom. She mused what Alastair might be up to. She'd never really told Logan that she wasn't too keen on Alastair. Not that he had ever done anything nasty. In actual fact, in his own peculiar way, he'd always been nice to her pretty much since the moment she'd arrived on the scene. He was just up himself and totally unaware of the entitled existence he led, and that rubbed Cally totally up the wrong way.

Logan emerged from the bathroom, a towel slung low on his hips. Cally swallowed. The view wasn't too bad as he made his way to the wardrobe.

'Yes?' he teased, catching her eye in the mirror.

Cally rolled her eyes. 'Just get dressed, you muppet. We're going to be late.'

Logan chuckled and pulled out a white shirt and dark trousers. Unlike her, with a quick spray of aftershave and a jacket, he was ready in a jiffy. Cally slipped on her heels, and Logan whistled. 'You look gorgeous. I'm really glad you're here, Cal. I know all this can be a bit overwhelming if you're not used to it.'

'It is a bit. But I'm glad I'm here too. It really is beautiful up here.'

'I *knew* you'd love it. You just have to get through meeting everyone else this evening. Though if Aunt Agatha starts on about her stamp collection, you're on your own.'

Cally laughed. 'Noted.'

'Right, come on, let's go face the Henry-Hicks clan.'

L ogan closed the door behind them and Cally inhaled a sharp breath at the chilly evening, more than glad that she'd decided on the velvet jacket outfit. Although they'd had lovely weather, once the sun was on its way down, it was cool. All through the grounds, uplights lit up the ancient trees, and tiny little lights in the flower beds beside the path lit the way to the house. Lights glowed from every window, and there was a faint sound of music and laughter drifting in the breeze.

Logan squeezed Cally's hand. 'Ready? Warm enough? The temperature has certainly dropped.'

'I am, yep, I'm fine.'

A few minutes later, they'd hustled past the sunken garden, along a tree-lined path, and bypassed the main front entrance with its vast porch and steps. Taking a side path, they entered a large sitting room with a huge fireplace via a conservatory door. Cally tried not to let her chin drop to the floor as she was met with towering ceilings, panelled walls, beautiful old rugs, warmth, candlelight, wealth and breeding just about every way she looked. A buzz of conversation greeted them. Cally plastered on her best smile, flicked her "I'm okay" switch at the back of her throat, and reminded herself that she'd faced tougher challenges than meeting a few posh people for a weekend bite to eat. How bad could a Henry-Hicks family dinner really be?

She looked around at people chatting and quickly assessed how her outfit held up. Spot on by Cally de Pfeffer. She had most definitely got it right. Maybe she was getting used to how the upper class did things, after all. She chuckled to herself and mused as a tall, distinguished-looking man approached them with a smile. She'd learnt that faking it until she made it was half the battle. She was beginning to be a pro.

With a champagne flute in her right hand and her left hand tucked loosely into the pocket of her satin trousers, Cally most certainly looked the part. The important thing was, now she *felt* the part too. Not totally. Oh no. There was a little bit of her that still prickled when she conversed with the Henry-Hicks of the world, but most of her was now okay with it. She'd learnt to accept that she was different and that nearly all of the problem with that was hers and nobody else's. In actual fact, no one else was really interested, which in itself was surprising. The Henry-Hicks of the world were so elevated that they more or less didn't really care. They didn't have insight into a world like Cally's and they didn't want to. They were so very removed from it that it went right over their heads. Once Cally had clocked that, she'd run with it and, in many situations, had realised that it was more than true. Tonight, as people sat around on beautiful old furniture, drank too much, and chatted, it was exactly the same. No one gave a hoot about whether or not *she* felt out of place. She'd learnt to suck it up and bowl on in.

Pretending to be interested in Logan's aunt's stamp collection, she observed the beauty of the room around her, taking in the details of the ornate ceiling and gorgeous old rugs. Her eyes darted around the room as she nodded politely at Logan's Aunt Agatha's enthusiastic description of her stamps.

'I have one from the first postal run in the Highlands. Can you imagine, dear? A time when getting a letter might take weeks! I rather cherish that stamp.'

'I can imagine you must do. Fascinating,' Cally said as she gazed at the gigantic gilded mirror with a slightly spotted surface alongside the fireplace.

Agatha smiled. 'Of course, some say the stamp is cursed. There are those who believe that the stamp has brought bad luck to every collector who owned it. But that's just superstition. Do you believe in things like that?'

Cally nodded, not in the slightest bit interested. She played along and smiled. 'Oh yes, quite. Superstition, absolutely.' Cally's eyes drifted to a beautiful seafoam green sofa where Logan was deep in conversation with his cousin, Alastair.

'I also have a particularly rare one from up this way with a mistake on it. Only fifty were ever printed.'

'Really?' Cally tried to inject some enthusiasm into her voice, but all she really wanted to do was stand and gape at the exquisiteness of the room around her. A pair of large, pastel green antique lamps flanked the beautiful sofa, huge fresh floral arrangements were dotted around the room, and a thick plush rug felt amazing underneath her feet.

'It was quite the scandal when they realised the misprint.'

'How dreadful.'

'Are you alright, dear?' Aunt Agatha's voice cut through Cally's observations. 'You seem a bit distracted.'

Cally turned back to the older woman. 'Ahh, sorry. I was just taking in this room. It's so lovely in here.'

'Ah, right, you've never been here before! I see, yes. It is rather splendid, isn't it? All the bits and pieces have been in the family for generations. Every piece has a story. This room hasn't changed in all the years I've been coming here apart from the odd upgrade or two.'

'Oh really? I love that.' Cally gestured to a pair of floral armchairs tucked either side of the fireplace. 'Those chairs, for instance. They're beautiful. Are they very old?'

'Oh, those, gosh yes. They belonged to my grandmother. She brought them all the way from London when she married into the family. Apparently, the story goes that she caused quite a stir, I can tell you. She was heavily into fashion at the time. I suppose it's a classic style these days.'

As Agatha began to ramble on about her predecessor's arrival in Scotland, Cally saw Logan watching her from across the room in the reflection in the mirror over the fireplace. He raised his glass in a funny little toast and flicked his eyes upwards.

Just as Cally was hoping that someone, anyone, would come and save her, Logan strolled over, joined the conversation and nodded in the direction of the dining room. 'Time for us to move in there. I hope you two lovely ladies are hungry.'

Cally was ready to eat just about anything and run far from Agatha. 'I am.'

'Let the feasting begin.'

The dining room was just as good if not better than the sitting room they'd come from. Though Cally wouldn't have called it a dining room. In her opinion, it was more like a banqueting hall. Grand and opulent, it gave off a sense of historical elegance, refined luxury and cosiness all at the same time. No mean feat. Beautiful old panelled walls painted in a soft, pastel green, intricate high ceilings and coving topped the walls, and very tall windows were draped with heavy, pleated curtains in shades of green and gold. Running along the centre of the room, a long, polished wooden dining table showed off tall, slender candlesticks with white candles, a gigantic chandelier threw sparkles around the room, and each table setting held a small wrapped gift. A Little Chef this was not.

Logan pulled out a high-backed chair made of dark wood, its seat upholstered in a deep, rich fabric. Cally sat down, tucked herself in, put her feet together, inhaled and stared at an ornate painting in a gilded frame at the far end of the room. She thought about her tiny cramped flat over the deli in the little seaside town. She'd come a very long way indeed.

17

The dinner had been long and drawn out with many courses. As the last of the dessert plates were cleared away, a few people had pushed back their chairs, the candles had burned low, and Cally had started to visualise going to bed. As she sipped a glass of water, coffee arrived by way of a tall silver coffee pot and delicate little coffee cups were passed along the table. After trays of handmade chocolates from Lovely were placed at each end of the table, all of a sudden, Alastair pushed his chair away from him, rose to his feet and tapped his dessert spoon against his water glass. A sharp ding echoed through the room. Cally chuckled to herself. So Logan had been right. Alastair was up to something.

Logan rolled his eyes. 'Here we go.'

Cally turned her head and shifted in her chair to look down towards the end of the table.

'If I could have everyone's attention for a moment,' Alastair called out.

Logan whispered in Cally's ear. 'So dramatic. I told you. I can always tell when he's scheming.'

Cally whispered back. 'How did you know?'

'I know him inside out. We were stuck together as children. It comes from that.'

Alastair cleared his throat theatrically. 'My dear family. Octavia and I have an announcement to make.'

'He's like the town crier.'

Cally's eyes widened. Alastair didn't hang around. He was going to announce that they were getting married or propose. One of the two. She waited with bated breath and shifted her eyes to Octavia, who was looking up at Alastair fondly. Octavia's face lit up, and she reached for Alastair's hand, giving it a squeeze. Blech.

'We've decided,' Alastair continued, pausing for effect, 'to embark on a grand adventure. We're taking a year-long sabbatical to travel the world!'

Surprise rippled across the table. Logan snorted softly beside Cally. 'A year-long sabbatical from what exactly? He doesn't even work. I'm not sure what he's taking a holiday from. You *have* to love him. He's always been the same. He can't even get the horses sorted for a day without it causing all sorts of drama.'

'Good point.' Cally whispered.

'Did this really warrant a big announcement?' Logan wondered.

Cally wasn't sure whether to say too much. It was fine for Logan to criticise Alastair, but her not so much. She didn't need to go there. 'Sorry, has he ever had a real job?'

Logan rolled his eyes. 'He worked for Uncle Reg for a bit after uni. Officially, he still does.'

Cally watched as Octavia stood to join Alastair. 'We leave next month. We've decided to start here in the UK and then head straight to India and make our way east from there. We're going to wing it a bit and see where we end up.'

'Wing it a bit?' One of Logan's cousins called out. 'What? Are you roughing it and backpacking?'

Alastair grimaced and shook his head quickly. 'Gosh, no. We won't be in youth hostels or suchlike. Rather not.'

A smattering of applause broke out around the table. Cally joined in with the clapping and laughter. Inside however, she couldn't quite get her head around the fact that Alastair and Octavia were just going off on a whim for a whole year. As you do. Travelling the world wasn't something that had ever been an option for our Cally. The concept seemed so foreign to her that she wasn't sure what to think. To be able to just take off willy-nilly felt impossibly grand for someone like her. As the family began to pepper Alastair and Octavia with questions about their itinerary, Cally's thoughts drifted to Lovely Bay. She thought about the long hours at the chemist, the early mornings working on her laptop for the online retail job, and the week-ends spent helping Nina with decluttering projects. Each shift, each extra hour, another pound in her savings account. Another step closer to her own little piece of Lovely Bay. There were no year-long sabbaticals in the distance for our Cally. Does anyone have a violin?

Logan waved a hand in front of Cally's face. 'Blackcurrant? You alright?'

She turned and forced a smile. 'Yes, of course. Just thinking.'

'About?'

Cally hesitated as she glanced at Alastair and Octavia. They were beaming, accepting congratulations and well-wishes from around the table. 'Oh, I don't really know. Just how different lives can be, I suppose.'

Logan rolled his eyes. 'For him, maybe. I suppose Alastair's lifestyle is a bit different from what we mere mortals are used to. I guess I don't really see it...'

Cally nodded, tracing the pattern on her coffee cup with her finger. 'It's not just that. It's the freedom, I suppose. The ability to just get up and go.' She shook her head and inhaled.

'What do you mean?'

'I've literally never had that.'

Cally imagined what it might be like to pack a bag and set off into the unknown, to wake up each morning in a different country, to experience new cultures and ways of life. To not have to worry about holding up the sky. To not have a job and to have to constantly keep checking bank accounts. Not that she wanted to jetset around the world. It hadn't ever really floated her boat. Or so she thought. She had her own very nice, tight little dream of owning her own place in Lovely Bay. She didn't need to gallivant around the globe, but the option to have it might be nice. Logan didn't get it. Not that she expected him to. It was sweet that he tried.

'We could travel too, if you wanted. Not for a year, but we could see some of the world together.'

'You'd want to?' Cally narrowed her eyes.

'I'd love to. We'd have a great time.'

Cally allowed herself to imagine strolling the streets of Paris, or watching a sunset over a beach. Palm trees, cocktails, sunbeds, nothing to care about. It didn't take long for reality to intrude: work schedules, chatbots, and savings accounts. 'It's a lovely thought, but...'

'Something to think about...'

'Yes.'

The grandfather clock in the corner chimed and Cally stifled a yawn and checked the time on her phone. The events of the day, the rich food, and the long walks in the fresh Scottish air had caught up with her.

Logan seemed to read her thoughts. 'Shall we call it a night? I've had enough.'

Cally nodded, pretended she didn't mind when really she wanted to go back and stopped herself from biting his hand off at the mention of going home to bed. She pretended to be casual and that it was up to him when really she couldn't wait to get out of her clothes, scrub off her makeup, and get into bed. She shrugged. 'If you like.'

Logan pushed his chair out and she followed suit. They made their excuses and said goodnight to the family, she smiled and chatted for a bit with Octavia.

Walking back to the cottage via the sunken garden, they stopped for a while on a bench by the water fountain. Because everyone has a water fountain in their garden.

Logan put his hand on her leg. 'How was that, then? Not too bad? You survived, so there's that.'

Cally nodded. 'I really enjoyed it.'

'Did you?'

'I actually did.' She gestured to the house. 'I've fallen for the house. It's so comfy and grand at the same time. Weird really. There's something about it up here, too.'

'Like what?'

'Like an aura or I don't know, a pull or something. Is that a thing?'

'I know what you mean. It's enough to have made Alastair announce his grand plans.'

'Yup. I wonder if there will be wedding bells with those two next.'

Logan widened his eyes. 'I don't know.'

'Feels like something's in the air.'

'Does it? How'd you mean?'

'I don't know really. A feeling in the water about those two or something. I can't put my finger on it.'

Logan joked. 'Ooh, intrigue.'

'Ha.'

Logan patted her leg. 'Well, you survived another Henry-Hicks bash.'

'I did.'

As they got up and strolled in the direction of the cottage,

Cally was surprised about how much she'd enjoyed the evening. Her mind flashed back to her first Henry-Hicks family event she'd attended at the races. She'd been a ball of nerves and unsure what was what. Now it was almost as if she was part of the woodwork of the actual inner circle of the family. It was odd and sort of nice at the same time. She couldn't shake a strange feeling, though, that something with, about, or to do with the family was going to happen soon. As they arrived at the door of the cottage, she winced a little bit as a thought went through her head that whatever was in the air it wasn't going to be nice. She wasn't wrong.

18

As per usual with Cally's body clock she'd woken very early and it was chilly. Not freezing wrap-yourself-head-to-toe-in-a-duvet chilly but Logan's-jumper-over-your-pjs chilly. Unlike the other mornings when Cally had woken up before Logan and crept downstairs in just her pyjamas, this morning, because she'd been prepared the night before, Cally had laid out one of Logan's jumpers to deal with the cold.

After tiptoeing down the creaky old stairs, she flicked the kettle on and stood looking at the mist hanging over the beautiful old conservatory adjacent to the garden. Then, after putting the jumper on over her pyjamas and with a mug of tea in her hands, she opened the back door, stood for a bit watching the mist and padded down the path in the direction of the conservatory. Morag had told her to pop in at any time, and with the foggy morning casting the whole garden in a sort of ethereal shroud, she was feeling its pull. In her slippers, she trudged along the path with the morning air nipping at her exposed skin. Despite the warmth of Logan's Fairisle jumper, she shivered as goosebumps rose on her arms. She clutched her steaming mug of tea close to her chest, felt the heat in her palms, and took in the mist hanging low over the landscape.

As she approached the conservatory, it seemed to emerge from the fog as if materialising from a dream. Pausing at the door, she inhaled deeply and took in the heavy-with-moisture air and scent of early morning dew. Somewhere in the distance, a bird called out and little droplets of condensation clung to the window panes, glistening drops catching the light and sparkling like diamonds all around her. A sudden rustle in the nearby bushes made Cally turn and look over to her right. Expecting to see another deer, she strained her ears as the sound came again and a rabbit emerged from the undergrowth. It froze as it spotted Cally and looked at her as if to ask her who she thought she was to be out so early. Its ears twitched, and as quickly as it had arrived, it darted away, disappearing into the mist. Deer, rabbits, eagles, she'd seen them all.

A few seconds later, Cally strolled through to the end of the conservatory, and sat precisely in the little spot Morag had told her about. Not quite Marbella. Much better. Sitting lost in thought with her tea, she pondered about how the Scottish estate had surprised her and how much she liked it. Her mind wandered to her thoughts the night before and all the conversation about Alastair and Octavia taking off for a year to travel the world. She imagined what it would be like to go off into the sunset without a plan to follow with no real destination in mind. How strange it would be to her to have a no-plan plan.

The more she thought about it the more she didn't like the idea at all. She thought about how excited Alastair's face had been when it had lit up at the prospect of trotting off on an adventure without a plan. She realised, as she stared at the leaf of a philodendron, that she didn't want that at all. What she wanted, in fact, was probably the opposite: a comfy blanket of stability and familiarity that would allow the rest of her to thrive. What she truly needed was to feel safe, to settle down and to build a life in Lovely, to further put her feet under the table of the community that had welcomed her. In fact, the thought of gallivanting here, there, and everywhere didn't really fill her with glee at all. In a funny sort of way it was the stay in the cottage in Scotland that had shown her that. For sure she wouldn't mind a trip to New York one day, ditto any other major city in the world. A nice little Greek island wouldn't go amiss, an Italian beach, perhaps a road trip across the USA. But really, what she wanted was to feel secure. She'd be quite happy living in Lovely Bay and getting on a train once a year to take her to the other end of the country to stay on the estate and spend a few weeks in a wax coat tramping around the country-side in wellies.

As she sipped her tea and pondered, Cally got lost in a world of her own as a drip of condensation from the leaves of a few exotic-looking plants plopped onto the ground beside her. Gorgeous early morning light filtered through the glass panes, and a few dappled shadows danced here and there on the tiled floor around her chair. A thick, earthy, damp soil smell filled the air, and a quiet so dense it was almost hypnotic surrounded her thoughts.

Thinking about what had happened the night before and how it had cemented her thoughts on what she wanted in life, she pondered being offered the promotion. The more she thought about it the more she realised that it was exactly what she wanted; it had just taken her a while to realise it. Just as she didn't need to be scooting around the world on a jet plane, the same was true for what she did for a job. She didn't need a power suit and a big career. She would be quite happy doing her thing with Birdie, in fact, it suited her down to the ground. The weekend at the estate had somehow shown her that as clear as day. She nodded and made up her mind. She would message Birdie that she would love to take the job. Sorted.

Just as she was thinking about going back into the cottage to make a hot blackcurrant and have a little read in the sitting room, a crunch of gravel outside the conservatory caught her attention. Leaning on a potting table she craned her neck to see one of the old Land Rovers pulling up outside the conservatory. She leaned out further to see a figure approaching through the thinning morning mist and realised it was Morag, the estate's head gardener. She was bundled up against the early chill in a thick jumper under dungarees, a green estate cap pulled low over her ears.

Cally looked down at the state of herself; old pyjamas with Logan's jumper over the top, slippers and bed hair. Not the best look. She tugged self-consciously at the hem of the jumper as she stood up when Morag entered the conservatory.

Morag beamed, her breath fogging in the cool air. 'Oh, hiya! I didn't expect to see anyone up and about after last night. You're up with the lark today.'

Cally smiled. 'Morning. Yes, I'm a bit of an early riser.'

Morag's eyebrows rose in surprise. 'Really? Not many of the lot that come up from down south can drag themselves out of bed at this hour.'

Cally chuckled. 'Force of habit, I'm afraid. My body clock's set to getting up for work these days.'

'Ah, that's right. You mentioned you work in a chemist. Must keep you busy.'

'It does, but that's not what I get up early for. I do some online work too, for a retail chatbot. It means early mornings or late nights. Usually mornings. I do the super early shifts to get it done and dusted.'

Morag whistled. 'Right, so you're up with the birds. You have two jobs do you? You must be busy.'

Cally chuckled and rolled her eyes. 'Actually, I have three.'

'Ah, well, no rest for the wicked, I always say. Better to be doing things.' Morag tapped the side of her head. 'No use in keeping this idle as far as I'm concerned. Asking for trouble if I sit around doing nothing but that's just me. This place sorts out my mental health.'

'I know, right? It's good to be busy.'

'Mmm. As long as you get the balance right. Anyway, how did it go last night over at the main house there? Fun evening, was it?'

'Really good, actually. The food was fantastic. Yes, I had a nice evening.'

'Excellent. I hear there was a bit of an announcement.'

Cally smiled. 'News travels fast up here.'

'That it does. There aren't many of us so we gossip, ha! Alastair is off on his travels, then?'

'Yes.'

'Alright for some. How about that then? A year off globe-trotting…'

'I know. Have you ever travelled much? Outside of Scotland, I mean.'

Morag straightened up. 'Can't say that I have. Since I've been up here, I've more or less stayed put. Can't be bothered with trekking all over the place when I've got what I want right here on my doorstep. You know? I mean, what's the point? I've been to London once or twice for gardening shows. I took a wee trip to the London Flower Show a few years back and that wasn't all it's cracked up to be. But other than that, I've stayed pretty close to home. Yeah, it sounds a bit boring, but there you go. I'm not trying to impress anyone.'

'And you're happy with that?' Cally asked.

'Aye, that I am. As I said, I don't see much need for galli-vanting about when I've got all this beauty right here.' Morag gestured around the conservatory and beyond to the mist outside. 'I don't really want anything much these days either.'

'I hear you.'

'Yeah, it's not for everyone living here, but it works for me. I've never really understood the need to travel to far off lands.

It's a thing though, for sure. I mean, who doesn't want a week in the sun every now and then, but going off for a year and that whole van life thing? Nah, not for me, thank you. Van life? Pah!'

'I haven't quite had the opportunity.'

Morag chuckled. 'Ach, I don't reckon it's all it's cracked up to be. Some folks, like young Alastair, need to roam a bit to find themselves. Others don't need any of that. They find themselves by putting down roots. At least, that's what happened to me.'

Cally nodded. 'That's it exactly. I've spent so much of my life feeling unsettled. Now that I've found a place in Lovely Bay, the thought of leaving it behind just doesn't feel right to me. Does that sound a bit bonkers?'

'Not at all. There's something to be said for knowing where you belong. For building a life somewhere, becoming part of a community.' Morag winked. 'Ask me how I know. I won't be leaving this place anytime soon.'

'Mmm, interesting. Don't get me wrong, I'd love to see Paris or somewhere like that someday.' Cally wrinkled her nose up. 'But the idea of constantly moving and never settling. I don't know, it's just not for me.'

Morag's eyes crinkled at the corners as she smiled. 'Sounds to me like you've got your head screwed on right, lass. There's no shame in wanting to build a life in one place. And who says you can't have both? A home to come back to, and the occasional adventure to broaden your horizons. If you ask me, that's the way to do it.'

'You're right. That's exactly what I want. A home in Lovely Bay, with maybe a trip here to Scotland now and then, and the odd holiday abroad. That would suit me well enough.'

Morag nodded. 'You can do a lot worse, I do believe. Half the problem in life is finding out what you *actually* want.' Morag swept her hand around the conservatory. 'Messing about in here all day with plants works for me.'

Cally nodded as she picked up her mug from the table and

little dust motes danced in the air as Morag started to fuss with a plant. She didn't need to gallivant all over the show, nor did she want to. She *did* want to throw herself into finding her own little flat and accepting the promotion at work. Yes, that was what she wanted. Her heart was set on cultivating her own little corner of Lovely. That was an adventure in itself. Too easy. What she didn't know was that in her little corner, there were still a few more surprises for our Cally to come.

19

It was the next day. Cally and Logan had spent the whole day out in the countryside and had clocked up many thousands of steps. They'd discussed everything and anything including moving in together properly with Logan being keen and Cally talking about buying a flat and the ins and outs of doing that. As they'd stomped along in nature taking in the beauty of the estate, they'd put the world to rights.

After the long outdoors day, Cally had fancied nothing other than tucking up on the sofa in the cottage under one of the tartan blankets, popping a film on Netflix, sloshing a measure or three of gin into hot blackcurrant, and dozing her way to bedtime. Unfortunately, Logan and Alastair had other ideas, and a plan was in place for the family to stroll down to the town pub for dinner and a few drinks. At least it was casual, and Cally didn't have to dress up. After being outside all day, including a long walk through the forest, faffing around with fancy clothes, and getting ready was the last thing she wanted to do. On coming in from the walk, she had peeled off her jumper and welly boots and headed straight up to run a long, deep bath.

About an hour later, she'd emerged, pulled on jeans and one of her ruffle top shirts, popped Logan's cashmere jumper over the top, and, as they'd headed out the door, she'd shrugged on her Lovely coat. Putting her hands in her pockets, she nodded; she was happiest in easy clothes and not being dressed up to the nines. She couldn't be doing with that every day of the week.

They stopped at the main house to meet everyone and then set off in the direction of the town. Cally walked along next to Logan and alongside Cecilia and Reg and as they made their way through the woods Cally felt the steps of the day like lead in her legs. After emerging on a lane and then taking another country path over some fields, they reached the little local town. Cally peered in shop windows as they walked along the pavement and ambled along the main street.

'It's a bit nippy out for this time of year, isn't it? Once that sun goes down, you know about it.' Cecilia remarked, her breath visible in the cool air. 'If there's one thing I've learnt it's that you never can tell what the weather is going to be like up here.'

'It is, but it's a fine evening for a walk to the pub,' Reg replied.

Cally nodded as they walked past the shop fronts lining the street. Little lights glowed in windows, a shop with beautiful handmade knitted jumpers and a large bay window was fogged up from the warmth inside and Scottish flags fluttered in the breeze. A chalkboard sign outside a little coffee shop advertised 'Homemade Scottish Tablet' and 'Freshly Baked Scones' and a few doors down, the deep blue sign of a Bank of Scotland branch stood out against the smaller shopfronts. Cally stopped and peered up at the building's grey stone exterior and large arched windows.

'That building's been there since the 1800s,' Reg chimed in. 'Used to be the only bank for miles around. Still is, for some services.'

Strolling casually further along, Cally loved the quaint little town. She stopped and looked in the window of an outdoor clothing shop showcasing a plethora of things to brace for when exposed to the Scottish elements: waterproof jackets hung alongside hiking boots, rain coats and cosy-looking fleeces. A vintage timber mannequin dressed in full hiking attire, complete with a backpack and walking poles, stood sentinel in the corner of the window. Cally cupped her hands over her eyes and peered in further. Cecilia stood beside her and followed her gaze.

'MacGregor's,' Cecilia said. 'They've been kitting out hikers and hunters for decades. I think the boot room at the house is almost like a secondary shop of theirs and let me tell you, you need it if you come here when it snows.'

Next door to the outfitters, a tartan shop with a stunning window display took Cally's breath away. The bay window and shop behind it reminded her of the coat shop in Lovely, with its old-fashioned display units, bolt upon bolt of tartan fabric, and a large cutting table dominating the centre of the room. In the far corner, a man in a white shirt and waistcoat was carefully measuring out lengths of fabric.

'That shop has been here for as long as I can remember,' Cecilia remarked. 'They can tell you the history of every tartan in the place. Fascinating, really, when you think about it.'

They passed by a traditional butcher's shop with strings of sausages hanging in the window, a small art gallery showcasing works by local painters, and a cosy-looking bookshop with stacks of novels and local history books visible through its quaint bow window.

'It's all so charming and cosy.'

Logan squeezed her hand. 'Hmm, I guess it is. I've never really thought about it.'

'It reminds me of Lovely.'

'I suppose it's very similar, yes.'

Getting to a small green, Cally was beginning to wonder

where the pub was. Her stomach very much needed to find it. Reg had other ideas as he stopped at an ancient stone war memorial and peered upwards. On its weathered surface, a way too long list of names of local soldiers lost in conflicts was listed on plaques lined up from top to bottom.

Logan shook his head. 'It's unbelievable really. Gosh, some of these were so young. The sacrifices made by these small communities all that time ago. Terrible.'

Reg shook his head and whooshed in air through his teeth. 'Imagine that.' He pointed at a list of five names all with the same surname. 'A whole family of young lads gone in one fell swoop.'

'Awful.'

As they neared the second section of the high street, the sound of conversation and clinking glasses grew louder from The Stag and Thistle pub on the corner. Cally was more than glad to see its whitewashed walls, dark slate roof, hanging baskets bursting with flowers and a chalkboard detailing the menu nudged outside. She couldn't wait to sit down. 'I didn't realise how hungry I was. My legs feel like I have cement in them.'

Cecilia chuckled. 'All that fresh air and walking will do that to you.'

Cally smiled as she stepped into the old Scottish pub and nodded at what greeted her; low dark beamed ceilings, lovely old worn timber floors, walls adorned with a mix of local memorabilia and hunting trophies and the smell of wood smoke, ale, and heather in the air.

A massive stone fireplace sat right in the middle of the pub and little clusters of tables here and there were chock full of people. Conversations in thick Scottish accents swirled around her, punctuated by bursts of laughter and the occasional clink of glasses. Cosy, comfortable and somehow just right.

Cecilia shrugged off her cardigan as they walked across the

pub. 'Ah, there they are.' She gestured towards a large table in the corner where Alastair, Octavia, and several other Henry-Hicks clan members were already seated. Cally followed Cecilia and Logan, took her coat and bag off and as they got to the table, she sat down on a bench seat with a long leather cushion between Logan and Octavia. Octavia kissed her on the cheek and smiled.

'What did you get up to today?'

Cally beamed. 'Walking. Loving it. It's beautiful up in the forest. Scotland is so pretty.'

'Oh, I know. Isn't it just divine?' Octavia gushed. 'Alastair and I are thinking of including it in our travel plans. A sort of farewell tour of the British Isles before we jet off to more exotic places, you know? We were thinking of getting a small plane out to the islands before we head south and then get on our way to India. Sometimes the heat is a bit much in the tropics if you know what I mean?'

Cally wasn't quite sure how to respond. She *didn't* actually know about jetting off to more exotic places. The idea of getting a small plane was completely and utterly alien to her. Octavia didn't need or want to know that. 'Yes, sounds good to me.'

'Right then, what are you drinking, Cal?' Alastair interrupted.

'What's Logan having?'

'A local ale, I think.'

'I'll have the same but only a half, or, umm, maybe just a gin and tonic?'

'Nonsense!' Reg interjected. 'You can't come to Scotland and not try a wee dram of whisky in the pub.'

Feeling slightly out of her depth but not wanting to seem impolite, Cally nodded. She didn't fancy whisky in the slightest. 'Okay, I'll give it a try.'

Cally chatted away to Octavia, who mostly rattled on about herself, her life and her travels. Cally didn't really care. She was tired, happy to be resting her legs and couldn't wait to order some food. She nodded, smiled and made the appropriate sounds here and there as Octavia told her all about how much she was looking forward to visiting Fiji and how they'd decided to take a year off because you never knew what was around the corner.

Alright for some, Cally thought and instantly chided herself for being mean.

Just after they'd studied the menus and were still waiting for Alastair to come back from the bar, Logan's aunt Agatha arrived. Logan got up so that she could squeeze in on the bench seat. Cally grimaced internally, not enamoured with the premise of having to listen to Agatha's twaddle as Agatha wriggled along the bench seat and sat down right next to her.

After a bit of small talk about the weather, Agatha smiled. 'Logan tells me you're a chemist. How fascinating! I've always been interested in the history of pharmacy. Did you know that the Scots were pioneers in the field?'

Cally internally rolled her eyes. Course they were. Before she could respond, Agatha launched into a detailed history of Scottish contributions to modern medicine. Agatha's eyes gleamed with enthusiasm as Cally's glazed six times over. She wanted to top herself at the thought of having to listen to Agatha droning on for the whole meal.

'...and of course, there's the famous story of the discovery of chloroform as an anaesthetic. Quite by accident, you know.'

Cally loved learning new things, but tired and starving, she couldn't have cared less. She tried and failed to look interested. 'That's quite something.'

'Oh yes, he was the one who introduced pain relief in childbirth.'

Cally wasn't sure whether she could stomach another long, boring conversation with Logan's aunt. Thankfully, Alastair returned at that moment, distributing the drinks around the table. Cally wrinkled her nose as a small tumbler of amber liquid was placed in front of her. She picked it up and inhaled a strong smell. Maybe downing it in one was an excellent antidote to boring old aunts.

'There you are, Cally,' Reg raised his own glass. 'Take a small sip, just to wet your palate. Then, take a larger sip and let it roll around your tongue before swallowing. You'll get all the flavours that way.'

Cally really wasn't that interested in the correct way to drink whisky. She just wanted to eat. The carton of blackcurrant in her bag would have done her fine. She pretended she was into the whisky and played the game. Lifting the glass tentatively, she brought it to her lips inhaled deeply before taking a tiny sip as instructed. *Disgusting.* Absolutely vile. The liquid burned slightly as it touched her tongue.

'Well?' Reg asked with raised eyebrows.

'It's, umm, interesting,' Cally replied diplomatically. 'I think it might take some getting used to.'

Reg chuckled. 'It's an acquired taste for some. But give it time. By the end of your stay, you might love it.'

Cally doubted that but maybe it was another thing about being in Scotland she might come to like. She took another sip, hid a wince and studied the menu as all the while Agatha rattled on.

A few hours later, Reg had consumed way too much whisky. Cally had finished hers and moved on to soft drinks. She had practically vacuumed up an Aberdeen Angus steak pie and after watching Octavia chase her chips around her plate and leave half of her pie, she'd wolfed Octavia's down, too. As she sat with Logan's hand on her leg feeling happy, full, and content, she felt pretty pleased with herself to be sitting happily with Logan's family. When she'd first stepped into the Henry-Hicks world, she'd been unsure of her place, embarrassed about her past and had spent way too much time and brain power constantly second-guessing herself on repeat. Now, she slotted in with them and their funny ways as if she was part of the furniture.

Logan's mum, Anne, chatted across the table. 'Logan said you're looking at property.'

Cally nodded, not sure whether or not Logan had mentioned to Anne about them living together properly. Knowing how casual Logan was about them living together officially he'd probably not even covered it with his mum. 'Yes.'

'How nice to be buying a house.'

Cally shook her head. 'It will be a small flat.'

'Oh, right, yes. You prefer a flat and not having to have all the upkeep. Right.'

That wasn't it at all. Cally would give her right, or left, arm for a house in Lovely. Unfortunately, the bank was having none of it. 'Mmm.'

'So, have you found anything?'

'I'm just in the looking stage at the moment to get a feel for the market.'

'I see. You've got a lot going on. What about the promotion you were telling me about? Have you decided on whether to take that or not? Logan said you were thinking about another career? Taking another path as it were…'

Cally really couldn't be bothered to go into the ins and outs of it with Anne. Anne was nice enough but she doubted she'd ever really worked a day in her life or had a job, let alone three. 'Umm, not really. I just need something to, you know, pay the bills.'

'Rather tedious, really, isn't it?'

'I guess so.' Tedious and *required* for Cally to exist.

'So have you had a chance to think about the offer a bit more since you've been up here?'

Cally nodded. In actual fact the break in Scotland had been great in giving her the clarity to see that Birdie's job was just what she wanted. Being away from Lovely had sealed what she now realised was a very special deal. 'I have, actually. Being up here has made me see that I think I'm going to give it a whirl.'

'Ahh, that's good news.'

Cally smiled. She really hoped she'd made the right decision. She'd soon find out.

20

The afternoon when Cally had laid on the sofa recharging and reading, she'd also flicked through quite a few pamphlets and old history books detailing all sorts about the estate. Her appetite regarding the estate had already been whetted just by strolling around and lapping it up, but learning more about it had really opened her eyes. She'd read with interest about the history of the house and its inhabitants, learnt more about the walking trails and read up on the wildlife, trees and many different plants on the doorstep. As she'd flicked through the books, she'd stopped with particular interest at a chapter about stargazing at the estate and the clarity of the skies.

Estate stargazing had piqued her interest, she'd noted the best-recommended spots and had planned on their last night to make the most of a clear sky and good weather. She'd planned what to eat, had walked down to the town to get supplies, and now stood in the kitchen over a huge bowl of chilli, spooning overloaded ladles into insulated Thermos bowls.

Across the other side of the kitchen, Logan had two open picnic baskets on the table and was putting a small gas cooker ring, a saucepan, and various other accoutrements into them. Cally put the two insulated bowls in one basket, went into the sitting room, grabbed a few of the tartan blankets from the back of the sofa, folded them neatly, and added them to one of the baskets.

Logan closed a basket and adjusted the little leather straps on the front. 'Okay, are we all set? Do you think the chilli will stay warm enough?'

'Yeah, it should do in those Thermos bowls. We'll use the cooker thing if we need to.'

'Excellent. Okay, we're done. I just need to put the milk, chocolate powder, and marshmallows in.'

'Yep, done.'

'Are you sure you're going to be warm enough?' Logan asked, eyeing Cally's layers critically. 'It can be cool up the top there, even at this time of year.'

Cally nodded, adjusting her scarf. 'I've got a few layers on. Do you think I need my coat? Nah, I think I'm good.'

'You definitely need your coat. Why risk it?'

'Right, yes, true. You're the expert in these matters. Pop that in, too.'

A few minutes later, each with a basket and a camping chair, they stomped out of the house, headed across the grounds, around the sunken garden, and made their way up the hill to the higher ground area detailed in the book. Logan carried a picnic basket in one hand, the bundle of tartan blankets in the other, and Cally clutched a bottle of wine and a smaller bag containing extra supplies. Chatting all the way, mostly about Birdie's promotion offer, once they'd arrived at the top of the hill, Logan put down the stuff and looked around. 'This is the best spot. We've got a clear view of the sky, and the fire pit is just over there. This is the one the book said, wasn't it? I haven't been up here for a while.'

'Yeah, it said this one for this time of year.' Cally nodded, taking in the breathtaking panoramic view. The sun had just dipped below the horizon, painting the sky in shades of pink and orange. In the distance, she could see the silhouette of the main house, its windows already glowing against the sky. 'I'm so glad we made the effort to do this.'

Logan smiled as he started to lay the blankets on the ground. 'Wait till you see it when it's properly dark. The stars up here are like nothing you've ever seen. It's amazing. Alastair and I used to come up here often back in the day.'

Arranging their spot, they opened the chairs, put out the blankets for warmth and unpacked the food. Logan pulled dry kindling and wood out of a little brick cubby area by the firepit and got a fire going as Cally took the Thermos pots out.

Cally shook her head. 'The days have flown by up here. I can't believe we're leaving tomorrow and I've got to go back to work. It's gone by so fast.'

Logan nodded. 'We can come back any time you want.'

Cally sat down on one of the rugs, leaned back on her elbows, and tilted her head to look up at the deepening twilight. 'Ahh, the colours are so pretty.'

Logan sat down and wrapped his arm around her shoulders. 'It'll only get better as it gets darker.'

'Hope so. In a funny way it reminds me of when we went in that hot air balloon. It must be because we're high up. Remember that? I loved it. Imagine doing that over here...' Cally remarked as she opened a basket and laid out cheese, French bread, and a jar of chutney she'd helped herself to via Cecilia at the main house.

As they sat eating the cheese and bread, it got darker and more and more stars winked into existence above them. The fire popped and hissed, Logan poured a couple of glasses of wine, and Cally wrapped one of the blankets over her shoulders.

The darker and later it got, the more stars came out. Cally sat with her head up looking at the sky. 'Incredible. The stars in

Lovely aren't too shabby, but these are something else on another level.'

'I think there's more light pollution down where we are. That's one of the things I love about coming up here – you can see the night sky in all its glory.'

Cally got lost in the sky, the air, the scenery, and the twinkles. 'When I first came to Lovely, I never imagined I'd end up here stargazing in Scotland with you. Weird.'

Logan chuckled. 'Funny old world, eh?'

Cally nodded. 'When my grandma passed away, I was so focused on surviving I didn't know what was what. I was just getting by day to day. I never really let myself think about the future and now I'm here.'

'You most certainly are and I love it and you.' Logan smiled.

'Things feel different now. I feel like my eyes have been opened. Before I was so bound up with caring, there wasn't any time for anything else. God, I was so sheltered and unworldly. Do you know what I mean?' Cally asked even though she was fairly sure Logan had no clue what she really meant deep down. He was far from unworldly.

'Yeah. You're different even from when we first met.'

'Am I? How?'

'I don't know.' Logan shrugged. 'Lighter.'

Cally sighed and looked up. It was a good way to put it. He wasn't wrong. 'There's so much to explore up here. It makes me realise how little I've seen of the world. This island we're on alone...'

'We'll do it all if you want to. Whatever you want.'

'That's the thing. I don't really *want* to do that much. I was chatting to Morag about it. Things like this are just amazing to me. I don't need to go gallivanting all over the place.'

'That's why I love you.' Logan winked. 'Easy to please.'

'Right back at you. You don't want to jet off like Alastair and Octavia?'

'Nah, not really. I mean I wouldn't mind a few weeks in the sun if someone offered it to me on a plate.'

'True.'

'It's been great up here, hasn't it? Really good to get away.'

Cally nodded. 'Definitely.'

'What's been your best bit?'

'Hard to choose. The pub night was fun. I think I've got a long way to go before I love whisky, that I do now know. I think my favourite part has been just being here, on the estate. I've really loved the walks and all the nature.'

Logan chuckled. 'Not the fancy dinner? You didn't love that?'

Cally widened her eyes. 'It was a lot better than I thought it was going to be.'

'Good. I know my family can be a lot sometimes.'

Cally laughed. 'They can. They've been so welcoming, actually when you think about it. I mean, really what more could I ask for?'

'Even Aunt Agatha?' Logan teased.

'Give me strength.'

'I did warn you.'

'You certainly did.' Cally's eyes widened as a shooting star streaked across the sky. 'Oh! Did you see that?'

'You have to make a wish if you see one. That's what we always used to say when we were up here when we were little.'

Cally closed her eyes for a moment and wished that a flat she could afford would come up in Lovely.

'What did you wish for?'

'Can't tell you.'

Logan laughed. 'Ha. Right, I'll get the chilli, shall I?'

'Yes, I'm famished.'

As they sat and ate the chilli, they talked about everything and anything, discussed what a nice time they'd had and how good the weather had been. Cally had thoroughly enjoyed herself, and it showed all over her face. Her heart wasn't far behind it. She'd needed a bit of time off from her three jobs and constant saving. She gestured in the direction of the main house. 'I can see why you love it so much and why it's a big part of the family.'

'Some people think it's too boring and too cold. Honestly, we've had visitors and guests who've said never again.'

'I bet it's chilly in the winter.'

'Yep. We'll have to come up. It's magical when everything is white.

'Aww, I'd love that. I really love snow.'

'Autumn's good too. When the leaves change colour, everything is red and gold,' Logan nodded. 'And, yes, winter. You haven't seen the estate until you've seen it in the snow, Cal. It's amazing but it is really cold. Speaking of cold, how are you holding up?'

'It is getting nippy but I don't want to go down yet.'

Logan stood up, pulled the chairs closer to the fire, began to rearrange their blankets and wrapped another one around both chairs and over their shoulders like a cocoon.

Cally snuggled into his side. 'Much better.'

They sat back, gazing up at the sky. Cally held up her finger and traced the constellations. 'I'm going to miss it up here but not Aunt Agatha and her stamps. Definitely not.'

Logan chuckled. 'I'm with you on that.'

'You're really lucky to have family. I've never had this before, you know? This sense of belonging to a place, to a family. It really is worth a lot if you ask me.'

'Get used to it. The Henry-Hicks clan have kidnapped you.' Logan joked. 'Just wait, though, so far you've only seen the good bits. We've got lots of old skeletons lurking in cupboards all over the place.'

Cally pulled the blanket over her shoulders and stared down at the silhouette of the main house and thought that the Henry-Hicks family didn't have any bad bits as such. From what she'd seen nothing bad *ever* appeared to happen to any of them. In a way, it didn't seem fair.

Logan rubbed his hands together. 'We should probably think about heading back soon.'

Cally nodded, but didn't make any move to get up. 'I think I could stay here all night and just sit and dream.'

As she tucked her feet up underneath her and stared at the sky, she thought about the weekend with the Henry-Hicks family and how she was now part of it. She winced a little bit as she thought about Logan's family and Alastair as he'd made his announcement. She couldn't put her finger on it but she had a strange feeling inside that something was going to happen. That after they'd left the estate and made their way back to Lovely things were going to change. She brushed the thought away. Ridiculous. The Scottish air was doing funny things to her head.

21

C ally was back in Lovely Bay sitting on a bench by the river doom scrolling through her socials. She shook her head and dropped her phone in her lap. She was meant to be deciding on Birdie's job offer, but for some reason or another, something kept stopping her from completely making up her mind. She'd gone over it so many times she had decision over-load. Truth be told, despite feeling in Scotland as if the job was the right path for her to take, a little part of her didn't want to make the choice and so she'd stalled. A section of her brain told her to stay in her lane and keep safe. Stay down, Cally de Pfef-fer. Someone like you doesn't deserve good things. Continue to do your three little jobs. Stay small. Wave at us from down there.

The feeling would also explain why, despite having looked at potentially every course in the country, from Land's End to John O'Groats, she'd not pushed the button on committing to anything in that department either. The same scenario had happened when applying for jobs before she'd received Birdie's offer; she'd looked at all sorts and had been surprised that her qualifications and work experience qualified her for quite a few different opportunities. However, none of them had taken her fancy enough for her to actually go for gold. She sighed and rubbed her temples. The constant back-and-forth in her mind was exhausting. On the one hand, the job offer represented everything she'd been working towards - stability, security, a chance to prove herself. On the other hand, she wondered if it was right.

'Come on, get a grip,' she muttered to herself.

She stared at the river for ages, waved as Clive went past on the riverboat, and watched as a woman walked along on the path in front of her and juggled a pram with a baby, a toddler, and a dog on a lead, all at the same time as chatting on her phone. A multi-tasking mum right there in front of her eyes. Opening the email from Birdie again, she then whipped out a small wire top notebook she kept in her handbag and made a list of the pros and cons of the job the old-fashioned way with paper and pen.

By the time she'd got to the end of the list and had sat and pondered for a bit longer, it really was a no-brainer. The job offer was just too good to turn down. The only thing on the cons list that made her think twice was putting all her eggs in one basket and doing a full-time job for the person in Lovely Bay you had to keep on the right side of. If anything ever went badly wrong with Birdie or they fell out, Cally was well aware that she'd be toast in Lovely. Or six feet under.

The list in her notebook stared at her as she reiterated all the pros of the job; there were many. The rational part of her brain knew that accepting Birdie's job offer was the logical choice. The benefits were undeniable - a steady income, healthcare, paid leave - all things she'd dreamed of having in the back of her mind. Yet, despite thinking she'd wanted an opportunity for years, a peculiar, nagging voice told her just to continue on as she always had. Stay in your lane.

She frowned at the thought. *Stay in my lane? Since when have I had the opportunity for anything else?* She thought about all the challenges she'd faced and overcome, all the things she'd had to juggle like the mum she'd just watched walk past. Maybe it was time to change lanes altogether.

She watched as a pair of ducks glided past, their little feet going ninety to the dozen under the water. A bit like her, really. She'd always felt as if she was swimming against the tide, struggling to keep her head above water at the same time as holding up that big old sky. Birdie's job would undoubtedly change that.

Picking up her notebook again, she ran her finger down the list of pros. They really were too good to turn down: financial stability, career growth, meeting new people, furthering her knowledge and experience, driving a little van - it was all there, laid out in black and white. No more juggling multiple jobs, no more worrying.

Her gaze drifted back to the river, and she watched as a few leaves floated by on the surface. A fish jumped creating ripples and as she watched the circles, her mind reiterated how long she'd been stuck in one place, doing the same jobs, living the same life. Logging onto the same chatbot portal for years. She sighed at the thought that even *that* had changed, updated and embraced new technology in the time she'd been working on it. She, however, had pretty much stayed the same. Always there, logging on in the early hours doing her same old thing.

A group of teenagers walked by with school bags over their shoulders, laughing and giggling. Cally thought about her youth and how it had been tied up with looking after her mum and her brother. No dreams for our Cally, nothing too ambitious or unrealistic. All the times she'd had no choice but to hold herself back, all the opportunities she'd let slip by because she'd been unable to dedicate the time because her responsibilities at home had always come first.

She picked up her pen again and tapped it against her notebook as she considered the cons she'd written down. Most of them, she realised, were, in actual fact, excuses stemming from her insecurities rather than real obstacles. The concern about putting all her eggs in one basket and things going wrong with Birdie really were just manifestations of self-doubt. She wondered about being risk-averse and if it was fundamentally about the job or about being afraid to succeed. The answer hit her like a tonne of bricks. She'd spent so long just trying to survive, to keep her head above water, that the idea of actually thriving was almost foreign to her. But wasn't that what she'd come to Lovely Bay for in the first place? A chance at a better life?

She looked at the word 'security' and thought about how the full-time job with benefits would give her that. How long had she lived without that feeling? Always worrying about the next bill, the next unexpected expense, and never able to plan for the future because she was too busy struggling to get by day to day. The job would lift a weight from her shoulders. No more survival.

Flipping back through the pages of her notebook, she came across an old to-do list scribbled on one of the pages. "Research local courses," it said, followed by "Look for new job opportunities." Both items were checked with little blue ticks. Yes, she'd researched courses and looked at jobs more than a few times. That was more or less as far as it had gone, though. She thought about all the courses she'd researched, all the job listings she'd pored over. How many times she'd been on the brink of this, that, or the other only to not take the leap and talk herself out of things at the last moment. Way too many times.

She nodded to herself. The job offer from Birdie was the universe giving her a big old poke in the side. A jab in the ribs. Practically shoving an opportunity in her face and daring her to take it. Telling her to pull on her big girl's pants and get the heck on with it.

She closed her eyes and took a deep breath. The Lovely smell and scent of the river filled her nostrils; earthy, fresh and familiar all at the same time. A few minutes later, she nodded. No more overthinking. Time to grab the opportunity with both hands and hang on for the ride. Our Cally was going to take the plunge. See what it was like on the other side.

22

It had taken Cally quite a bit of time to make up her mind, but she had finally decided to *officially* take the job; it was just too good not to. After again spending way too much time weighing up the pros and cons, she'd decided that she would be crazy not to take it. Logan had told her that he didn't really think she could go wrong and that the job would open up lots of doors. So she'd decided to go for her life.

With a spring in her step that she'd finally made a decision, she walked down the steep steps from her flat, strolled over the first floor of the deli building and down the next flight of stairs and just as she was heading for the back door, she bumped straight into Alice coming the other way.

'Morning, our Cally, how are you?' Alice asked.

'Good, thanks. Everything is fine with me,' Cally replied. 'How are you?'

'Yep, great. I'm looking forward to a week off.'

'I bet.'

'How was your time up in Scotland? How did the weather treat you?'

'It was just right. I had a really nice time. Much better than I thought it was going to be. You live and learn.'

'I've heard it's nice. It's been on my bucket list for a long time.'

'Right. It wasn't on mine, but I will definitely go back. It would be nice to see it at Christmas time.'

'I reckon.'

Cally looked in the direction of the door, 'Anyway, I must get going.'

'Have a nice day.'

'You, too. See you.'

A few minutes later, Cally smiled at the sound of the Shipping Forecast as she walked into the back of the chemist. She always knew when Birdie was around by whether or not its dulcet tones could be heard from the street.

On hearing Cally come in, Birdie put her head around the dispensary door. 'Morning, our Cally. How are we? Keeping out of trouble, I hope.'

'Good, thanks, very good.'

'Ready for our important strategy meeting,' Birdie joked with a wink.

'Yes, I am,'

Birdie wiggled a little white box. 'I have Lovely chocolates for us to indulge in.'

Cally chuckled. 'Trying to bribe me, are you?'

'Of course! I know how the world works. Bribery has performed wonders in my business.' Birdie laughed. 'Let's get the kettle on.'

Cally stripped off her coat and made her way to the staff room kitchen. Birdie followed in behind her, shut the door and put the little box of chocolates on the table. After waiting for a pot of tea to brew, Cally sat down.

Birdie raised her eyebrows. 'Let's cut straight to the chase, shall we? What have you decided? Remember, no pressure at all

– if you'd rather just keep things as they are here, that's fine by me. If so I'll start putting the feelers out.'

'I'd love to take the job. Thanks for giving me some time to think about it. Sorry it took a while.'

'Excellent!' Birdie clapped her hands and pulled the chocolate box away. 'I don't need to bribe you, then, ha ha!'

Cally laughed. 'You need to pay me in Lovely chocolate.'

'Okay, what I'll do is get the proper offer of employment sent and then we'll get started as soon as possible. I can't see any point in hanging around.'

'Nope.'

'Any questions?'

'Will it be in at the deep end, or will there be training or what?' Cally asked. 'The email mentioned a few things...'

Birdie smiled. 'Well, there's the new system for you to have a look at, and the training modules can be done online if you want to do it that way. I thought you could start with that and see how you get on. To be honest, the more I've thought about it, the more I think it's a bit suck it and see.'

'Yes, right, okay.'

'You've done so well here that it might be best for you to just go with that and run with it.'

Cally thought that might be the case. 'Mmm.'

'The main issue I have, as you know, is as I've taken on more shops, I've lost control of some of the day-to-day stuff. For a fact, I know that Peaceton isn't running quite as smoothly as everywhere else. I just haven't had time to get to the bottom of it, and it's a mess.'

'Maybe I should start there then.'

'The pharmacist working there at the moment is managing everything because it's quite a small store, but I think it needs some looking into. The storeroom needs sorting out just for starters...'

'Okay. Well, it sounds as if that might be a good place to begin. I like a challenge.' Cally laughed and sipped her tea.

Birdie popped a chocolate truffle in her mouth. 'As long as you don't mind being in the deep end a little bit.'

'Of course not,' Cally nodded, while inside feeling slightly nervous. *How hard could it be, though?* she thought to herself.

'I'll talk to the pharmacist there and brief her that you're going to take over everything regarding the ordering and deliveries.' Birdie opened her phone and made a note. She looked up with her eyebrows raised. 'So, we get on with this as soon as possible, as we said, yes?'

'Yes,' Cally nodded.

'Fabulous.'

'Thank you, Birdie. I cannot believe how generous you've been.'

'Nonsense! What about your other job? What are you going to do about that?'

'I'll phase that out,' Cally said with a smile, feeling strange that she would at last be finished with the chatbot job. Unknowingly, it had been a big part of her life.

'And Nina, working for A Lovely Organised Life. She's going to miss you.'

'She will. She's already apprehended me for evening shifts and weekends if I can fit them in. We'll see.'

'I thought she might. She knows what she's doing.'

'She does. I'll see how I go.'

Birdie pushed her chair back. 'Right, well, welcome to the company! Here's to the start of a new road, our Cally.'

Cally nodded. She couldn't wait to see where the road took her. She hoped it was nice around the corner. There were a few surprises to come.

23

Cally had spent most of the day in the staffroom online taking part in the training module for the new system. She was now under one of the counters in the shop trying to locate a part of a payment dongle that had cracked off, bounced across the floor, and skittered under the counter. She frowned as she heard the Shipping Forecast get closer and saw Birdie's pristine white shoes appear next to her head. The tone of Birdie's voice made her stop on all fours mid crawl. She didn't like the sound of Birdie's voice *at all*. With a massive surge of adrenaline, she panicked, knowing something was very wrong and edged out backwards as fast as she could.

'Is your phone off?' Birdie asked. Her tone tight, abrupt, and snipped.

Cally patted her pocket. Her phone wasn't there. 'Err, I left it out on the back. What's up?

'The manor is trying to get hold of you.'

'What? The manor? What for?'

'It's Doreen,' Birdie replied by way of explanation. It didn't explain anything.

'Oh right. What's wrong?'

'I don't know. She sounded harassed.'

'Weird.'

'I said you'd call,' Birdie said flatly.

Cally picked herself up from the floor and brushed herself off. 'Okay. I hope it's nothing serious. I wonder what's happened?'

After walking into the back room and locating her phone, Cally frowned to see loads of missed calls from a few different numbers including Logan's mum.

She called Logan's mum, Anne. 'Hey, sorry I missed your calls, it's Cally. Is everything okay?'

Anne sounded *terrible*. 'No, no, not at all. There's dreadful news.'

'What? Oh my god, is Logan okay?'

'No, I mean, yes, it's not Logan. Do you know where he is?'

'He said his phone was playing up. He'll be on the train back now if he made the one he said he was rushing for. He was out of battery just as he was getting to the station. What's happened?'

'There's been an accident.'

'What. Who with?'

'Alastair and Octavia have been involved in a plane crash. Alastair is not in a good way. He is in surgery at the moment. I'm sorry to say that it's touch and go. I don't know what to do.' Anne started to ramble. 'He was airlifted there. We need to get in touch with Logan. Right, he's on the train. I'm going with Cecilia and Reg now. Someone has to make sure the horses are sorted out. Doreen will have to ask one of the gardeners.'

Cally took charge. 'Oh God! Oh, okay. I'll go to the station. Don't worry. I'll sort it here and tell him. I'll text you to keep you updated. I'll talk to Doreen, and we'll work out the horses.'

Anne swore. 'Logan needs to get to the hospital. You two need to come. It's very serious, Cally. It's not looking good. We are leaving now.'

'Right. Understood. You go. Don't worry. I'll do everything. Just text me the details of where we need to go.'

Cally listened as Anne continued, then said goodbye, put her phone on the counter and raised her eyebrows.

Birdie stood with a concerned look on her face. 'What's happened?'

'Alastair and his girlfriend have been involved in an accident.'

'Doreen said it was an accident, but I didn't want to alarm you.'

'Alastair's in surgery. They couldn't get in touch with Logan. He spoke to me just before he was getting on the train. I think it might be best if I go there now and wait for his train to come in. Is that okay?'

'Of course! Do you want me to drive you?'

'Umm. No, I'll scoot around there and see if Logan took his car. If not, maybe you can come and pick us up?'

'Sure. I'll keep checking my phone.'

'Yep.'

'Let me know how you get on.'

Cally grabbed her bag and jacket as she headed for the door. 'Will do. Thanks, Birdie.'

Cally's mind turned over as she hurried towards the train station, weaving through the familiar streets of Lovely Bay. Anne had sounded *awful* on the phone, and Cally's brain struggled to process the information that Alastair had been in a plane crash. As she approached the station, she could hear the distant whistle of an approaching train. She hoped that Logan had made it and she quickened her pace, practically jogging the last few yards to the entrance.

Just as she was hustling through the station approaching the waiting room and then the ticket barrier, Nancy came out of the office, her arms full with a towering pile of box files. Nancy frowned at Cally's face. 'Everything okay, our Cally? You don't look at all good. What's up?'

'There's been an accident.'

'What? Where? In the chemist?'

'No, Alastair.'

'What up at the manor?'

'No, he's gone away. Long story.'

Nancy looked confused. 'Sorry, so why are you here? Where is he? Can I help?'

'Logan's on the train, but his phone was out of charge because it's on the blink. I've been on to him to get another one but he hadn't got around to it. Now he's on the train, or at least I think he is and no one can get in touch with him. I presume his phone is dead.'

Nancy balanced the files and checked her phone. 'Yeah, that's the train from London just outside the station now. Platform two.' She clicked a button on the gate, pulled it open, and waved Cally through. She indicated to the gate, 'I'll leave this one on the latch, just push it back on your way back. I hope everything's okay.'

'Thanks.' Cally hurried through and made her way to the platform just as the train pulled into the station. She scanned the disembarking passengers anxiously and spied Logan right at the end of the last carriage as if he'd just made the train. She swallowed. He had his bag slung over his shoulder, his suit jacket in his hand, his tie loosened, and he looked tired after a long day.

'Logan!' Cally called out, waving to catch his attention.

Logan craned his neck at the sound of Cally's voice, smiled, then narrowed his eyes as she got closer and he took in her expression. His smile faltered. 'What's wrong?'

Cally took a deep breath. 'There's been an accident. It's Alastair and Octavia.'

Logan's face drained of colour. 'What? What kind of accident? Are they okay?'

Cally shook her head. 'They were in a plane crash. Your mum called. Alastair's in surgery. I'm sorry, it doesn't sound good.'

Logan swore. His face looked as if the news had physically struck him. 'A plane crash? But they've only just left. Where are they?'

'Your mum said Alastair's been airlifted to hospital.' Cally explained.

Logan's eyes were wild, he nodded and fumbled for his phone. He waved it and swore. 'It died when I got to the train.'

'I know that's why I'm here.' Cally squeezed his arm. 'I don't have all the details. Did you drive here and park in the car park?'

'Yep.'

Cally turned, taking control. 'I'll text your mum so she knows what we're doing. I told her we'd go to the manor first and sort stuff out with Doreen. She didn't seem to know what was what. Then I'll drive us to the hospital. Actually, no, let's just call her. She was, err, a bit, umm, hysterical and not making much sense.'

Cally pressed Logan's mum's number and put the phone on speaker. It rang three times. 'Hello.'

'It's Cally, Logan's here. We're at the station making our way to the car. I've just told Logan.'

'Mum! What the hell? What happened?'

There was a shaky exhale on the other end of the line. 'Oh, thank goodness. Logan, darling, we need to get up there as soon as we can.'

'What happened? How bad is it?'

'It's not good, sweetheart,' Anne said, her voice breaking slightly. 'They were in a small private plane. Something went wrong during take-off. We don't know all the details yet.'

Logan made a choked sound. Cally wrapped an arm around his waist.

'Alastair's in surgery now,' Anne continued. 'He has multiple injuries. Internal bleeding, they said. Octavia's in better shape, thankfully. She's got a concussion and a broken arm, but she's conscious and stable.'

'Which hospital, Mum?' Logan asked, his voice barely above a whisper.

'St. Lucy's in London,' Cecilia replied. 'I'm driving Cecilia and Reg now. Cally said you'd do everything. You follow on behind when you're done.'

Logan nodded. 'Right. We'll be there as soon as we can.'

'Drive safely, darling,' Anne urged.

'Okay,' Logan agreed. 'We'll see you soon.'

Logan's face was ashen as they hurried through the train station and made their way to the car park. Of course, Logan's car was parked about just as far away from the station as it could be.

'I'll drive,' Cally said firmly, holding out her hand for Logan's keys. He handed them over, climbed into the passenger seat, plugged his phone cable into his phone, and stared blankly out the windscreen.

As Cally started the engine and pulled out of the car park, Logan shook his head, his voice hollow. 'I can't believe this is happening. They were so excited about their trip. They've not even left the country yet.'

Cally squeezed his hand. 'I know. Try not to assume the worst. Alastair's tough.'

Logan nodded but didn't look convinced. 'Was anyone else hurt?'

Cally shook her head. 'She didn't mention anyone else. The call was very rushed. I left the chemist and came straight to the station. We can ask when we get there.'

Cally didn't say anything else as she drove through Lovely.

The tension in the air wasn't pleasant as Logan jabbed at his phone and swore repeatedly. As Cally drove past Lovely lighthouse, she cringed. She'd been right all along. A feeling inside had told her there was something around the corner, and here it was, hitting her right between the eyes. There was no way she was going to say anything aloud, but she had a horrible sense of doom that wherever they were headed it was not going to end well. She tried to quell a sensation in her stomach that really bad news was coming their way.

24

The car was silent as Cally navigated through the traffic on the motorway. Her mind turned over and over as she silently went through a mental checklist about her work commitments and she realised as she'd thrown a few things in a bag that she'd forgotten to put in any clean tights. As they hit traffic and slowed to a crawl, Logan tapped his hand repeatedly on the centre console as if somehow him doing that might speed the traffic up. It was as if tension and stress streamed out of him. Cally had never seen him like it and never wanted to again. His phone buzzed with a text. He read it and frowned. 'It's from Mum. They've arrived at the hospital. No news yet. Alastair's still in surgery.'

Cally nodded, keeping her eyes on the road. She didn't have much clue about surgery, but the little she did know told her that Alastair had been in for a while. 'I'm not sure what to think. Is that a good thing or a bad thing? That's good, isn't it?'

'I suppose. I just keep thinking, what if he doesn't make it, Cal? What if the last real time I saw him was at that stupid pub in Scotland, and I was annoyed because he was going on and on about his travel plans? Remember afterwards when I was moaning about how spoilt he was? I went on about it for ages, didn't I? I was slagging off how entitled he was.' Logan swore and sighed.

Cally had had similar thoughts as they'd driven along. 'Don't think like that. He'll be fine. Honestly, we don't even know the full story yet.'

'I'm trying. I just can't believe it. It was the sound of Mum's voice. It's serious.'

Cally had thought exactly the same. 'Hmm. Let's just wait and see.'

'He's not just my cousin. I've like grown up with him.'

Cally felt her heart ache at Logan's voice. 'I know. I know.'

The traffic cleared again, and they drove on in silence for ages. The motorway felt way too busy and endless as far as Cally was concerned. She kept checking the map on the screen to her left, feeling as if they were never going to get there. After about another hour had passed in excruciatingly slow traffic, Cally's phone buzzed with an incoming call. 'Can you check that? It might be someone from work. I left in a rush. I was halfway through an order out the back.'

Logan picked up Cally's phone and flicked open the cover. 'It's Nina.'

'Can you answer? I was going to text her about that evening job tomorrow when we got there.'

Logan answered the call, putting it on speaker. 'Hello?'

'Logan?' Nina's voice came through, sounding worried.

'I'm here, Nina,' Cally called out. 'I'm driving. We're on our way to London.'

Nina sighed. 'I heard what happened. Birdie told me. Are you both okay?'

'We're fine. Just worried.'

'Of course, of course,' Nina said. 'Is there anything I can do?'

'No. I'm not sure when I'll be back. I might not make it to that job.'

'Don't worry, I've already thought about that.'

'Great. Thanks. Sorry if I let you down.'

'Don't be silly! If you need anything at all, just shout.'

'Thanks, Nina,' Logan said, his voice thick with emotion. 'Appreciate it.'

After they ended the call, Logan leaned back in his seat, and closed his eyes as Cally slowed down as another gnarly rush hour traffic spot had them almost stationary. Cally gripped the wheel tightly and wished they could be transported to the hospital in any way other than via the horrors of the M25. The whole atmosphere in the car reminded her of the many times she'd made her way to the hospital for her grandma. It had been a very similar scenario when she'd been in the hospice, too. The feeling as if you were about to enter something you had no clue about, at the same time as being racked with emotion.

Logan's phone trilled. He snatched it up. 'Hello, Mum? Any news?'

Cally watched Logan's face anxiously, trying to gauge the news from his expression. She sat silently with her hands still gripping the steering wheel.

'Okay. Yes, we're about halfway there. The traffic is a joke. Thanks for letting us know.' Logan tapped his phone and put it into the centre console, ran a hand over his face and swore. 'He's out of surgery but he's not out of the woods yet. He's going to intensive care now.'

Cally sighed. 'That's good news, isn't it?'

'Yeah. Yeah, it is. She said they've just been told the next twenty-four hours are critical...' Logan's voice trailed off.

'Right.'

Logan swore again. 'I can't believe this. One minute he's going off to see the world and now this.'

Cally patted Logan's hand. 'It'll be okay.' Inside she wasn't sure if she believed that it would. The horrid inner nagging voice brayed at her.

As they crawled along, silence and tension filled the car. 'Do you want me to drive for a bit?' Logan offered. 'We can pull in at the next petrol station.'

Cally shook her head. 'I'm okay. It's fine.'

As they neared London, the traffic began to pick up again, and it finally felt as if they were getting nearer to the hospital. Cally wasn't big on driving, and considering she'd never ventured very far from home, she wasn't doing too badly. She kept her eyes glued to the road and waited for the instructions from the speaker as she navigated carefully through the busy streets, following the GPS directions to St. Lucy's Hospital. After taking a wrong turn and going around in circles past an NCP car park for what felt like hours, they finally pulled into the hospital, waited at a barrier and followed a tight road to an underground car park. After locking the car, they hurried into the building, following signs to the intensive care unit, navigated their way through the huge hospital and arrived at a bright and oddly cheerful ICU reception area.

Cally blinked as she took in an overly lit bright pink wall behind the main focal point of a shiny white curved reception desk. The cheerful-looking area felt totally out of sync with how Cally felt. As they waited in a short queue, the smell, the staff, and the lighting made her feel as if she'd zoomed back a few years. As she stepped to the side while Logan spoke, her eyes roamed around the reception area; a sign encouraged donations via text to support the hospital, a bright red bin denoted something serious inside, and various signage above the desk barked instructions and hospital-related information. A couple of friendly-looking staff in bright uniforms bustled around behind the desk, and a few minutes later, Cally and Logan were on their way to an outer waiting room.

As Logan held the door open for Cally, the smell in the

waiting room hit her full-on, making her want to gag; a mixture of too-hot yet air-conditioned stale air, cheap coffee, and very stressed people. Cally knew the smell only too well. She'd been part of it many times before. The smell sat alongside a memory she would rather have forgotten. Cecilia, Reg, and Logan's mum were sitting awkwardly upright on horrid green and purple plastic chairs. Logan's mum rose as soon as she saw them and gave Logan a tight hug.

'Oh, darling. I'm so glad you're here.'

Logan hugged her back fiercely. 'How is he? Any change?'

Cecilia stepped forward and hugged Logan then pulled back, her face etched with worry. 'He's stable for now.'

Reg kissed Cally and then clasped Logan's shoulder. 'He's fighting, hopefully.'

Logan nodded, his jaw clenched tight. 'And Octavia? How is she?'

'She's okay,' Cecilia said. 'They're keeping her in for observation because of the concussion, but she should be able to go home soon.'

'Can we see him?' Logan asked.

Cecilia shook her head. 'Only immediate family are allowed in ICU and not even us at the moment.'

Logan's shoulders slumped. Cally wrapped an arm around his waist. They sat down, Logan asked a tonne of questions, Cecilia cried, Cally forced herself to be strong, Anne shredded a tissue in her lap, and Reg looked as if he didn't know what to do or say for the best. Logan leaned his head back against the wall and closed his eyes. Cally stared at a set of two drinks machines wedged precariously in the corner. 'Does anyone want a cup of tea?'

Cecilia nodded to the machines and screwed up her lips. 'We had some coffee earlier. It was rank. Absolutely disgusting.'

Cally shifted to the front of her seat. 'How about I go off and find us all a nice cup of tea? There must be a little shop somewhere.'

Reg exhaled and nodded. 'I'd love one.'

Cally stood up. 'Right, I'll be back with tea.'

Cally was more than pleased to get out of the waiting room. As she went through the hospital in search of a decent cup of tea, she felt as if she'd rather be anywhere else than in the horrible room with the sickly smell, humming drinks machines, and overly bright lights. After following a coloured line on the floor in and out of corridors for ages, eventually, it led her to a line of lifts. She studied the floor directory for a second, pressed the button to go down with her elbow, stepped in and a few minutes later found herself in the hospital café. Realising that she was starving and that everyone else probably was too she bought a few rounds of sandwiches, five cups of tea, grabbed a cardboard cup holder, shoved the sandwiches in her bag and made her way back up to the waiting room.

The tea and sandwiches, despite the severity of the situation and the tense atmosphere, went down well. Eventually after they were long gone and what felt like hours, a doctor in scrubs appeared at the waiting room door. 'Family of Alastair Henry-Hicks?' he called out.

Everyone in the room sat up straighter. Cecilia and Reg stepped forward. Cecilia flicked her hand between herself and her husband. 'We're his parents,' Cecilia said, her voice tight with anxiety. 'How is he?'

The doctor's face was serious. He beckoned Cecilia and Reg out into the corridor. Cally watched through the slim pane of glass in the door and saw all sorts of emotions cross Cecilia's face. In a flash she remembered being the one standing in front of a doctor listening to stuff she had no clue about. Standing there holding up the sky.

About ten minutes later Cecilia and Reg came back in as Logan paced around.

'He's still critical, but he's showing some positive signs.'

'What happens now?' Anne asked.

'We wait.'

Tears streamed down Cecilia's face and she let out a strange animal-like sob. Logan jumped up and hugged her. Cally bit her lip. She still had the bad feeling. She couldn't shake that there was more to come. She wasn't wrong.

25

It was the next day. The night before, Cally, Logan, and Logan's mum Anne had, in the end, left the hospital and made their way to the Henry-Hicks London house in Chelsea. Cally woke up and, for a second, couldn't get her bearings. She turned to her left to see the bed empty. Laying back on the pillows, she looked around the room for a minute and thought about the day before. It had been stressful, tiring, horrible, and tense in every way. On top of that, there had been the repugnant smell, the awful bright lights, and the feeling of being in limbo, desperately waiting for news. Plus, she'd hated the driving and the traffic. Nothing about the day had been nice. It had most definitely not been a perfect day.

In direct contrast to that, now, however, Cally found herself so very far from the hospital waiting room, it was comical. She blinked as she looked around at the elegant, opulent, and beautifully decorated bedroom surrounding her. It was so luxurious that it made her feel as if she was having an out-of-body experience. Walls with stately golden-yellow wallpaper looked back at her, a heavy peach throw blanket draped the foot of the bed and to the left, in a window alcove, a plush loveseat upholstered in rich velvet, and a comfortable armchair sat nudged up to the curtains. Little decorative cushions were perched here and there, and between the loveseat and the armchair, a small round table with a vase of flowers looked as if someone had polished it for a long time. Cally wasn't sure whether she wanted to get up or not. For a good few minutes, she just stared at the windows dressed in their swathes of luxurious, heavy cream-coloured curtains, and their elaborate draping and tassel details. On the far right, against the wall, a stylish cabinet with a glass front held two matching lamps with cream-coloured shades and a grandmother clock ticked in the corner.

Cally shook her head; she was a long, *long* way from the dreary rental house she'd lived in the last time she'd been anywhere near a hospital. In the guest room in Chelsea, the overall feeling swallowing her was like everything else to do with the Henry-Hicks lot: decadent yet understated luxury, and timeless elegance to the max.

Not sure whether to go downstairs or leave Logan alone and not really totally aware of where she was, she slipped out of bed, pushed the door open to the en-suite, and stood at the double sinks staring at her reflection. When she'd hastily shoved a few things in a bag in the cottage, she'd not bothered with anything from the bathroom – she needn't have worried. The en-suite was stacked with all sorts of fancy high-end lotions and potions; Asprey soap and matching cream stood by both sinks, a white robe with its belt tied up neatly hung in a little cabinet, and a massive stack of white towels and flannels was perfectly folded underneath the sinks. Cally sat on the loo and peered at the rolltop bathtub, picked up a bottle of Kiehl's soap, examined its ingredients and put it back down again.

She'd mused it many, many, *many* times since she'd met Logan, but the same thought again filtered through her brain: how the other half lived. The "London" house as the Henry-

Hicks clan always referred to it, served as a base for when any of them were in London. Like Doreen at Lovely Manor and the housekeeper in Scotland, the London house had staff which explained how when they'd rocked up the night before exhausted, they'd found food in the fridge and fallen into freshly laundered beds.

On the side of the sink, Cally realised that clean clothes were neatly stacked and ready for her: a navy blue luxury top and matching casual bottoms together with clean undies and a plain white pressed t-shirt. She vaguely remembered Logan saying something to her about it the night before when she'd undressed. He'd whisked her underwear, tights, and shirt away saying he'd take everything downstairs to be sorted. Half asleep by that stage, she'd not really taken much notice. She shook her head and pondered what it was like to live in the lap of luxury. A glimpse into the life of the elite. When the going got tough, other people washed your underwear.

After showering and luxuriating in how even the shower-head and water felt like a whole other world from her tiny flat above the deli, Cally pulled on the clothes and admired how the fabric felt on her skin, not really understanding how a simple top could be so soft. Had a little fairy spun the top in silk? How was it screaming luxury at her? How did it make her feel as if she might float? She had no idea but wanted in on it somehow in her life. Logan was more and more a keeper every single day.

Once she got down a few sets of stairs and navigated her way through a large hall to a kitchen, she definitely wasn't float-ing. The look on Logan's face put paid to that. He was sitting at a large, long, ornate marble kitchen island looking at his phone. He looked worse than dreadful. He sighed and closed his eyes as Cally walked in. 'Morning.'

'Morning. Any news?'

'Nothing really.' Logan slipped off his stool. 'Tea?'

'Yep, please'

'Toast?'

'Don't worry I'll make it.'

Logan gestured to the stools, 'No, sit down. I'll do it.'

A few minutes later, he passed Cally a mug of tea and a plate with buttered toast and proceeded to pace back and forth, the polished floor squeaking slightly with each turn. Cally didn't know what to say or do for the best. There was a tension in the room she wasn't quite sure how to deal with. Not only that, she still had the feeling in her water that very bad news lurked just around the corner. She *did* know she'd be keeping that little morsel of knowledge under wraps. As she sat eating the toast and drinking her tea, minutes seemed to take hours.

About twenty minutes later, she'd gathered her jacket, been to the loo, and they were outside the house, walking across the road to Logan's car. As he fumbled in his pocket for his keys, Cally peered over at four-storey Grade II listed Georgian prop-erties and gulped at their magnificence. Tall, white, beautiful old houses stood on all four sides of central gardens and just behind where the car was parked, a huge iron gate with a lock led the way inside. Through wrought iron railings, lush well-kept lawns were maintained with crisscrossing gravel pathways. The paths divided the space into neat sections of greenery with benches strategically placed here and there surrounded by flower beds. The scene was completed with mature leafy trees, Victorian-style lamp posts, low boxwood hedges, and a statue in the middle. Very, very nice.

Logan didn't even give it a second glance, clicked the remote control for the car, opened his door, leant over and pushed Cally's from the inside. She hopped in, kept her mouth shut, and sat looking out the window as Logan slowly inched the car around the fancy London square. After navigating their way through the traffic, the same as the night before, they found themselves in the hospital car park and took the same route they'd hurried along the previous evening. Arriving in the ICU reception, Cally continued not to say much as Logan paced in the queue to speak to the staff behind the desk. Once through the main entrance, Logan opened the door to the inner waiting room and gestured for Cally to go in first. Seeing no one in the waiting area, Cally immediately felt as if something was very wrong. For a long time, no one walked past the door. There was no sign of Reg, Cecilia or Anne and no news via their phones.

Just as Cally was thinking about doing a coffee run, she peered down the corridor through the sliver of glass in the door and saw Reginald come out of a door with a doctor. Cally read the situation instantly; she could see by Reg's body language that the news wasn't good. His face was grave, as if every little part of him sagged and had gone grey. Cally remained where she was, didn't pass on her observations to Logan, kept quiet, and watched as Reg and the doctor disappeared again. Half an hour or so later, the waiting room door opened. Reg stepped in, Cecilia behind him. Reginald's face was ashen, his eyes red-rimmed.

Logan was on his feet in a flash as Anne came in behind Cecilia. 'What's happened?'

Reg's voice was barely above a whisper. 'He's gone.'

Cecilia sobbed and Anne said nothing.

'What?' Logan's voice cracked. 'What do you mean? It can't be right! They said he was stable!'

Reg shook his head, his eyes unfocused, he mumbled, not very easy to understand. 'His brain. They couldn't... there was nothing they could do.'

Reginald and Cecilia looked shell-shocked. Anne's face was streaked with tears. Reg seemed to have aged years in the span of minutes. His whole face looked as if its skin had somehow deflated.

'Our dear, sweet boy.' Cecilia's words dissolved into weeping as Reginald pulled her close.

Cally focused on Logan not quite sure what to do. He stood

slightly apart from the others, his face a mask of shock and grief. Feeling somewhat detached, as if watching a particularly surreal and very unpleasant film, she stepped beside Logan. His face was stony as he looked down at the floor and gripped Cally's hand. Anne began to sob.

26

Early the next morning, Cally had left Logan asleep and crept out of bed after a very unsettled night of tossing and turning this way and that. After finding herself awake in the early hours, she'd grabbed her pile of clothes from the chair by the door, padded down the hallway to one of the main bathrooms, and locked the door behind her. The same as in the ensuite guest bathroom, in the main bathroom there'd been no lack of high-end toiletries to see Cally through. She'd showered, pumped a ridiculous amount of posh shower gel onto her skin, washed her hair, done the same with the conditioner, rinsed off, dried herself with the plumpest towels she'd ever got close to in her life, and then tiptoed down the stairs to what the family referred to as the "drawing room" at the front of the house.

The room, the same as everything else in the house, was comfortably luxurious and quietly opulent. For a second, Cally just stood in the doorway looking at it all: a huge old fireplace and mantel, thick, heavy curtains perfectly aligned in beautiful folds pulled back over floor-to-ceiling shutters, lamps nearly as big as her on highly polished tables, two oversized, overly plush sofas, so many expensive cushions the dents in their tops just so.

Strolling over a beautiful rug with plaited edges that topped a herringbone floor, Cally sat in one of two wingback chairs by a wide, deep window nook looking out over the square. A soft pitter-patter of rain doused the window panes in tiny speckles of light, and a swish of cars passing around the square filled the air. Cally looked past two exquisitely manicured bay trees on the marble front steps and watched as the rain fell onto the pavement. A heavy sky full of grey clouds draped the whole scene in a muted wash of faded colours in perfect sync with what was going on in the house.

Cally pulled her MacBook Air onto her lap, flipped up the lid, pressed the button in the top right-hand corner, and checked into the chatbot portal to make sure her shifts were covered for the rest of the week. Then, resting her chin on her hand on the arm of the chair, she idly watched the rain and thought about how long she'd worked on the chatbot. She'd found the jobs years before on a job board and had made the application along with hundreds of others. She remembered the ghastliness of the online video assessment via a pre-recorded woman from some remote HR department. Then came ridiculous multiple-choice questions in the next round. After that had involved role playing, again via a pre-recorded session of videos. Finally, at the end of the tests she'd had a video call with a human in a call centre in Ireland and eventually a job offer in her inbox.

She shook her head as she watched a woman with an umbrella and a little girl in a yellow raincoat and pink wellies stroll to the gate of the garden opposite in the middle of the square, open the gate with a key and walk in. Here she was in a very posh house, logging into the portal and looking at her shifts just as she had done for a long time. Albeit in very different circumstances and by way of a fancy MacBook Air, she was still there with the chatbot in her life. Sometimes, she felt as if the customer service job was ultimately a crutch, a stable part of her life that, no matter what she did or where she was, simply was always there for her on the other side of her screen. She'd told herself that she hadn't yet given notice for the job because she wanted to keep the extra money for a bit longer. Really, she wondered if that was true. She knew deep down it wasn't.

Just as she was pondering when she'd give up the chatbot job, she saw the doorknob turn, and the door quietly opened into the room. The housekeeper, Larissa, whom Cally had met the day before, smiled. 'Morning.' Larissa held up a tray. 'I thought you might be in need of a cup of tea.'

Cally smiled. 'Ahh, thank you so much! You didn't need to do that. I didn't think anyone was up yet. I was trying to be quiet and keep a low profile.'

'I don't think anyone else is. I started at five and heard you come down.'

Cally raised her eyebrows. 'That's an early start.'

Larissa put the tray on the small table beside Cally. 'There's a lot to do in a house of this size.'

'I suppose there must be.' Cally looked at the mug of tea and a little plate of pastries. 'So kind of you, thanks.'

'Couldn't sleep?' Larissa asked.

'Oh, yes and no. It's a habit. I've been getting up early for years.'

'What, for the horses?'

Cally chuckled. Larissa clearly assumed Cally was in the same boat as the rest of the Henry-Hicks. 'No.' She tapped her laptop. 'I work online and I regularly do a morning shift, so my body clock wakes up early. I've been doing it for years.'

'I see.' Larissa lowered her voice and gestured upwards with her left thumb. 'How were they last night? What a dreadful thing to happen.'

Cally pursed her lips for a second. 'Not great. Hopefully, they might have got some sleep.'

'It's terrible.'

'I know.'

Larissa shook her head. 'I don't think it's going to be a very pleasant few months for anyone involved.'

Cally nodded. She felt exactly the same way. 'No, it won't be. Not at all.'

～

A few hours later, Cally sat at the worktop in the kitchen of the London house. She took a sip of her tea, the warmth of the mug nice in her hands. She watched Logan move around the kitchen, his movements mechanical as if he was operating on autopilot. She felt small, insignificant, wary, and not sure what to do or say.

'How are you feeling?' She knew it was a ridiculous question even as she heard the words come out of her mouth.

Logan paused his hand on the kettle. 'I don't know. It still doesn't feel real.' He turned around and leant against the work-top. 'I keep expecting my phone to buzz with some ridiculous meme from Alastair or for him to burst through the door. Do you know what I mean?'

Cally nodded. She knew the feeling exactly – she'd had it with her grandma. When her grandma had passed away, Cally had felt as if she'd actually lost not just someone in her life but a job, too. Which, to be fair, she had. Her whole existence had involved caring. Not just the physical side of it but the full and hefty mental load had always been at the very centre of her life. When it had been removed, that alone had felt like a loss. As if someone had chopped off her arm. 'I can't say anything other than it's very hard.'

Logan sighed and ruffled his hair, making it stand up at odd angles. 'The thing is, I can't stop thinking about how much he irritated me at that dinner. What a thing to focus on! I feel so guilty.' Logan's voice broke slightly on the last word.

Cally had felt similar things when her mum had died. 'I know it's not easy.'

'How is it possible that a funeral is being planned? They were meant to be going around the world...' Logan trailed off.

Cally put her mug down. She was well aware of the feeling of grief. She also knew that it had to be navigated with care. 'I wish I could do something to help.'

'You're already doing it by just being here. I'm sorry if I'm miserable.'

'Don't be ridiculous! What about Octavia? Has there been any update on her condition? What did your mum say?'

'She's being discharged today, apparently. I can't even imagine what she's going through.'

'I know.'

Logan watched a couple of pieces of toast pop out of the toaster, buttered them, and pushed a plate in Cally's direction. Cally pulled the plate towards her. 'I need to let Birdie know I won't be in.'

Logan looked up, frowning slightly. 'God, Cal, I'm so sorry. I didn't even think about your new job.'

Cally shook her head. 'Don't apologise. It's fine.'

'What about the customer service stuff?'

'I've covered them all until next week. Maybe this will be the end of it...'

'Thanks for doing that.'

'What's the plan for today?' Cally was of the opinion that Logan should head back to Lovely, but she intended to keep quiet about what she thought unless she was asked.

'I don't think there is one. I don't know, really.' Logan gestured around the house. 'I suppose see what happens. There's not really a lot I can do here.'

'Why don't we go for a walk?' Cally suggested. 'Get some fresh air before things, well, you know. It might do you good.'

Logan hesitated, then nodded. 'Yeah, I could do with some fresh air.'

Half an hour or so later, they stepped out into a dreary London morning, the streets still damp from the early-morning rain. Cally took in her clearly affluent surroundings: the towering white townhouses lining the square and the luxury cars parked in designated bays. It was a far cry from the cosy, slightly shabby charm of Lovely Bay but nice all the same.

'This must have been an interesting place to be when you were young,' Cally noted.

Logan strolled along with his hands in his pockets and glanced around as if seeing the street for the first time. 'I suppose so. Though we didn't spend that much time here, really. It was more of a base for when we had to be in London.'

Cally peered at a beautiful tall house with heavy black window boxes dancing with box hedges and white flowers, a huge brass knocker on a front door, and marble steps. 'Right, yes, I see.' She didn't see. Not even close.

'Look, I'm sorry about this, Cal. It must be bringing back stuff for you.'

'It's fine.'

'Is it doing that, I mean?'

'A bit. It would be weird if it didn't.'

'Right.'

'It's different, though. I sort of knew what was coming. I had a *lot* of time to prepare.'

'Hmm.'

'You didn't have that.'

'No.' Logan swore. 'I just don't know how to deal with it.'

Cally sighed and squeezed Logan's hand. 'Just prepare yourself for it to be tough. It's really the only thing you can do.' Cally silently swallowed, more than aware of just how horrible it was going to be. She wasn't looking forward to the coming few weeks. There she'd been thinking how lucky and gilded the Henry-Hicks lot were. How that had changed.

27

A week or so later, things were back to semi-normal as much as they could be. Cally had been busy at the chemist, continuing with the training course on the distribution system and Logan had gone back to work. After she'd finished work, Cally had realised she'd left her iPad at the cottage before the accident and had decided a walk and some fresh air would do her the world of good to clear her head after a few days of learning the ins and outs of the system. She'd made a hot blackcurrant, taken her time and strolled up to the manor. Having not been to the cottage for a few days, she'd let herself in and was surprised by what hit her; a horrible mess as soon as she stepped in the door.

Cally frowned and shook her head. The cottage was usually cleaned by one of the Manor cleaners from an agency in the next town, but by the way it looked the cleaners had not been near nor by it. Logan's shoes were strewn in the hallway, his work bag looked as if it had been dropped on the floor, and when she got to the kitchen, she raised her eyebrows. The sink was littered with dirty dishes and a pint of milk on the worktop looked as if it had seen better days. Loads of dirty mugs stood by the kettle, and the kitchen table was scattered with all sorts. The microwave door was open, showing a bowl of congealed baked beans that appeared to have been heated up and then forgotten. A bottle of wine with a third left in the bottom stood with the top off besides a dirty glass. Cally wrinkled her face in surprise. It was not like Logan at all to live like a slob. In fact, he was usually fairly meticulous about things. Right in front of her, she could see grief doing its thing.

Taking off her cardigan and rolling up her shirt sleeves, she got to it right away, opened the dishwasher, started to methodically unload the clean dishes and one by one put them away. As she dumped the baked beans in the bin, turned on the tap and began to rinse the plates and load them neatly into the empty dishwasher, she thought about all that had happened since she'd arrived back from Scotland. The image of Reginald's face as he'd come through the hospital waiting room door was scorched into the frontal lobe of Cally's brain. She'd never be able to unsee the unfiltered pain and she hoped that she'd never witness it again in her life. Reg's face had been half horrified and half shocked. Cally had never seen a look like it. Since then, she'd seen Reginald at the London house and at the manor and he aged twenty years in a few days. He'd appeared as if he was in freefall, flailing around not sure what to do or say. As if he would never hit the ground again. Cecilia wasn't far behind.

Cally sighed as she removed everything from the worktops on either side of the sink, unplugged the kettle, put it on the kitchen table, and copiously sprayed the sides with kitchen cleaner. Working from the wall out, she systematically cleaned the worktops until they were sparkling, plugged the kettle back in, popped a tablet in the dishwasher, and pressed go. The microwave was not giving off good vibes; she cut up a lemon, squeezed the juice into a bowl of water, dropped it in, closed the door, and pressed the button for three minutes on high. Fiddling with her necklace as she watched the bowl spin around for a second, she puffed a huff out of her lips. At least she was doing something useful in the midst of the terrible time. There was that.

Just as she was taking a bag out to the bins behind the stables, she saw Doreen coming the other way with a jumble of empty recycling containers in her hands.

'Hey, our Cally. How are you?'

'Not too bad. You?'

Doreen shook her head and sighed. 'I've been better. Not good times. I'm keeping my head down and staying busy.'

Cally lowered her voice. 'How are things?'

'Cecilia is *not* in a good way. She's going downhill fast now rather than the other way. Grief is a funny old thing.'

'Hmm.'

'What are you doing? How is Logan?'

'I'm fine. Yeah, Logan is struggling.'

'I thought so. I saw him yesterday. He didn't want to talk.'

'No, it seems to be his way of dealing with it. I came up because I'd left my iPad here a while ago and it's got a list on it I need.' Cally gestured in the direction of Logan's cottage. 'I've spent the last hour cleaning. It was a right mess in there.'

Doreen clucked her tongue. 'Logan said he didn't want anyone there. It was cleaner day for the cottages today and so I told them not to go in.'

Cally shook her head. 'I gathered that. It's very unlike him to be messy. In fact, he's usually the other way.'

'Grief does strange things.'

Cally nodded, her heart heavy. 'I suppose it does. I'm worried about him.'

Doreen sighed and put down the recycling containers. 'It's not easy losing someone so suddenly. Especially someone like Alastair. He was always here, there, and everywhere.'

Cally thought about her mum and her grandma. 'I know. I've been through it a couple of times but not like this and as suddenly. I think a lot of it is the shock.'

'Who would have thought? You just don't know what's coming your way, do you?'

'No. Logan's trying to put on a brave face. He and Alastair were close...'

Doreen nodded. 'They were more like brothers than cousins, I sometimes thought.'

'From what I saw, I guess so.'

'Thick as thieves when they were little. Always getting into some mischief or other. When they were about eight or nine, they decided they were going to run away and join the circus.'

Doreen chuckled. 'They packed their little rucksacks with sweets and comics, and snuck out in the middle of the night. We found them asleep in the old treehouse by the lake covered in bites.'

'Aww, sweet.'

Doreen tutted. 'It's hard to get your head around it.'

'I wish there was more I could do to help.'

'You're doing plenty, love. Just being there for him, that's what he needs right now. I mean, what else can you do?'

'Not a lot. How are the funeral preparations coming along? You've taken on a lot of that from what Anne said.'

Doreen pressed her lips together. 'As well as can be expected, under the circumstances. They were talking about it being in London, did you hear that? I didn't think that was a good idea, but it's not up to me.'

'Yes. I thought the same.'

'I'm glad they settled on the church in Lovely for the service. It seemed more fitting in my humble opinion given the family's history with the place.'

'Agree.'

'The reception in the marquee near the summer house

surrounded by the beautiful poppy fields will be nice. If "nice" is a word that can be used in this situation.'

Cally nodded and raised her chin in the direction of the summer house. 'It's a beautiful spot.'

'Who wouldn't love those poppy fields, especially when they are in full bloom like this?'

'True. The funeral is going to be a lot of work.'

Doreen sighed and rubbed her forehead. 'Yes, there are loads coming which is why the marquee is also a good idea in my opinion. The family alone is extensive, as you know, and then there are all of Alastair's friends and colleagues. We're looking at a lot of people turning up, if you ask me.'

'I reckon so. Do you need any help?' Cally offered.

'I might need some help here and there and at the church. Everything here is mostly covered with the staff. I was going to mention it, actually. I just know you'll get your head down and get on with it. I can't be doing with any, well, you know what I mean.'

'Of course. Just let me know when and where.'

'I'll let you know the details. I'll message you.' Doreen lowered her voice. 'I just thought I can rely on you. You know? I phoned Birdie earlier. She's going to rally the troops.'

'Of course. I'll make sure I'm available.' Cally lowered her voice. 'Have you heard anything about Octavia?'

'Not well, I'm afraid. She's still in shock. Can't quite believe it's real.'

Cally nodded. 'I can't even imagine.'

Doreen clicked her fingers. 'All those dreams and plans, gone in an instant.'

'It's strange, isn't it? How life just goes on,' Cally gestured towards the fields. 'The flowers are still blooming, the birds are still singing. It feels like the whole world should stop, but it doesn't.'

Doreen nodded. 'That's the way of things, I'm afraid. The world keeps turning, as they say.'

'I suppose.'

'Speaking of life going on,' Doreen said, glancing at her watch, 'I'd better get back to work.'

'I hope you're okay. I know it can't be easy organising all of this.'

'It's the least I can do.'

With that, Doreen picked up her recycling containers and headed off towards the main house, leaving Cally standing by the bins. After depositing her recycling, she walked back to the cottage, her mind full about the funeral. When she walked back into the kitchen, it was a vast improvement from what she'd found. The dishwasher hummed away, the worktops gleamed, fresh air came in through the window, and she'd put away stuff that had been all over the kitchen table. Strolling into the laundry room she put a load of whites on and started to fold things from the tumble dryer. Then in the sitting room, she wiped down the coffee table, plumped up the cushions, and went to the mantelpiece to dust. She sighed as she picked up a picture of Alastair and Logan in a framed photo she hadn't noticed before. Logan and Alastair, arms slung around each other's shoulders, grinning widely at the camera. They looked to be in their late teens or early twenties, standing in front of the stables. Both of them looked so happy and carefree. Putting the photo back down, she sighed, glanced at her phone, felt surprised to see how much time had passed, found her iPad, and made her way back out.

Walking down the long driveway as she stared ahead at the swathes of poppies swaying back and forth in the wind, she couldn't stop thinking about the funeral and how many people would be attending. How sad it was going to be. She squeezed her eyes together at what it would be like for Cecilia and Reginald dealing with the unthinkable task of burying their child.

As she reached the main gates, Cally paused and looked back towards Lovely Manor. The grand old house stood as it always had not looking any different. It appeared seemingly untouched by what was going on in and around it. Shouldering a loss that had shaken the Henry-Hicks family to its core. Cally sighed. Perhaps their life wasn't quite as gilded after all.

28

Cally blinked one eye open, frowned, puffed out her lips and rolled over. No Logan. She propped herself up onto her elbows and frowned. She was not, in fact, dreaming. It was correct that she'd woken up to the smell of bacon, eggs and frying onions. Was there the smell of croissants, too? Whatever it was, she liked it. She checked the time on her phone. It was still *very* early. Pulling on her pyjama top and slipping on the matching bottoms, she twirled her hair into a bun on the top of her head and made her way to the kitchen, where the bacon smell just got better. She could hear pots clanking and the coffee percolator bubbling. Logan was barefoot and bare-chested, leaning against the tiny worktop with his phone in his hand. Cally let out an inner sigh of relief that he looked a bit better.

Logan glanced up. 'Morning, Blackcurrant.'

'Morning. Sorry, what are you doing?' Cally asked, gesturing around the kitchen.

'Putting up some wallpaper.'

'Funny.'

'What does it look like I'm doing?'

'I don't know, but I *do* know it smells amazing.'

'I am making you a good luck breakfast for your first real day in your new job. Now you've got the training thing over with and you're going to be out on the road, I thought I would see you off.'

Cally shook her head. 'You *really* didn't need to do that.'

'I *really* did. I know I've been a nightmare to be around...'

'Your cousin just died.'

'Still.' Logan gestured into the sitting room where the table was laid with a white tablecloth, a little jug of flowers and a carafe of fresh orange juice.

Cally raised her eyebrows. 'Wow, do I get this every day now?'

Logan widened his eyes and swore. 'Pah, no you don't, this has nearly killed me. You might have to live off the memory of this for a while. It's been a task in coordination.'

About ten minutes later, Cally sat at the table with the table-cloth and the flowers, a glass of freshly squeezed orange juice in her hand, the coffee pot in front of her and a plate of food ready to be tucked in. Rashers of bacon sat artfully arranged next to a little gathering of avocado and rocket, a poached egg sat on top of fancy sourdough bread, tiny little circles of bright red chilli and snips of chives winked at her, and a round of homemade hash browns was nudged up on the side. Cally smiled. Not quite home-brand cornflakes. A high-ranking trust fund breakfast if ever she'd seen one.

'So, thoughts about today?'

Cally felt a flush of heat run up her neck. She switched the flick in the back of her throat. The one she hadn't used for a very long time. 'Nothing, really. It's fine.'

Logan frowned. 'The voice is back.'

'No, it's not.'

'Let me tell you: it is.'

'I just feel a bit scrambled, as it were.'

'Totally natural. You would do.'

'I guess so.'

'What's the brief from Birdie?'

'I'm going to the shop in Peaceton to see what is what out the back. Birdie said it's a disaster there because she's not all over it and hasn't got the time.'

'To do what?'

'She wants me to just start at the bottom in the back room and see what's going on. It makes sense to start from there. Then I'm going to have to implement what we do in the Lovely shop and change some of the systems and think about what I learnt in the training sessions.'

'Sounds challenging.'

'Yep.'

'Is that why you did the voice?'

'I'm just nervous.'

'I'm not. You'll walk it, Blackcurrant.'

Cally nodded, but inside, she wasn't quite as sure. As the reality of going to another shop loomed, she wondered what she'd taken on.

Cally drove along a dual-carriageway with the radio on low and her phone clamped in a holder beside her. It had taken a bit of time to get used to the small company van. Vans had clearly come a long way. Not that she'd ever driven one before, but this one had all the mod cons and was easy enough to drive. What was interesting was that the seat was comfier than the one in Logan's fancy pants car, and the mirrors were better, too.

After the big breakfast with Logan, she'd popped down to see Birdie and set off with instructions from Birdie that she'd be fine and that the pharmacist Estrella would be waiting for a quick meeting and to show her the ropes. Birdie had said that she'd briefed Estrella that Cally would be taking over the stockrooms and ordering and delivery systems right from day one. As she drove along with a vague idea of where she was going, Cally thought about what she was going to do first. Butterflies fluttered around in her stomach, but she told herself that she would be fine. She had little choice but to get stuck in.

About half an hour later, after navigating a particularly nonsensical one-way system and following the instructions to find the allocated parking space behind the shop, Cally grabbed her travel cup, slipped her laptop into her bag, locked the van behind her, and made her way to the Peaceton chemist. Punching the code into the lock on the back door, she let herself in and looked around. The setup was fairly similar to the Lovely Bay store. Though the building was slightly more modern, the premise was the same: a front-of-house shop area, a dispensary to the back, a small staff room and various storerooms. As if someone had been expecting her, a woman with tight white trousers, high red shoes, and a white dispensary coat poked her head around the door.

'Yoo-hoo! You must be Cally. I'm Estrella. Lovely to meet you. Welcome!'

The woman's voice was loud and happy with a distinctive, what Cally thought was Spanish, accent. Cally smiled at the same time as the hackles on the back of her neck stood up. She pushed down the feeling. 'Hi. Yes, I'm Cally. Happy to be here.'

Estrella beamed. 'So, nice to meet you. Congratulations on the new job. I've heard so much about you from Birdie.'

'Thanks.'

Estrella started to unbutton her pharmacy coat. 'I thought we'd go to a coffee shop for a chat. Yes?'

'Oh, right, okay.' Cally gestured to the small staff room, where she could see a coffee machine the same as the one in the

Lovely Bay shop. 'We're fine here. We don't need to go out, do we?'

Estrella was adamant. She wrinkled her nose and made a funny face. 'No, no. Let's go out. The company is paying so that's always a good thing.'

Cally didn't like that *at all*. 'Rightio. I don't mind.'

Cally followed Estrella out of the chemist and down the street to a small, independent coffee shop. The smell of freshly ground beans and baked goods wafted out as Estrella pushed open the door. 'This place makes the best coffee in town, and the cakes are to die for.' Estrella led Cally to a table by the window. As they settled into their seats, a waitress approached to take their order. Estrella smiled and waved her hand back and forth in front of her. 'We'll put it on expenses, of course. Perks of the job, I say. It's your first day, so we need to welcome you properly. Cake is always better when it's free.'

As they waited for their drinks, Estrella continued to gush and wave bright red polished nails around in front of her. Cally blinked at her enthusiasm. 'So nice to meet you finally. I feel like I already know you from all Birdie's said. It sounds like you've done a great job in the Lovely shop. Tell me more.'

Cally shifted in her seat. Maybe she'd led a very sheltered existence, but Estrella seemed not only intense but completely over the top. 'Well, there's not much to tell, really. I've been working for Birdie for a while now, and this promotion just sort of happened.'

'Oh, don't be modest!' Estrella exclaimed. 'Birdie doesn't just hand out promotions to anyone.'

Cally blushed. 'I don't know about that. I just try to do my job well.'

'Don't we all.' Estrella flicked her hand out in front of her a little bit. 'It's all about hard work here too, isn't it? It suits me – my culture is a hard-working one.'

'Oh, really? Where are you from then?'

Estrella launched into a detailed account of her journey from Ecuador to England, her pharmaceutical studies, and how she'd eventually found her way to Birdie's company. Cally listened, nodding at appropriate intervals, but found herself slightly overwhelmed by the torrent of information from the gushing woman. She sat back and listened, not able to get a word in edgeways, so much so that she found herself tuning out for a second.

'Birdie is the most wonderful boss you could ask for. So understanding, so supportive and just leaves well be. I like that. Keep away is my motto, ha! The benefits are out of this world. Health insurance, dental, paid holidays, and don't even get me started on the gym.' Estrella lowered her voice. 'Plus, you know all the other unspoken benefits here and there.'

Cally nodded, not able to get a word in edgeways. 'Mmm.'

Estrella patted Cally's hand. Cally had to stop herself from recoiling. Estrella felt *way* too familiar as far as she was concerned. Cally shrugged it off as a difference in culture thing. Estrella, however, didn't seem to notice and continued unabashed. 'I've been so looking forward to you working here. It'll be wonderful to have someone new on the team, someone with fresh ideas.'

Cally smiled, but inside, she felt more than a twinge of unease. Whatever her intuition was telling her, she didn't like it. She tried to push the feeling down, telling herself she was being unfair, and not very nice. Estrella was doing absolutely *nothing* wrong.

'You'll have to come for after-work drinks!' Estrella lowered her voice and made a mock-whisper type sound. 'Don't tell anyone but we might have a few of those on the company, too.'

'That sounds nice.' Cally wasn't sure if it *was* nice. She couldn't shake the feeling that something was *very* off. Estrella's enthusiasm appeared almost too perfect, too rehearsed.

Estrella seemed to clock what Cally was thinking. 'Oh, goodness! Sorry! I'm not being too much, am I? People say I can be a bit intense when I'm excited. It's the way we do it where I'm from.'

Cally shook her head. 'No, no, you're fine.'

Estrella nodded. 'I'm just so *thrilled* to have you here. It's going to be wonderful.'

After finishing their coffees, Cally tried to shake off her doubts. She was being silly, she told herself. Estrella was just being friendly and welcoming. It was perfectly normal to be excited about a new colleague. But as they walked back to the chemist, with Estrella's red shoes clipping on the pavement and as she chattered away about the various projects they'd be working on together, a little voice said things in the back of Cally's head. She couldn't quite silence it. It sat in the back of her mind, warning her that something wasn't right. Not a great start to her first day out and about with her new job.

'Right then,' Estrella said as they re-entered the shop. 'Shall we get started in the stockroom? I'll show you how I do things here and tell you what I need done. I have my own way of doing things. No reason to mess with that.'

Cally nodded and the penny dropped. Estrella thought that she was in charge and that Cally was working *for her* and not the other way around. It had all been a power game. She kept her mouth shut and followed Estrella into an overwhelmingly messy, disorganised stockroom where she couldn't see the wood for the trees. Listening as Estrella rambled on, she didn't say anything but just quietly took it all in. Internally, our Cally nodded. It wouldn't take her long to get the room shipshape and see what was what. Estrella had a shock coming; that she knew for free.

29

It was a day or so later and Cally had just left the manor house. She'd spent most of the day with Doreen, helping to prepare for the funeral. When she'd first offered to help Doreen, to be honest, she'd expected Doreen to say no. Despite the number of staff at the manor, Doreen, however, as the funeral had approached, had leant on Cally for all sorts of little jobs here and there. Cally had been running around all day, tying up loose ends left, right, and centre. You know those little flies with blue bottoms? She was one of those.

With a takeaway hot blackcurrant in her hand Doreen had made for her just before she'd left, she walked away from the manor on a path beside the edges of the perfectly manicured lawns. A long line of well-cared-for trees swayed back and forth in the wind, and coming from the direction of the marquee that had been erected for the funeral, she could hear the distant chatter and occasional laughter from some of the manor workers. The laughter in the air was at odds with what was going on with the family inside the manor. There wasn't much to laugh about in there at all.

Cecilia had become more and more distressed as the funeral

had approached and was barely getting out of bed. Reg had turned to the bottle, and Logan wasn't far behind him. Cally shook her head as she thought about it and reached the area of the garden where the path narrowed and led down a small hill in the direction of the main gates. She took careful steps towards the bottom and as she pondered what was going on, she felt that, as usual, the same old familiar thought that the Henry-Hicks family was entitled and didn't even know it. She thought about Cecilia staying in bed all day. Yes, it was *more* than terrible what had happened, but Cally couldn't stop herself from thinking about how when her grandma had passed away, she certainly hadn't had the luxury of staying in bed, far from it. She had, in fact, had to get up and get on with what was left of her life. She'd teetered on being homeless and had been racked with constant worry. Shuddering at the thought, Cally ploughed on in the direction of Lovely Bay and thanked her lucky stars, she was closer to buying her own place.

From the road, she could hear the sound of the bin man coming up the lane and, faintly on the breeze, the sounds of Lovely Bay Primary School at playtime. Life outside the manor continued, while inside, it felt as if everything had stopped with Alastair's passing. Cally shook her head as she got closer to the gates, and just as she was about to press the button for them to open, she bumped straight into one of the gardeners who was kneeling down weeding a bed.

'Afternoon, our Cally,' the gardener said, standing up and placing his hands on the small of his back. 'How's everything going up there at the house?'

Cally raised her eyebrows. 'Not great. I've been helping Doreen. She was in a bit of a pickle with it all.'

'Yes, I thought that when I went up for lunch earlier.' The gardener's weathered face creased with concern. 'What a sorry old state of affairs, eh?'

Cally nodded. 'It's been awful. The whole family is in shock. I suppose you would be...'

The gardener leaned on his rake. 'I remember when Alastair was just a young lad, running around these gardens, getting into all sorts of mischief. Always had a smile on his face, that one. You can't believe it...'

'I know.'

The gardener nodded. 'It just goes to show, doesn't it? You never know what's around the corner. One day you're planning a grand adventure, and the next, well, the next, you're not.'

'Logan's been saying the same thing. How fragile life is, how quickly everything can change.'

'That it can.'

Cally swept her hand across in front of her. 'The gardens look beautiful. The poppies are so pretty. Everything always looks lovely here.'

The gardener waved off the compliment and sighed. 'It's the least we can do for the family. They've always been especially good to me. Alastair always had a kind word or a joke to share when he'd see me working, too. Well, I'd best get back to it.'

'Yep. See you at the funeral, I guess, if not before.'

'Will do. And, our Cally?'

She looked back. 'Yes?'

'You take care of yourself, too, you hear?'

'I will. Thank you.'

As Cally waited for the gates to open, she could hear the scrape of the rake behind her. Strolling along the road in the direction of Lovely she thought about the gardener's words and rolled her eyes. She didn't need to take care of herself. She'd seen it all before.

30

Cally was back in Peaceton for the day. She stood with her hands on her hips in the doorway of the stockroom at the shop, and surveyed the very chaotic scene before her. Boxes were stacked haphazardly from floor to ceiling, shelves overflowed with a jumble of products, and layers of dust coated every surface that didn't have a teetering pile of boxes on it. She let out a long exhale. She wasn't in the least daunted by the task but it was going to be quite the undertaking.

'Right then, best get cracking,' she said to herself as she shook her head.

Rolling up her sleeves she put her experience with Nina to good use and did a quick first sweep of the room. The first thing would be to create some semblance of order out of the initial layer of mess. She'd need to group similar items together, take a proper inventory, and compare it all against what was listed in the system. Then she'd be able to make sense of stock levels and take it from there. She began methodically working her way through a towering stack of containers in one corner and tutted over and over again. As far as she was concerned, the mess and disorder were completely unnecessary. She frowned; it was so haphazard and jumbled, it was almost as if it had been done on purpose. None of it made any sense. She knew from how things were ordered and how products came in from the delivery vans that the stacks and piles were so out of sync that it defied logic. That had been her first red flag.

Starting at the top of a tall disorganised stack of boxes, she sorted items into categories – medicines, toiletries, first aid supplies, and so on. As she worked, she compared the state of the room to the tidy, well-organised area she was in charge of back in Lovely Bay. It was a very startling contrast. No wonder Birdie had wanted her on board. She would certainly be earning her pay that day.

Wondering how on earth the place had got in such a state in the first place considering it had only been open for a while, she tutted as she worked. In amongst orders and stock, it looked as though years of clutter had accumulated resulting in what felt like a muddle of chaos. After a good few hours of sorting, she'd made a small dent in the clutter and perched on a rickety stool, she booted up her laptop and pulled up the inventory spreadsheets and delivery system to have a look and see if she could tell what was what. She shook her head in quick little movements and frowned as she went down the spreadsheet. Right away she didn't need a calculator to tell her that it didn't add up. The second red flag had appeared.

Delving further into the stock and boxes she cross-referenced the physical count against what was listed in the system to try and start to organise things. The simple cross-referencing was how she'd first started to work and organise things in the Lovely shop. As she tallied up an open carton of Cold & Flu sachets with the date on the accompanying order sheet, she noticed an error. Assuming that it was just a data entry mistake, she moved on with her head down and started to work her way through box after box.

By the end of the day, she wasn't liking what she was finding at all. As she tidied, sorted and worked her way through more products, a distinct pattern began to emerge. Time and again, the physical count came up just short compared to what was listed in the system. It was cleverly done, too, and if you weren't as fastidious as our Cally, it might possibly have been overlooked. It wasn't huge amounts either - a few items here, half a dozen there - but it was consistent.

It hadn't taken much more for Cally to decide that things were wrong. What she'd found had gone beyond simple mistakes or possibly sloppy record-keeping. What she hadn't realised before she'd got stuck in in the Peaceton shop was that her experience working in Lovely had given her a keen eye for inventory management. She knew how stock levels typically fluctuated and what constituted normal shrinkage and what was what at different times of the retail year. This felt different.

Moving back from the cardboard boxes to her laptop, she delved deeper into the spreadsheets, pulled up historical data, looked at stock levels and sales figures over the previous few months, and came up with more duds. The more she dug, the more alarmed she became. There were odd spikes in certain product sales and orders that didn't align with the seasonal patterns or promotional periods she'd come to know well. Items would show as fully stocked one week, then inexplicably depleted the next, with no corresponding spike in sales figures. It was as though bits of inventory here and there was vanishing into thin air.

'Something's not right here,' Cally muttered, shook her head and squeezed her eyes tightly together as if somehow that might help.

She was so engrossed in her analysis that she barely registered the time and it wasn't until she realised she was starving that she saw she'd been looking at the figures for hours.

'Everything alright in here?' Estrella called from the corridor. 'You've been holed up for ages. I know it was a mess so I thought I would leave you to tidy up, then the next time you're in, I will show you how I want things done.'

Cally hastily minimised the spreadsheets on her laptop screen. She'd let Estrella believe whatever she wanted for the time being. 'Fine, thanks. I just lost track of time getting stuck into the tidying.'

Estrella was still of the opinion that she was in charge. Cally let her continue to think that. 'No rush. Take as long as you need. I'm heading home now – don't forget to set the alarm when you leave and I'll see you the next time you're in.'

'Will do. Have a good evening!'

Cally waited until she heard the jingle of the shop's front door and flipped her laptop open. The discrepancies she'd found went well beyond normal fluctuations and errors. What she'd not been aware of was that her experience in Lovely had made her a bit of a master at stocktaking and the corresponding figures on a screen. Everything was screaming at her that something was very wrong in Peaceton. It wouldn't take her long to prove it, either. She would need more evidence which meant she had a lot more digging to do but she'd get there, of that she was sure. She looked around the cluttered stockroom, still largely in disarray despite her hours of work and couldn't stop thinking about how cocky and sure of herself Estrella was. Also: the red shoes.

Shaking off her unease and time to call it a day, she stood, stretched and winced as her stiff muscles protested. She'd be back after the funeral to continue her investigation, keep schtum and head down, and put herself on a secret little mission to find out just what was going on. Estrella needn't be any the wiser.

Just as she was getting her bag from the other stockroom, she passed a jumbled pile of boxes behind the door she hadn't even started on, and something caught her eye. Peering closer, she turned her head to the side and noticed a label with the day before's date. Odd. Very odd. She shifted a few boxes aside to get a better look. As she dug deeper, she uncovered more recent postage labels. An entire stack of newly delivered stock had been buried beneath and in between a load of old promotional items behind the door. Cally more or less knew what was in the boxes because she knew the labels on the cartons. From what she could see, they were a mix of over-the-counter medications – painkillers, allergy tablets, heartburn remedies, and the like. All items that sold steadily and wouldn't raise suspicion if they went missing in small quantities. It would explain some of the discrepancies she'd been finding between the physical counts and the system records. She wondered why anyone would shove new deliveries behind the door in the back room. It went against all logical stock management practices to put new stock away unseen. The way Cally worked, new deliveries were properly logged and shelved, not hidden away. It was exactly what you would do if you wanted to deliberately conceal things. Red flags waved from everywhere.

Cally swallowed as she closed the door, walked to the back, punched in the code on the alarm and walked out; her new job wasn't going to be quite the walk in the park she'd assumed. She wasn't wrong.

31

A few days later, Cally was at the church. She had walked past the blue nave door of Lovely Bay Church many, many times on her walks to the manor. She'd never been inside, though, until now. She'd arrived to help Doreen with the final few bits of the funeral setup. Stepping into the porch, she inhaled as she looked around with a strange, sick sensation in her stomach. The preparations for Alastair's funeral had made her reflect on the lead-up to her grandmother's funeral, which had been a completely different kettle of fish but just as horrid nonetheless. Her grandma's funeral had been an end-of-life, natural passing that had been sad, yes, but not distressing. This felt very different. Full of trauma and grief and a life that had ended too soon. The horror of a plane crash. Stricken parents unable to cope and a whole family plunged into distress. All around, in every aspect: *dreadful.*

Cally paused just inside the inner door, allowing her eyes to adjust to the dim light and stood on the ancient stone floor for a second. High above a centre aisle, vaulted ceilings soared, stained glass windows lined the walls, and beautiful timber pews led the way to the altar. Everywhere she looked, white roses and lilies looked at her. There had been none of the 'no flowers' malarkey for the Henry-Hicks family. Doreen had been instructed, by way of Cecilia, to fill both the church and the marquee with as many white flowers as possible.

As Cally walked further into the main church, she noted that Cecilia's instruction had been followed to the letter. The ends of the pews drowned in elaborate arrangements of white roses and lilies tied with long satin ribbons, shimmering in the light coming in through the stained glass windows. Baby's breath, ivy vines, and sprigs of greenery fell from the pews to the aisle, and in every nook and cranny, roses and lilies jostled for space. Cally shook her head and raised her eyebrows. Simple, elegant, serene and timeless. Just like everything else to do with the Henry-Hicks family. A plethora of whites and creams appeared to almost dance in front of her eyes. Sadness right there for all to see.

Cally's mind flicked back to her grandma's funeral. A small, simple affair in a modest church. A few odd bunches of flowers here and there. A scavenge of random relatives. No support. Just as Cally was bending down and looking at the beautiful embroidery on a kneeler, the door creaked open behind her. She stood up to see Doreen, her arms hanging with gigantic lanterns.

Doreen put the lanterns down, smiled and walked over. 'Hey, our Cally. How are you?'

'Fine, thanks.' Cally gestured to the flowers. 'It looks amazing. I don't think I've ever seen as many flowers in one place.'

Doreen pursed her lips and nodded. 'They've followed the brief, that's for sure.'

'They have.'

'Just this last part and we're all set. Thanks for all your help.'

'No worries.'

'Everything is done now. There's nothing left to do here apart from the candles.'

Cally lifted her chin in the direction of the door. 'Birdie should be here any second.'

As if on cue, the church door opened again, and Birdie shuffled in, weighed down with cardboard boxes.

'Ah, Birdie, there you are. We were just saying…'

Birdie piled the boxes on a table at the back of the church. 'Sorry, I'm a bit late. Took me a while to get the rest of the order in the car.'

Doreen shook her head. 'Not to worry. We've plenty of time yet.'

Cally peered into one of the boxes, her eyes widening at the sheer number of tea lights stacked inside. 'Wow, that's a lot of candles.'

'And there are more in the car,' Birdie added, stretching her arms. 'I think we've enough to light up half of Lovely Bay.'

Doreen nodded approvingly. 'Good. Cecilia was very specific about wanting candles and flowers. Thanks for letting me use your delivery company. That express service is unreal.'

Birdie nodded. 'Not a problem. I thought they'd deliver and they did.'

Doreen smiled. 'It's really helped us out.'

Cally listened as Doreen instructed them on the plans for the tea lights and lanterns. Each pew end was to have a cluster of lanterns, with more candles scattered along the aisle and at the entrance.

Cally began to slit open the inner boxes of tea lights and Birdie started to slot them into lanterns.

'How's Logan holding up?' Birdie asked in a hushed voice as they worked.

Cally slid another box of tea lights in Birdie's direction. 'Not great, to be honest. He's struggling.'

Birdie clucked. 'Poor lad. It's never easy, losing someone so young. More like brothers than cousins, really.'

'Yes, I suppose so.'

As they worked, light streamed through the stained glass windows, an overpowering scent from the flowers filled the air, and a quiet sound of three women, heads-down getting a sombre job done. After a good hour or so, Birdie put her hands on her hips and looked up at the windows and mused. 'It's beautiful in here. I've lived in Lovely Bay for a long time and it never fails to amaze me how pretty it is.'

'It is. I've walked past it so many times, but I've never been inside...'

'It's seen a lot of history, this place,' Doreen piped up. 'Christenings, weddings, funerals. You name it, I've seen it. Generations of Lovelies have passed through these doors.'

Cally smiled. 'It's funny, I fell over just outside there on the cobblestones when I was on my way to the manor to work for Nina. It feels like that was ages ago now.'

'What, right out here?'

'Yes, I had a cup of blackcurrant and I tipped it down my blouse. It was freezing that morning.'

'Those cobbles can be slippery over this side of Lovely.'

'Indeed. I fell over and then bumped into Logan that very morning on the driveway. Hence, the nickname Blackcurrant.'

'And now, here you are...'

'I know.'

'The world goes in circles as they say.'

'It certainly does.'

As they worked their way down the central aisle, creating clusters of lanterns at the end of each pew, Cally became more and more emotional. Another hour into their work, the pew ends flickered with the soft light of dozens upon dozens of candles, the white flowers seemed to glow in the candlelight, and the whole place took on an ethereal feel.

'It's going to be a beautiful service. Sad, of course, but beautiful.' Birdie noted.

Doreen stood beside her, put her hands on her hips and nodded in agreement. 'It is. I think we've done Alastair proud.'

Cally joined them, and they all stood looking at the decorated church. It had been transformed. The soft glow of hundreds of candles looked back at them. Doreen started to pick up random empty cardboard boxes from the pews. 'Well, I think that's us done. Unless you can think of anywhere else, we could squeeze in a candle?'

Cally and Birdie both chuckled. 'We've covered every available surface. Good job they're not real or we might be in danger of setting the place alight.'

'True enough. The wonders of technology, eh?'

Cally imagined the church as it would be when she next saw it. The pews filled with mourners, the air heavy with grief, the scent of flowers, the casket at the front testament to a life cut tragically short. She wasn't looking forward to it at all. The sooner it was done and dusted the better.

32

Cally stood in the bedroom in her flat and looked at the dress hanging on the mirror in front of her. A sombre black affair with matching velvet headband. She hadn't counted on going to a funeral in the slightest. It hadn't been in her plans, and just as everyone else had constantly reiterated, she couldn't quite believe it. The outfit in front of her told her she would most definitely be attending a funeral. The dress, with its slashed neckline, sleeves to the elbow, and fitted bodice, was nice, at least. After going to her grandma's funeral, she hadn't thought that she would be attending another one quite as soon, and certainly not one for somebody as young as Alastair. Who ever really thought that they would be going to a funeral for a young person, though? But here she was, about to dress herself from head-to-toe in black and spend the day trying to be of some use to Logan.

There was no doubt that Alastair was gone and that she was about to go to his funeral. She was well aware of that. After a bit of deliberation, she'd spent the night alone without Logan. When he'd said that he was going to be getting home late, part of her had been secretly and selfishly pleased. She'd thought that some time on his own would do him good and set him up for the next day. Maybe she was wrong…

Slipping the dress over her head and smoothing it down as it settled into place, she popped on plain black shoes on top of tights with a little heart on the ankle, then gathered her hair at the nape of her neck, twisting it into a neat, low bun. A few strategic clips secured any stray bits, and a liberal spray of hairspray went over the top. As the heavy scent of the hairspray filled the air, Cally was suddenly transported back to the day she'd first properly met the extended Henry-Hicks family at the races. She remembered the nervousness that had knotted her stomach and the feeling of being utterly out of place among Logan's posh upper-class relatives. She'd spent most of the day careering between loving the pomp and fuss of the event with feeling as if she was a fish out of water. There had also been her very awkward encounter with Logan's ex-wife. Being in a marquee with Logan's ex flashed through her mind; that little episode hadn't helped her inferiority complex at all.

As she gazed at her reflection and looked herself up and down, Cally realised how much had changed since she'd met Logan. Even how she was dressed gave evidence to that. At this event, unlike the first few she'd attended, she'd had no worries about her attire in the slightest. In fact, she'd gone straight online and ordered the dress, found the sweet tights with the heart on the M&S website, and ordered the shoes at the same time. She no longer worried about how she was dressed and the fish-out-of-water feeling had faded over time, replaced by a growing comfort with the Henry-Hicks clan. She wasn't quite one of them, never would be, but she no longer felt like a complete outsider, and she'd grown fond of their funny ways.

The memory of the day at the races, which felt as if it had happened yesterday at the same time as if it had been years before, was a real stake in the ground at how different she was now. That race event was a marker of how far she'd come in her relationship with Logan and his family. Now, she was an intrinsic part of it all with a role to play. As she prepared for a much more sombre family gathering, she felt a bittersweet feeling of belonging. She'd mentioned to Logan in Scotland how lucky he was to have a good family. Here, now, they were being put to the test. The funeral was probably going to be up there with one of the darkest hours for the Henry-Hicks family, and whether she liked it or not, she was right in the thick of it.

Tucking a beautiful padded black headband into the front of her hair, she wondered what the funeral was going to be like. She was no stranger to funerals and had been to a few in her time and as far as she was concerned, funerals were never a good thing. None of the ones she'd attended had been even close to pleasant. Her grandma's had been a low-frequency, sad, grim affair with not many people in attendance at all. From her perspective, it had floored her with just about every emotion imaginable; mostly, she'd been flooded by pure and utter relief. Said relief had, in turn, made her feel guilty.

As she fiddled with a very fine, narrow strip of veil on the velvet headband, she swallowed at the thought of what was going to happen that day and how Logan was going to cope. This funeral was a whole different kettle of fish altogether to any of the ones she'd ever been to. A funeral for an older person was bad enough, but a young man in his prime, a venue ready to be swarmed by mourners, the manor, and everything that came with that made Cally unsure what was going to eventuate.

She winced as she thought about Logan as she traced the outline of her lips with a nude lip liner. He'd been in a sort of numb vortex since they'd entered the hospital and Reginald had told them the news. Right from the word go, he'd been quiet and distant and not really wanted to talk about or do anything much. It was almost as if he'd been pretending it hadn't happened at all. Here and there he'd made an effort to snap out of it but it hadn't really worked.

Cally hadn't been sure what to do or how to handle it. She'd tried to just fumble her way through, hoping that he would get better with time. What she had noticed and kept quiet about was that more and more Logan was using alcohol to numb the pain. He had been drinking way too much, using wine as a crutch to make himself not feel what was going on around him. Part of Cally felt that a tiny part of Logan had died at the same time as Alastair. She perished the thought.

Finishing her lips, she went into the kitchen, bent down to the cupboard beside the fridge, grabbed a mini carton of blackcurrant, and put it in her bag. Clicking the magnetic clasp on her bag, she tapped the back of her hair to make sure it was still in place, grabbed her phone, picked up her blazer, and made her way out of the flat. After going down two floors, she sent Logan a text message:

Cally: *Hi, how are you?*

Logan: *Yes, okay. You okay?*

Cally: *Not too bad. How about you?*

Logan: *I'm fine. Are you on your way here?*

Cally: *Yes, I'm just heading down now. Birdie is dropping me off.*

Logan: *Okay, I'll see you soon.*

Cally: *Is there anything you need me to get you?*

Logan: *No, I'm fine.*

Cally: *Do you want me to bring you something from the deli?*

Logan: *I'm good.*

Cally: *Are you sure?*

Logan: *Yes.*

Cally: *Have you eaten anything?*

Logan: *No, I've just had a cup of tea. I'll do a coffee when you get here, just before we leave.*

Cally: *I think you should have something to eat.*

Logan: *I can't even look at food.*

Cally: *See you soon.*

Putting her phone back in her pocket, Cally walked out of

the back of the deli and along the lane to the little parking spot behind the chemist, where Birdie was just pulling up in her car. Birdie got out and raised her eyebrows as she took in Cally. Birdie looked sombre head-to-toe in black. The Shipping Forecast came from inside the car.

'Morning. How are you?' Birdie asked.

'Good, well, not good, but fine. Considering the circumstances, I'm okay. You?'

Birdie nodded. 'Yeah, I'm fine, too. I have to say going to a funeral is never my favourite way to spend a morning.'

'Nope.'

Birdie lowered her voice. 'Well, you scrubbed up well. Nice dress.'

'Thank you.' Cally took in Birdie's beautifully cut trouser suit. 'Same to you.'

Birdie stepped closer and peered at Cally's headband. 'Gosh, that's really effective. Where did you get it?'

'I googled "headband for funeral," and it was the first thing that came up. 'Given the people that will be there, I felt as if I needed a hat or something. This does the trick, doesn't it?'

'It does, and it's beautiful. You nailed it. What is it? Like padded velvet knotted with a little gauze veil?'

'Yeah. You just pop it in your hair.'

'Nice.'

'I wonder how this funeral is going to go?' Cally shook her head and exhaled.

'The actual service itself will be impeccable. I know Doreen has worked her socks off for everything to go well, but when someone so young passes away, it's not great at the funeral, in my experience.' Birdie sighed and shook her head. 'Horrible and I wish I didn't know how I know that, but there you are.'

'Yep. I'm setting myself up for it to be *awful*.'

'How's Logan doing?' Birdie asked.

Cally shook her head again. 'Yeah, not great. To be frank, he's been getting worse as this day has drawn closer.'

Birdie screwed up her lips and made a funny face. 'I'm not surprised.'

Cally paused for a second. 'He's been drinking way too much. I *really* don't like it.'

Birdie swore. 'That's the way he's dealing with it then, is it?'

'It is.' Cally sighed. 'I don't know, but I'm hoping today will give some closure or something. I don't mean that in a nasty way.'

'No, no, of course not. I get you. He'll be fine; he's a good lad. He just needs to put today behind him and go through the stages of grief.'

'Mmm. True.'

'What about you? Are you alright? You're right in the middle of it all.'

Cally nodded. 'I'm managing. It's not easy.'

Birdie gave a sympathetic smile. 'It's tough. Give it time. Come on, let's get going.'

Cally walked around and climbed into the front seat of Birdie's huge car, smoothed her dress over her knees and tucked her bag in the footwell. They chatted as Birdie drove through Lovely, out past the lighthouse, and down into the lanes as fields of green stretched out on either side. A few grazing sheep dotted the fields here and there, and the occasional ancient oak tree lined the road. In the distance, Cally could just make out the outline of Lovely Manor, its imposing silhouette surrounded by a sea of red poppies.

'I've always loved this drive when the poppies are out. It's so peaceful out here.'

Cally nodded. 'It is beautiful. I can see why the Henry-Hicks family chose this spot for their home back in the day.'

As they got closer, signs of the day's event became more apparent. A few cars lined the long driveway, dots of men in dark suits and women in sombre dresses made their way towards the house. To the left, Cally could see the large white marquee she'd helped Doreen to prepare. Cally swallowed at the sheer scale of the event, and as they pulled up to the ornate iron gates, one of the ground staff, not in his usual work gear but smartly dressed in a black suit and tie, approached the car. Birdie rolled down her window.

The man recognised them instantly. 'Oh, morning, our Cally, Birdie.'

Birdie nodded. 'I'm just dropping off our Cally.'

'Right you are. You'll need to go left there and around the back. We're keeping cars off the main driveway as much as we can.'

Cally shook her head and reached for the door handle. 'No, no. I'd prefer to walk if that's alright.'

'Of course.'

Cally turned to Birdie. 'Thanks for the lift. I'll see you at the church.'

Birdie reached over and squeezed Cally's hand. 'See you later. Give my best to Logan. Tell Doreen to just shout if she needs anything. I'll keep checking my phone. Colin is on standby, too.'

'Will do.' Cally lowered her voice as she got out of the car. 'To be honest, I can't wait for this to be over.'

'I don't think you're the only one.'

33

C ally could see Logan standing near the entrance to the house. In a flash, she was on the stairs of the riverboat, her brown paper bag having fallen away at the bottom, a chicken breast at his feet. He didn't look anything like he had then; his face was pale and drawn in his dark suit as he scanned the approaching guests. When his gaze landed on Cally, she saw a very evident flicker of relief cross his face. Quickening her pace, she tucked her bag under her arm, weaved in and out of a few people and made her way towards him. He didn't smile. The closer she got, the more she could see the strain in his eyes and the tension in his shoulders. Without a word, he reached out and took her hand.

'Hey,' Cally said softly. 'How are you holding up?'

'I'm fine. That's about all I can say right now. I can't tell you how pleased I am that you are here. It was a big mistake for me not to be with you last night.'

Cally nodded, not sure what to say for the best. 'Right.'

Logan's grip on her hand tightened as they stood for a moment, surrounded by people in black clustered here and there. Cally could see Logan's parents near the entrance to the house, greeting guests with solemn nods and murmuring thanks. Octavia was there too, looking pale and fragile, supported on either side by family members.

Cally felt Logan stiffen beside her. Following his gaze, she saw a group of young men approaching, their faces grave.

'Alastair's friends from university. I should go and say hello.'

Cally watched as Logan moved to meet the group, accepting their condolences with nods and thanks. Even from a distance, she could see the effort it was costing him to maintain his composure. She turned to see Doreen in a black dress and hat coming out of the main door of the house.

Doreen raised her eyebrows. 'Our Cally.'

'Hi. Do you need any help with anything?'

'No, we're all set. I've been making tea and coffee and croissants all morning.'

'How was it last night?'

Doreen lowered her voice to a whisper. '*More* than dreadful. Honestly, Cally, I've seen some bad times, but it was *horrendous*. Cecilia had to, well, err, she had to be put to bed with, you know, a pill before I even left, and Anne wasn't much better.'

Cally swore. 'What a sorry old state of affairs.'

'I know. At least you are here now. Logan needs all the support he can get. He's certainly not going to get it from anyone else.' Doreen tutted and shook her head.

Cally nodded, her eyes still on Logan. 'I just wish there was more I could do.'

Doreen patted her arm gently. 'I've had the same thought many times these past few weeks. It's going to be a difficult day.'

Logan strolled back in their direction. 'Morning, Doreen.'

'Logan. I hope you've had something to eat. I didn't see you in the kitchen earlier.'

Logan shook his head. 'Couldn't stomach it.'

Cally interrupted. 'Let's go and get a coffee.' She checked the time on her phone. 'We've got plenty of time before the cars arrive, and we leave for the church.'

Doreen gave Logan a nudge on his elbow. 'Do as she says. The last thing we need is you collapsing. Go and have a coffee. Do you want to come into the kitchen, and I'll make you one?'

'Nope. We'll pop back to the cottage.'

Inside the cottage, Cally was pleased to see it wasn't in a terrible mess. She pulled a coffee plunger out of a cupboard, flicked the kettle on, poured coffee beans into the top of a coffee grinder, and pushed the button on top. Logan sat down and sighed. He swore. 'I keep saying the same thing over and over again: I can't believe it.'

Cally shook her head as she poured ground coffee into the bottom of the plunger. 'I know. I don't know what to say for the best. Nothing anyone can say will help you.'

'I'm not looking forward to seeing the coffin.'

'You wouldn't be.'

'My mum and Cici were awful last night.'

Cally felt bad that she'd been pleased to keep away. 'Yes, Doreen said. You might feel a bit better after today, in a way. I know it doesn't feel like that, but, you, well, you get this bit out of the way, as it were. Not in a horrible way.'

Logan sighed. 'I hope so. I can't feel much worse. Do you know what? I could down a bottle of wine to get me through this.'

'Not happening.'

'I know.' Logan attempted a joke. 'A shot in my espresso?'

Cally smiled. 'Sorry, not a good idea.'

'Can I just say?'

'What?'

Logan smiled. 'It's not the time, but you look *so* pretty, Blackcurrant.'

'Thanks.'

'How do you even do that?'

'What do you mean?'

'Turn up looking like that and make me feel better?'

'Ahh, I'm a master.' Cally joked, glad that the tension in the air had eased a little bit.

'You are. I don't know how I'd be doing this without you.'

'I wouldn't be anywhere else.'

34

Logan's grip on Cally's hand was so tight as they walked out of the cottage in the direction of the funeral cars she thought one of the bones in her hand might fracture. The sight outside the main entrance of Lovely Manor wasn't the best, as far as Cally was concerned. She gulped as they walked across the gravel drive. They then stopped by the hedge to the left of the steps and she drew a breath as she stood next to Logan and watched Cecilia and Reg come out of the front door. Both of them appeared as if, in the space of a few weeks, they had aged *many* years. Cecilia not only looked old, tired, grief-stricken and drawn, but she also had a look on her face Cally couldn't quite fathom. There wasn't even a word for it, as far as Cally could make out. She narrowed her eyes and squinted at Cecilia as she got into one of the huge black funeral cars. The look on Cecilia's face was worse than distraught; it said that she would never be the same again.

A funeral director in a black morning suit came up to them, held out his hand and directed them towards the correct car. Once they were in the back of the car, Logan gripped Cally's hand again as if hanging on for dear life. As the gravel crunched when the car pulled away, Cally gazed up at the bright blue sky above Lovely Manor and the swathe of poppies in the distance. The blue sky and pretty scene felt all wrong. Slipping her sunglasses out of her bag and onto her face to use them as a bit of a shield, she sat staring out of the window as silence strangled the car and nobody said a word.

The car remained silent, Logan's grip didn't lighten, and Cally continued to stare out of the window as the funeral procession made its way through the main street of Lovely. A few people stood outside shops with their heads bowed, cars pulled to the side, and as they stopped at some traffic lights in the High Street, Cally let her eyes rest on the red brake lights of the funeral car ahead and couldn't quite believe that Alastair had passed away. She felt tears prick at the corner of her eyes as she realised it could have been any of them. She could have been the grieving partner. Her life could have been ultimately tipped upside down. She could be the one in Octavia's shoes. It made her want to wrap Logan in clingfilm and never let him go. It all felt very unfair. As the traffic inched along the road, it fleetingly went through her mind that it didn't matter where you were in life, how much money you had, or whether or not you had family – bad things *could* and *did* happen at any time.

The silence still draped the car as it approached the church, where a sea of traffic and a long line of vehicles parked in the surrounding lanes indicated that there were a lot of people at the funeral. Even that, however, did not prepare Cally for the number of people inside the church as they entered through the blue nave door. As they walked in, Cally's heart pounded at the sight of hundreds of mourners in black facing towards the altar. An organ played from a balcony behind them, the little tea lights glowed from every nook and cranny, and every inch of the church was tightly packed with people. Additional chairs down the side walls were also occupied, the gallery area to the back right was full, and people were standing anywhere there was an inch of space.

As the procession made its way through the centre aisle of the church, Cally took in the beautiful stained glass windows and watched as little sparkles of light caught dust motes in the air. She averted her eyes from the coffin and tried to keep a neutral look on her face as they passed the rows and rows of mourners dressed in black. Logan still gripped her hand tightly, the tension radiating from him to her. As they slipped into a pew at the front marked with a reserved sign for family, the organ music swelled and then faded away, leaving a heavy silence in its wake.

We are gathered here today to celebrate the life and mourn the passing of Alastair Henry-Hicks.

The service continued, a blur of hymns and readings. When it was Logan's turn to speak, Cally held her breath. He stood slowly, making his way to the front with measured steps. For a moment, he stood silently, his gaze sweeping over the congregation. Then he began to speak in a very sad, low voice. By the time he had finished speaking, there wasn't a dry eye in the church and when he sat back down, Cecilia reached out along the pew and squeezed his hand, tears streaming down her face.

Half an hour or so later, the last notes of the organ faded away and the congregation began to file out of the church. Cally blinked rapidly as they stepped outside, her eyes struggling to adjust to the beautiful day, relieved that it was over. With emotions high, she felt drained and sad. Logan was worse. As she glanced up at him, he looked *utterly* exhausted, as if the weight of his grief was a physical burden sitting squarely on his shoulders.

She smiled at him and put her hand on his back. 'You did brilliantly.'

'I couldn't have got through it without you.'

'You should be proud of yourself. That was *not* easy.'

Logan shook his head. 'I want to get the rest of this over with. I don't know how much more of this I can take. It all feels so final now, you know? Like this is really it. Alastair's gone, and he's not coming back.'

Cally felt as if her heart was cracking at the pain in Logan's voice. 'It won't always be like this.'

Logan nodded. 'Thank God I've got you. I wouldn't have made this otherwise.'

35

Cally needed a blackcurrant. Hot Blackcurrant. Possibly, with four hundred measures of gin sloshed in the top. A time machine might go down well, too. Meaning that she could hop in, flick a few switches, and transport herself and the rest of the Henry-Hicks family back to Scotland and stop Alastair and Octavia from going on their travels. Which in turn would mean that Alastair would still be alive. That would then mean that Logan would not be wading around in the depths of grief and trying to counteract it by consuming copious amounts of white wine. Unfortunately, there weren't any time machines at our Cally's disposal. Nor was it a good idea for her to join him in the numbing qualities of alcohol by drinking too much gin. It would not be good for her to get hammered. One of them needed to keep their wits about them.

It had been a long day. Cally had started the day dealing with complaints on the chatbot where she was doing her last few shifts, spent the middle of the day cleaning the cottage and the end of the day wondering what she could suggest to Logan that might, firstly, take his mind off Alastair, and secondly, stop him from sitting on either her or his sofa and working his way down a bottle of wine or two.

Logan had been with her all day. It was as if he was stuck to her side. Whilst beside her, he didn't *do* or *say* much at all. He'd followed her out of bed when she'd got up for the chatbot shift, silently made them both a cup of tea and sat more or less as close as he could get to her without sitting on her laptop as she'd worked. He'd done the same when they'd gone to the cottage, shadowing her while cleaning. It felt more than weird to Cally that she was the one in the lead. Ever since she'd met Logan, he'd been dynamic, buzzy, full-on, and had very much played the alpha role. Now, he was in the depths of zeta mode. Cally didn't like how it felt at all.

Despite being stuck to her like glue all day, Logan had said all of seventeen words to her. *Want a coffee from the deli? Done with the chatbot?* And her favourite: *What did you do with the bleach?*

Now, they were back at the flat and Cally had suggested all sorts of things to get them out. She'd even included going bowling as an idea. That was a new low. Not that she really wanted to go out, and certainly not bowling. Before the accident, she'd been more than happy to snuggle up on the sofa, tucked in and intertwined with Logan, and have a few drinks. Now, with him in his current state, not so much.

Whilst Logan was in the bath, she slid her laptop over and did a search on "tips for when someone is going through grief". She felt as if, with her own experience, she should know. However, oddly, she felt the opposite and had no idea. Even weirder and really nasty she'd felt a couple of times like telling him to suck it up. That in itself horrified her. She read the first article and nodded. The first tip spoke of precisely what had happened in her day. It said to be present and that simply being there for someone, even in silence, could be comforting. As she read further, she agreed that grief was isolating. She knew how that felt for sure.

The article's second point was to listen actively and let the person talk about their feelings, memories, or thoughts without interrupting or trying to fix their emotions. Cally made a funny face. So far, there hadn't been much chance of talking in Logan's case. His lack of conversation all day had been tantamount to that. All week, in fact. He was hardly saying much at all. Cally read down the article and took on board that she needed to avoid clichés such as "they're in a better place". She was supposed to offer practical help, be patient because grief didn't have a timeline. The person may have ups and downs, and it was important to understand that emotions change frequently in the world of grief.

Cally nodded in agreement as she read that everyone grieved differently and took on board that some people may want to talk about their feelings, while others might need space or prefer distractions. The article said to follow the lead of the person grieving. She continued to read, tried to take the suggestions on board, and finished by rereading a few times that

compassion, patience, and understanding were key. Grief was deeply personal, and support could make a difference just by being present and available. Cally shook her head that there was no "suck it up and get on with it" option and resolved to be patient and present.

She rapped on the door of the bathroom. 'Is everything okay in there?'

'Yes.'

'Need anything?'

'No.'

As they had been all day, Logan's responses were short and sweet. He, again, didn't appear to be in the mood to chat. Cally thought about the advice in the article and left it. She was present; that would, hopefully, be enough.

Leaving him to it, she bustled around the kitchen, checking on the pork she'd put in a low oven that morning. Inhaling an amazing smell of caramelised onions, apples, herbs, and pork, she pulled open the oven door and checked on the meat. That morning, before she'd wondered if going out was a good idea, she'd thought Logan might do well with a home-cooked meal. She'd put a loin of pork on a bed of onions, apples, and herbs, sloshed in a bath of wine, and left it to do its thing. She'd stopped in the bakery for tiger bread and bought some olives from the deli as a little starter. Now, taking baby rocket, spinach, and chard out of the fridge, she tumbled it onto a plate, finely sliced pear and fennel, squeezed on lemon juice, tossed it all together then added grated pecorino and a smattering of walnuts. She envisioned that a nice meal might do things to help a grieving partner but didn't hold out much hope. Pottering around, she put an old cutwork tablecloth that had been her grandma's on the table, snipped some lavender from the bush she had growing in a pot on the balcony, popped it in a jam jar, and added it to the centre of the table.

As she heard the bathroom door handle go, she swallowed as Logan came out the bathroom with a towel slung around his waist. He might be sad but other things about him had not changed. Wowzas. He just about managed a smile as he went into the bedroom and came out a few minutes later in soft blue shorts and a white polo shirt. Cally closed her eyes for a second as he went straight to the fridge, took out a bottle of wine, pulled two oversized glasses out of the cupboard and filled his almost to the brim.

Cally was more than concerned that the night would plunge into him drinking too much, but didn't let it show. 'Dinner's almost ready.'

Logan looked up, his eyes slightly unfocused. 'Oh, yeah. Sure,' he mumbled and looked at the salad on the table. 'Thanks.'

'No worries.' Cally bit her lip as Logan gulped a big mouthful of wine. 'Can you grab the cutlery?'

Logan nodded as he fumbled slightly with the cutlery drawer and gestured around the kitchen. 'Sorry. You've done all this. I should have helped. I'm a bit...'

'Don't be silly. It's been a tough week.' Grabbing a pair of oven gloves, Cally opened the oven door and pulled out the tray of pork. Steamy, fragrant air billowed around the small kitchen. She transferred the pork and onions onto a serving dish, popped the pan on the hob and stood making the gravy.

Logan reached for the bottle of wine and topped up his glass. Cally was concerned but unsure about whether or not to broach the subject of how much he'd been drinking.

'This looks great, Cal. Thanks for taking care of me.'

'You don't need to thank me. How are you feeling?'

Logan shrugged, taking another large gulp of wine. 'Fine, I guess. As fine as I can be, considering what happened. I don't know, it just doesn't seem real. I don't know what to do.' He trailed off, and gazed out the window.

Cally tried to keep the article she'd just read in mind. 'It's okay not to be fine. What you're going through is difficult.'

Logan nodded. 'I know you've been through this. I just keep thinking about him, you know? I wish I'd been *nicer*. Hindsight is a wonderful thing, eh?'

Cally wrinkled up her nose. 'Try not to think that.'

'Easier said than done.'

'Yup.' Cally poured the gravy into a little white jug, put the serving dish on the table, and sat down. Logan got up to get another bottle of wine out of the fridge. Cally couldn't not say anything. 'Umm, do you think you should slow down a bit with the wine?'

Logan looked up, a flash of anger in his eyes. 'I'm fine,' he said, his tone sharper than usual. 'It helps to take the edge off.'

'I'm a bit worried about you. This isn't like you. I don't think it's a good idea. Sorry, but I'm calling it. I can't just sit here and let you drink too much again. I don't think it will help in the long run. The opposite, in fact.'

Logan sighed and put the bottle back. 'I know. I'm sorry. I don't know how else to deal with this.'

Cally felt her heart ache. At least Logan was sharing how he felt. She'd take that as a plus. 'I wish I could make it better.'

'It's not *fair*. He had so much life left to live.'

'Nope. It's not fair at all.'

'Sorry. I know it should be *me* being the one who looks after *you*.'

Cally shook her head. 'What? Where did that come from? Not at all. Where does it say that you have to look after me? Don't apologise. You're allowed to grieve, Logan. You don't have to be strong all the time. I was just pointing out that getting sozzled isn't going to help matters...'

Logan pushed his chair out, opened the fridge, and grabbed a can of lemonade. 'You're right. I'm going to dilute this.'

Cally smiled. 'I'm not telling you *not* to drink. I just think getting plastered might make you feel worse in the long run. I really don't think it helps.'

'Yeah, I hear you.' Logan gestured to the table. 'You've made this gorgeous meal. I'm not going to ruin it. I think I just need to, you know, hibernate for a bit. I don't really want to do anything.'

'I've noticed.'

'Are you okay with that?'

'Of course!' Cally nodded. 'Of course, I'm okay with it. You take all the time you need. There's no rulebook for grief.'

Logan took a bite of the pork. 'This is good. Thanks.'

'I thought a home-cooked meal might be nice.'

'I keep thinking about things I did with Alastair. Nothing could keep him down for long. He was sort of annoying at the same time, too, which is making me feel really guilty.'

'I get it.' Cally let out a ginormous sigh. 'I've been there. You just have to work through it.'

'He loved you, Cal. He always said I needed someone to keep me on my toes, and you certainly do that.'

Cally begged to differ. However, there was no way she was going to say that she'd never really warmed to Alastair and that he had, on more than one occasion, totally rubbed her up the wrong way. She thought about her own experiences with grief, wondering if there was anything she could say that might help. 'When my grandma died, I found it really hard because I was relieved. Then, when I actually just admitted that to myself, it actually helped.'

'Right. I see. It just doesn't feel real, you know?'

'It does get easier…'

Logan was quiet for a moment. 'It's just going to take time, I think, or I just suck it up and get on with it. I just feel like I should be handling this better,' Logan admitted. 'I mean, look at you for instance. From what you told me you had so much crap going on after your grandma passed away and you got on with it.'

Cally shook her head. She'd had little choice but to get on with it. Yet another difference with the Henry-Hicks lot and especially Logan. He'd never been in this situation before and he was floundering around wondering what in the name of goodness was going on. In her case, she'd had no choice but to deal with it. 'You can't compare grief. Some people just put on a brave face.'

'Is that what you did?'

'Hmm. I guess so. It was different, though – she was old, and I'd had a lot of time to get used to it. Part of why you're feeling like this is perhaps because of the shock. I mean no one ever wants to get news like that.'

'I feel so *useless*. Like I should be doing something, but I don't know what. There's nothing to do.'

'You're not useless. It's okay to take time for yourself, to feel what you're feeling.'

'I keep thinking about when I spoke to Alastair. He was so excited about his trip with Octavia, talking about all the places they were going to see. I remember thinking he was being a bit over the top, you know? Like, it's just a holiday, mate, calm down,' Logan continued, his voice catching slightly. 'Now I wish I'd been more enthusiastic and asked more questions. If I'd known it was the last time I'd speak to him...'

'You couldn't have known.'

'No.'

'All your feelings are valid.'

Logan nodded. 'I don't know what I'd do without you. I love you, you know that?'

'I love you too.'

Cally sighed as she took a sip of her drink. She hoped that loving Logan was going to be enough.

36

Cally paused in front of the window display outside a Chinese restaurant in Peaceton and gazed at a row of upside-down golden-brown ducks on huge stainless steel hooks. Her eyes widened as she took in the sight of row after row of them glistening and shimmering under the lights and her stomach rumbled as she inhaled the scent of soy, honey, and spices coming out of the open door.

As an old man jostled past her muttering about his lunch, she stood and stared in the window for a bit, lost in thought about what she'd discovered in the Peaceton shop. It was quite clear as soon as she'd got her head down and was back at work after the funeral, that Estrella was swindling product, and possibly also money, from Birdie's shop. It hadn't taken Cally very long to work out, either. Once the stockroom was in order and she'd organised the mess, it was more than obvious to her that things didn't add up. Someone not quite as capable probably wouldn't have found the discrepancies quite as easily, but once Cally's strategies were in place she could see it as clear as day. Unless she was very much mistaken, Estrella was carefully filtering out orders here and there and often. Cally assumed that Estrella would then be selling them via online sales channels, a market stall perhaps, or something similar.

Continuing to stare into the shop window, Cally shook her head. She couldn't believe it. She was not that long into her job, and right away, she'd come across a *gigantic* issue. What she'd found was a big problem that she would need to get to the bottom of sooner rather than later. She was going to have to deal with it, there was no doubt about that. Her issue was that she wasn't really sure what to do or how to go about it. She had little to no experience of management, staff, problems or anything of its ilk at all.

Even though she was certain her figures were correct, a little bit of doubt whispered to her to hold her horses. She nodded as she made her way back to the Peaceton shop. She would perhaps talk to Logan about it and see what he thought before she did anything. Or maybe she would go straight to Birdie and come out with it right away. She really didn't have a clue.

On top of being worried about what to do, her blood boiled away to itself. She *hated* with a passion seeing Birdie being taken for a ride. She couldn't quite believe Estrella's cheek. Although, really, she'd known it right away. The woman had given her the heebie-jeebies from day one, and now she knew why. Cally shook her head. If there was one thing she hated, it was dishonesty. She thought about how generous Birdie was and how Estrella was clearly not only fiddling but also not pulling her weight, too. Cally had watched her leave early on more than one occasion, pretend she was working when really she was looking at clothes on the Next website, and she was late nearly every morning without fail. Estrella getting one over on Birdie made our Cally see red.

As she strolled along a busy pavement and reflected on the problem, she saw the benefits of her previous part-time jobs. Yes, they were low-level and hardly very exciting, but along with that came the simplicity of clocking on, clocking off, and that being the end of it. No problems and no responsibility. Her biggest problem in the past had been a dog eating a cashmere sock. Now, right from the start, issues were coming her way.

C ally had spent the rest of the afternoon cross-checking, sorting, and ordering and trying to not even look in Estrella's direction. By the time she'd got home, she'd more or less stripped by the front door, made a pot of tea, hopped in the shower, and emerged in a soft cosy tracksuit, ready to clarify everything she'd discovered that week. Sitting at her desk by the window, she popped on the little lamp, turned on the fire, lit a candle, and flipped up the top of her laptop.

Half an hour later, her mind fizzed with the discoveries she'd made as she'd further sorted the stockroom and put her systems in place. As she rechecked her numbers and what she'd found the evidence was clear: Estrella was *definitely* swindling money from Birdie's business in Peaceton. Cally had gone over the numbers countless times, hoping she'd made a mistake, but there was no denying it. Estrella was a thief.

As she heard Logan's key in the lock, Cally pushed her chair out and smiled.

'Hey, Blackcurrant,' Logan called out as he entered the flat.

'Hey.'

'You alright? You look a bit peaky.'

Cally wrung her hands. 'Not really. There's a problem at work.'

Logan shrugged off his coat. 'That didn't take long. Off to a good start. Come on, then. Out with it.'

'Estrella. You know the one I told you about who I didn't like the look of right from the word go? I think, no, I *know* she's been stealing from the business.'

Logan's eyebrows shot up. 'Stealing? Are you sure? That's a big call to make.'

Cally nodded vigorously and patted her laptop. 'I didn't really need to look because I could tell right away. But I've been going over the books, and there are discrepancies. Items missing from inventory, money not adding up. It's all very clever, but once you know what to look for, it's as clear as day.'

'Blimey. That's quite the bombshell. How long do you reckon this has been going on?'

'I'm not sure. It's hard to say without digging deeper. She was weird with me today, too. She kept poking her head around the door checking on what I was doing and asking about how much I knew about the ordering system. It's like she's clocked me.'

'So, what are you going to do?'

'I don't know *what* to do. I mean, I know I have to tell Birdie, but I've only been in this job for a bit. What if I've got it all wrong?'

'Don't doubt yourself. If you say the numbers don't add up, then they don't add up. You're good at what you do. That's why Birdie wanted you in the first place.'

'I never expected to be dealing with something like this so soon.'

'Welcome to the world of management,' Logan joked. 'It's not all spreadsheets and team meetings, you know.'

Cally chuckled. 'The chatbot is looking very attractive right now.'

'What? You love listening to women complaining about their French linen dresses shrinking in the wash. Not.'

'Ha.'

'You're best to just tell Birdie right away. The sooner the better, I reckon. No point in letting it drag on. I've been in this situation. Don't let it fester.'

Cally took a deep breath. 'I'll talk to her when I'm next in the shop downstairs.'

37

Cally sat on a rickety old chair at a worn timber table in a tucked-away corner of the lighthouse. She'd been to the lighthouse many times before, but it was very special being there for a chowder evening. Something exciting and very Lovely indeed. The room was dimly lit, with most of the illumination coming from mismatched candles in old jam jars scattered across the tables. It felt as if she'd stepped back in time or into some sort of parallel universe where people sat around in old lighthouses surrounded by candlelight.

She'd been invited to the speakeasy by way of Birdie and Nancy and had snapped up the tickets as soon as they'd come out. She loved the chowder speakeasies and there was no way she'd ever miss out on a pop-up event at the lighthouse.

Logan sat across from her, his face half in shadow, half-lit by the flickering candlelight. He looked as bemused as she felt. 'Well, this is certainly nice. Cosy.'

'Is it me, or does it feel *really* secret? Like more than usual?'

'It does.'

'Nancy said this one goes under the radar.' Cally giggled.

'We're lucky to be here, especially me being a Henry-Hicks

and all that. I'm only here because of you.' Logan joked. 'You open doors.'

'Are you saying that I'm more of a Lovely than you?'

Logan laughed. 'That may well be. It's your new coat and job.'

'Ahh, it's weird living here. There's always so much more to Lovely than meets the eye.'

'Coats, chocolate, and chowder.' Logan bantered.

As if on cue, Colin appeared at their table, wearing a striped fisherman's jumper and balancing a tray precariously in one hand. 'Evening, you two.'

Cally nodded. 'Evening. This is all very clandestine.'

Colin's grin widened. 'Ah, well, that's the beauty of it, isn't it? A little bit of mystery keeps things interesting. Now, what can I get you? Chowder or would it be chowder?'

Logan leaned forward and played along. 'What sort of chowder do you have?'

'Well,' Colin lowered his voice. 'We've got a smoked haddock chowder that'll knock your socks off. And for those feeling a bit adventurous, there's a curried crab chowder that's been getting rave reviews.'

Cally's eyebrows shot up. 'Curried crab chowder? That sounds... interesting.'

Colin laughed. 'Nah, just the usual. You get what you're given. Like it or lump it.'

Logan looked at Cally and played along. 'We'll try the usual, shall we?'

'Excellent choice. And to drink? We've got a lovely local ale that pairs well with the chowder, or there's wine if you prefer. That's your lot, I'm afraid, unless you want a soft drink. We have plenty of that. Or I can do you a cup of tea.'

'The ale sounds perfect,' Cally said, and Logan nodded in agreement.

As Colin bustled off, Cally took another look around the

room. The other tables were filled with a mix of familiar faces, candles flickered, and everyone seemed relaxed and happy. She felt the same, and thankfully, it appeared Logan did too.

'I wonder how long this whole chowder thing has been going on?' Cally mused.

Logan shrugged. 'Decades. I wouldn't be surprised if my great-grandfather used to sneak down here for a secret bowl of chowder.'

Cally smiled as she looked around. One of the things she liked about Lovely was how it seemed to have endless layers of history and secrets. Every time she came across a new bit of the past or a superstition, she fell in love a little bit more. Lovely, just as it had the first time she'd visited, was so different from the horrid grey, miserable world she'd grown up in, where everything had been about caring and the daily grind of getting by. It just didn't feel like that in Lovely, even when things were far from rosy. Even as Logan had flailed around grieving, Lovely had almost felt as if it had supported her.

Colin returned with two small glasses of amber ale, placing them carefully on the table. 'There you go. The chowder won't be long. Get ready to enjoy – it's a good one.'

Cally took a sip of her drink, sighed, sat back in her chair, and felt her whole body relax. 'This is good.'

Logan seemed more relaxed than he'd been for a long time. 'It is. It always seems to taste nicer when you're sitting somewhere like this.'

'So true. It's these little bespoke experiences.'

Cally sipped her drink and soaked in the atmosphere; the room was filled with the low hum of conversation, the occasional clink of cutlery against bowls, and from somewhere the faint sound of an old radio playing vintage jazz tunes. The sea glinted in the distance.

Logan lifted his chin in the direction of the view. 'It's beautiful this evening, isn't it?'

Cally nodded. 'I don't think I'll ever get tired of this view.'

'Me neither. Actually, speaking of views, there was something I wanted to talk to you about.'

'Oh?'

Logan went to continue just as Colin reappeared, carrying two steaming bowls of chowder.

'Here we are,' he announced, putting the bowls down in front of them. 'Two curried crab chowders, piping hot and ready to warm your souls. Joking, two regular old Lovely chowders. Though I have to say these are far from same old same old.'

Cally inhaled an incredible aroma wafting up from the bowls – a mix of seafood, garlic, and something uniquely, as far as she was concerned, Lovely. 'Amazing. Thanks.'

Colin beamed. 'Wait till you taste it. It's good. Shout if you want more.'

As Colin moved away to check on other tables Cally and Logan dug into their chowder. For a few minutes, neither of them spoke. There were more than a few appreciative nods. Cally dipped her spoon into the thick, creamy concoction: rich, velvety, and with just the right amount of garlic. It was one of the best Lovely Bay chowders she'd had, but she said that every time. 'Oh my god,' she mumbled around her spoonful, her eyes wide. 'This is fab.'

Logan nodded. 'And there Colin was having us on about curried chowder. You can't beat this.'

'It's so good.'

Logan nodded and wiped his mouth with a napkin. 'Funny really. I never would have tried chowder if it wasn't for living in Lovely.'

'Same. That's Lovely for you.'

Logan lowered his voice. 'It's all a tad weird, really.'

'I know. When I first worked for Birdie, I swear I thought everyone was a bit bonkers here, as if there was something in the water. And now here I am, part of it.'

'Speaking of surprises and back to what I was saying. I've been thinking. Now I'm feeling better about everything and a bit of time has passed...'

'Right, yep.'

'First, I want to say thank you for, well, you know, sticking by me.'

'Don't be ridiculous! I can't believe you'd even say that.'

Logan raised his half-full glass. 'I know I've been putting away much too much of this.'

'It's fine.' Cally pretended. It wasn't fine. Logan had been very sad and had dealt with it by drinking way too much way too many times.

'It's *not* fine.'

She decided to come clean. 'Okay. Actually, you're right, it's not fine.'

'You've stuck by me when I was far from my best.'

Cally joked. 'You're worth it. Just.'

'I mean it. Anyway, in light of all that, I thought you might like a trip up to the estate.'

Cally wrinkled up her nose and frowned. 'The estate? What in Scotland?'

'Yep. You said you wanted to see snow when we were there back in the summer. So if you want to, I'm going to arrange it. It's amazing up there when it's cold.'

'Do you mean for Christmas?' Cally frowned.

'I was thinking just before so we get all the best bits of the festive season but still get to spend time in Lovely for Christmas itself. Up to you.'

'Mmm, yep, good idea.' Cally's eyes lit up at the prospect of a pre-Christmas trip to Scotland. 'That sounds wonderful, actually.'

'I thought you might like the idea. The whole estate looks a picture when it's covered in snow.'

'I can imagine.'

'I was thinking we could invite a few others. Birdie, Eloise, Nina, some of my family.'

Cally raised an eyebrow. 'What? That's quite a group. Any particular reason? That's a bit out of the blue, isn't it? I thought you meant just us.'

Logan shrugged. Cally noticed a flicker of something in his eyes, but she wasn't sure what. Inside, she sighed. She didn't want to go to Scotland as part of some grief thing to do with Alastair. She was wholeheartedly behind Logan and was happy for his grieving to take as long as was required, but she drew the line at shrine-like reminiscing trips. Nope, she would not be partaking in that.

'No reason. Just thought it would be fun to have everyone together after, well, you know, the last few months or so have been grim. Plus, the estate can certainly accommodate them all, so I thought, why not? Time's ticking on.'

'True,' Cally nodded, still watching Logan closely. There was something he wasn't telling her, she was sure of it, or maybe he was just strange because he was finally through the initial part of the grief and feeling better. She decided not to push it. If he had something planned, she'd find out soon enough. One thing was for sure though; if Logan started to go on about Alastair, their family holidays up there and recreating past festive trips, she'd pull the plug. She was happy to support him, but that would be a step too far in her humble opinion.

'So, what do you think? Are you up for a Scottish adventure?'

Cally grinned. 'Absolutely. However, I'll need to do some serious shopping. I don't think any of my clothes are suitable for Scottish winter.'

'Don't worry, you know what it's like up there. You could turn up in a bikini and be kitted out in the boot room. It's practically an all-weather gear shop.'

'Good point.'

'When were you thinking of going?' Cally asked, already mentally rearranging her work schedule.

'Early to mid-December, something like that. That way we're back in time for Christmas in Lovely, but we still get the full winter experience in Scotland. I'll get it sorted.'

'It sounds perfect. You know, if someone had told me a couple of years ago that I'd be sitting in a secret chowder speakeasy in a lighthouse, planning a trip to a Scottish estate, I'd have thought they were pulling my leg.'

Logan chuckled. 'Lovely has worked its magic on you.'

'Sometimes I still can't quite believe this is my life now.' Cally swore. 'Now I look back, I was in quite the grim place before I moved here. Thank goodness for Birdie, helping me out with the flat.'

Logan reached across the table. 'Well, believe it because it's only going to get better from here. Now I've got past, you know what. At least, I hope I have. Yeah, we're on the up, Blackcurrant.'

Cally side-eyed. Logan was acting quite strangely. She wondered if he was now hiding stuff from her and had been day drinking. He didn't appear to be drunk, though, which was weird. There was something in his tone she didn't like. More than odd. She opened her mouth to ask what he meant about things getting better and closed it as Colin appeared at their table again.

'Everything alright here? Can I tempt you with seconds? Or perhaps cake?'

Logan didn't waste any time. 'Seconds, please. It's too good to pass up. Honestly, one of the best I've had.'

Colin's chest visibly puffed. 'On it. I'll be back.'

Cally took a sip of her ale. 'I read quite a lot about the estate in winter in those books in the cottage. What's it like?'

'Snow-covered hills, the loch sparkles and sometimes

freezes. Cal, you'll love the cosy evenings. The roaring fires up there are next level.'

As Cally sat and listened to Logan describe the estate, she loved the idea of another weekend there. Though Logan was acting a tad on the strange side, inwardly, she let out a sigh of relief. As the months had passed, he seemed to have turned a corner, which was welcome news. She thought about Scotland and snow and all things festive. The train ride alone would probably knock her socks off. Logan was correct. It would do *her* and *him* the world of good. She was going to jump in with two feet and see what happened.

38

C ally had been for a coffee with Logan in the deli before work. The point had been to give her a bit of courage, Dutch or otherwise, before she went in to tell Birdie about what she'd discovered in the Peaceton store. After discussing the ins and outs of it with Logan the night before at the speakeasy, he'd said there was nothing for it but to get on and tell Birdie as soon as possible. He'd also come up with the idea to soften the blow by inviting Birdie to Scotland at the same time. To say that Cally was nervous about having to inform Birdie about the Estrella problem was an understatement.

Unsure about why she was so worried, she'd spent the night tossing and turning, not able to get it out of her mind. In the end, she told herself that she had the evidence, that she knew she was correct, and once she'd told Birdie, it would be out of her hands. It just all felt a bit grubby and underhanded. Truth be told, it was something she didn't want a bar of at all.

With the problem swarming around her head, she walked into the back of the chemist to the sound of the Shipping Forecast with flutters in her stomach. As she shrugged off her coat, she decided she would not beat about the bush and would tell

Birdie right away. However, she didn't get a chance. As soon as she saw Birdie, she knew something was wrong. Birdie's face was like thunder.

'Morning. Everything okay with you?'

Birdie frowned. 'No, not really.'

'Oh, what's happened?'

Birdie wiggled her phone. 'I've just had a phone call from Estrella. She's resigned. Just like that, out of the blue! Talk about pulling the rug out from someone…'

Cally was totally thrown. For a second, her brain raced, and she didn't know what to do or say. She stalled for time, 'Oh.'

'Yeah, apparently, her mum is very sick back home, and she's decided she needs to go back right away, as in, *right* away, like tomorrow morning. She's booked a flight. Just like that.'

Cally quickly tried to analyse whether or not she should tell Birdie what she'd found. She decided to keep her thoughts to herself and see how it all panned out. She shook her head. 'Goodness!'

Birdie narrowed her eyes. 'It's all very sudden. I need this like a hole in the head.'

Cally wasn't sure where she stood. Estrella had never mentioned that her mum was sick. The plot thickened. From what she already knew, it all seemed suspicious. Cally decided she didn't really care as long as she was rid of her. It worked for her. 'So, now what?'

Birdie shook her head. 'Well, now nothing. She sent an email too to inform me of her resignation, and then she also messaged me saying that she won't be back. She cleared out her stuff and left the dispensary keys and everything. I can't believe it.'

Cally *could* believe it, alright. It was pretty clear that Estrella must have got wind of what Cally had discovered. Estrella was no fool. 'Can she do that? What about notice, her contract, and all that sort of thing?'

Birdie raised her eyebrows. 'That means nothing, really. Not worth the paper or digital signature it's on. I'm up the creek without a paddle. What happened to good old-fashioned loyalty?'

'What? Can she just leave like that?'

'Officially, no, but do you really think I'm going to chase her to Ecuador?'

'Good point. So, what do you do now?'

Birdie shook her head and tutted. 'Put my thinking cap on, cobble around with the other pharmacists to cover her hours, and draw a black line under the whole thing.'

'Right. I see.' Cally liked the idea of drawing a line under it all very much.

Birdie screwed up her lips and narrowed her eyes. 'I knew it! I *knew* there was something about her. I was desperate when I took her on, so I ignored my doubts, but you know when you know? I should have listened to what my inner voice told me.'

Cally remembered her feelings as soon as she'd set eyes on Estrella. She didn't want to say too much. 'Mmm.'

'Well, at least I'm well rid, there is that. I don't have to go through the aggro of getting shot of a bad egg if she was one.'

Cally let out a huge internal sigh. Oh, Estrella was definitely a bad egg. She decided she would keep schtum about the theft and what she'd discovered, at least for now. If Estrella really was gone, there wouldn't be much point in adding fuel to Birdie's stressful fire. It would all come up in the accounting at the end of the year anyway. For the time being, it would probably be good to just leave it be. 'Yup.'

'So, that's my news for this morning. What about you?'

Cally smiled and did a little waving movement with her hands. 'I actually have something a lot happier to tell you. Park that for a minute. Ha.'

'Oh, yes? I need good news.'

Cally started to laugh. 'What would you say if you got an invite to a certain little estate I know in Scotland?'

Birdie squinted. 'I would be there with bells on. I would kiss the person who invited me.'

Cally giggled. 'Be my guest then.'"

'What?'

'Logan's organising a trip and inviting a few locals. It's all very last minute. We thought you'd like to come.'

Birdie did a funny twerk sort of jig. 'Ooh, yeah, ooh yeah.'

Cally cracked up.

Birdie put her hands into fists, gyrated her hips, and made as if her fists were pom poms and pumped them in front of her. 'Give it to me.'

Cally burst into laughter. 'You're nuts.'

'No, I'm not. I have been anticipating and *praying* for this for a long time. Colin will be beside himself. Thank you, thank you, thank you. Who's Estrella again? Let me at the estate. I'm going to dine out on this for *years*.'

39

Cally had just come off the phone from the bank after a long conversation about her mortgage with a surprisingly nice and friendly mortgage advisor. After initially dreading the call and not being sure what was what about mortgages or the world of finance, the advisor had spoken her language and put her mind at rest. She'd had a really informative conversation which had told her loads of things she hadn't realised. Firstly, her deposit was a lot more valuable regarding the term of the loan than she'd thought, and secondly, her proof of stable income over the previous few years and her job meant she was in a good place.

Therefore, as instructed by the mortgage advisor she'd started the application and got the ball rolling on officially starting the *actual* journey to buy her own home. She'd spent a long time finding the correct forms, adding her details left, right, and centre, getting official documents together, and popping in what felt like the inside measurement of her left leg. After checking everything six times over, she'd pressed to submit and had wondered what would happen and when.

The mortgage advisor had given her a rough idea of the

amount of loan she might be granted and how much the payments would be each month. It turned out that what she'd inherited from her grandma had been more beneficial than she'd realised, and she would definitely have enough to buy a flat somewhere in the vicinity of Lovely Bay—something Cally was more than happy with.

So, that was one thing on the home front that was more or less sorted. The other thing was the moving-in or not with Logan thing. There had been a few more discussions with him about them living together, but ultimately especially in light of what had happened at the manor, they had not reached any cement conclusion. A plane crash had put paid to that. As the first time he'd mentioned it, Logan had been, in Cally's eyes, *way* too casual about the whole thing. Again, his attitude had irritated her a fair bit. Not that he knew that, oh no. She'd kept that little morsel to herself. To be fair, he already had enough on his plate without her whinging about the way he'd asked her to live with him.

In her eyes, though, officially moving in together was an *enormous* thing. For him, it was very clear, not so much. From his side of the fence, he seemed to act as if it was a given anyway. After initially feeling put out regarding his utter nonchalance, Cally'd decided not to make a mountain out of a molehill and to roll with it. She'd taken on and got used to him acting as if he could take it or leave it and had decided that she was fine with that. He'd said a couple of times that, as far as he was concerned, they were almost living together anyway, so what difference did it make? Which, if you actually analysed it, was true. Fair enough.

It's just that there was a severe lack of trombones playing in our Cally's ears or happy-clappy hot air balloons floating on by. You see, she had expected, wanted, and possibly *needed* maybe a bit more fanfare. To indeed feel special about it. However, that hadn't happened, and so she'd sucked it up.

In light of that and because of the accident, months had gone by and they'd just continued on as they were, living between the cottage and the flat, and bobbing along just as they had. Since going to Scotland, the job offer, the accident, and everything else that had come their way, the issue of them officially moving in together hadn't really been that important in the grand scheme of things anyway.

Despite all of that and the fact that Cally was busy, she'd been adamant about at least getting the ball rolling with the mortgage application before they went to Scotland and had started tentatively looking for a flat. Logan was of the opinion that whatever they ended up doing, they couldn't go wrong. Oh, how simple it all seemed to and for him. He was very black and white about everything; she would be able to fulfil her dream of having her own place, and if they moved into it together, that would be that. If they chose to do something else; she could rent the flat out. As far as he was concerned, it was a win-win. How easy everything was if you had the surname Henry-Hicks.

Taking all of the above on board, Cally was stalking the estate agents and online sites and starting to note prices, areas, and getting a real feel for what was out there. Her hunt for property had started in semi-earnest. What she hadn't factored in and nobody had told her was that the hunt for a flat in Lovely Bay wasn't likely to be a swift one. What she'd very quickly come to ascertain was that Lovely was very tightly held. There weren't many flats in the first place, and the market was so competitive that it was almost to the point where it was one out one in. Often by way of a wooden box.

And so Cally had found herself with not much to go on at all. She'd been to see a two-bedroom flat on the harbour side of Lovely Bay, not far from Nina's place, but had quickly realised it was too far out of her budget. She'd widened her net a little bit to the next town and gone to see a flat in a new building not far from a shopping centre. As soon as she'd arrived, she realised it was a no-go, and after quickly scooting around, she'd hurriedly crossed 'new build' off her list. Since living in the flat above the deli with its old fixtures and fittings and lovely boutique feel, she knew that an established building was a non-negotiable.

Opening her laptop and clicking on a property website, she selected the drop-down button to change her preferences to 'flat' and then changed the sort order to 'lowest price'. Only a couple of properties came up. She clicked on the first one and scrolled through the pictures. It fit the bill of one of her requirements in that it was in a beautiful old building with high ceilings and sash windows. That's where it ended. A horrible modern renovation, apparently reflected in the price, looked back at her from the photos—a vast walk-in shower instead of a bath, complete with black fixtures and fittings, and a modern acrylic shiny kitchen with an oven hood so large it nearly swallowed the whole flat. Cally tutted and moved on to the next one.

The next one was better in terms of its aesthetics and what she would have to play with, but it was a basement flat, and the security issues and lack of light totally put her off. Changing her preferences, she scrolled down to the bottom of the page, clicked on the next page, and again scrolled to the end where beautiful old Lovely Bay houses looked back at her. She made a funny little laughing sound as she clicked on one of the pictures and scanned through—exactly what she was looking for. In her dreams. A magnificent old Victorian house with a few floors, high ceilings, beautiful skirting boards, a basement, original features galore, fireplaces, sash windows, and ceiling roses. Divine. With a divine price to match.

Sighing a little bit, she clicked the cross in the corner to close the website, put her hand on her chin and thought about how it wasn't fair. Other people got to buy beautiful old houses with stunning gardens and all the things. She was stuck with a one bedroom flat. Swiftly following that she gave herself a stern old talking-to about feeling low about her property hunting. She was right on the cusp of being able to afford her own place, not only that, in the third smallest town in the country, too. She was no longer at the mercy of renting somewhere, no longer had to worry, no longer had to pour money down the drain.

She smiled about having a nice deposit in her bank account and how hard she'd worked for that. She needed to be happy, celebrate and be grateful for the good stuff. Cally de Pfeffer had reached her goal. What she didn't know was that more good things were on the way.

40

Cally sat at a small makeshift desk in the back room of the chemist, surrounded by a new delivery, staring at the spreadsheet on her laptop screen. Numbers swam before her eyes, each one a reminder of the discrepancies she'd uncovered way back when she'd first worked at the Peaceton store. Estrella's abrupt departure niggled at her like an itch she couldn't quite scratch. From the word go, in her bones, she'd categorically known something wasn't right with Estrella. Estrella wasn't as stupid as she'd thought, though, and had ducked out as fast as she could, playing her trump card before she'd been caught. That irritated Cally no end. Slimeball.

Cally had been turning over what she'd discovered for days, weighing up whether or not to bring it to Birdie's attention. She'd reasoned that with Estrella long gone, what good would it do to stir up trouble? It would all come out soon enough, anyway, when the accounts were correctly filed. But every time she tried to let it go, her conscience had prickled and poked her. It wasn't just about Estrella; it was about doing what was right for the business and the trust Birdie had put in her with the job. From her side of the fence, she just felt that Birdie should know.

With that in mind, Cally had decided to stop beating around the bush and had compiled all the evidence she'd gathered in an easy to navigate manner. She'd created a new spreadsheet, meticulously detailed each discrepancy she'd found, added notes about patterns she'd noticed, and cross-referenced everything with the records. As she'd worked, the scope of Estrella's deception didn't change; if anything, it shocked more.

Cally felt a knot in her stomach as she wondered how it had gone unnoticed for so long. It wasn't until she heard Birdie calling her name from the dispensary that she realised how she'd been head down on her laptop thinking about it for ages.

'Our Cally? Are you still back there?'

Cally blinked. 'Yes, I'm still here.'

Birdie appeared in the doorway. 'Everything okay? You've been tucked away in here for hours.'

Cally took a deep breath. It was now or never. 'Actually, there's something I need to talk to you about. Do you have a minute?'

Birdie's eyebrows shot up at Cally's tone of voice. She nodded. 'Oh, no. What now? Of course. I'll put the kettle on.'

A few minutes later, they were settled in the staff room with mugs of tea in hand and Cally perched on the edge of a chair at the small table with her laptop balanced on her knees. She could feel Birdie's curiosity radiating off her in waves.

Birdie took a sip of her tea. 'Right then. This looks serious. What's all this about?'

'It's about Estrella and the Peaceton store.'

Birdie's eyes narrowed. 'Estrella? Not even thought about her. She's long gone. I thought we'd seen the back of her. What about her?'

'Well, when I was first working on organising the stockroom and going through the records, I noticed some discrepancies. I think she got wind of what I was doing…'

'Discrepancies? What sort of discrepancies?'

Cally turned her laptop so Birdie could see the screen. 'At first, it was just little things. A few items missing here and there, and numbers not quite adding up. There was so much mess and chaos. But the more I looked into it, the more I realised it was part of a pattern.'

Cally felt butterflies swarm through her stomach as she walked Birdie through her findings. She pointed out the inconsistencies in the stock levels, the odd spikes in certain product sales that didn't align with promotional periods, and the mysterious disappearance of newly delivered stock. As she spoke and pointed, Cally watched Birdie's expression change from confusion to disbelief and finally to white-hot anger. Birdie's face became progressively redder and she pressed her lips into a thin line.

'Are you telling me,' Birdie said slowly, her voice low and controlled, 'that Estrella was stealing from me? Why am I asking that? I can see it.'

Cally nodded, relieved that Birdie had connected the dots herself. 'I think so, yes. And not just products. I believe she was manipulating the records to cover up cash discrepancies as well.'

Birdie swore. Cally blinked in surprise. 'That conniving little... I knew there was something off about her! But I never imagined she was a thief. Who does that? I was so good to her, too.'

'I'm sorry. I know this must be a shock.'

Birdie waved her hand dismissively. 'Don't apologise. You've done nothing wrong. In fact, you've done everything right. It doesn't matter now. We'll never see her again. Not heard anything from her...'

'I wasn't sure at first. I wanted to be certain before I said anything. And then, when Estrella left so suddenly, I thought maybe it wasn't worth bringing up. But it just didn't sit right with me to let it go. I couldn't just be here and not tell you.'

Birdie nodded. 'You did the right thing. Even if Estrella's

gone, we need to know the full extent of what happened. You know, when she first started, I had my doubts. But I was desperate for help, and she seemed capable enough. I should have trusted my instincts in the first place.'

'You couldn't have known. She was clever about it.'

Birdie tutted. 'I should have been paying closer attention.'

Cally sighed. 'I can't help wondering why she did it. Was she in some kind of trouble? Or was it just greed? I *do* know I wasn't keen on her from the moment I stepped in.'

Birdie shook her head. 'Some people just see an opportunity and take it, regardless of who it hurts.'

'I suppose.'

'Well, at least I know what is what now.'

Cally felt as if a weight had been lifted from her shoulders. It was good, like really, really good, to feel as if she'd done the right thing. She'd spotted something others had missed, had trusted her instincts, and had taken action. Here she was, adulting in a real job. Trusted, wanted, and conversing as a valued part of a team. How good did that feel? Me oh my, so very good indeed.

41

A good few months or so had gone by since the funeral. Logan had most definitely had his fair share of ups and downs, but overall, he was on the mend. Cally had navigated her way through it, seen the grief sequence she knew well come and go for him, and successfully made it through the other side. In a funny way, what had happened to Logan had made them much closer. Almost as if the shared knowledge of what it felt like to grieve was another connection between the two of them. Cally wasn't quite sure if connecting over what grief felt like was a good thing or not. She supposed she didn't have much choice in the matter.

After a nice long walk, she was on her way to view a flat on the other side of Lovely. As she came over the crest of a hilly residential area, she looked down at the bay in the distance. The sloping, tree-lined street she was on was oddly quiet with no cars and apart from a rustle of leaves and a few birds here and there, not a lot could be heard at all. As Cally walked along, she nosed at the white picket fences at the front of pretty houses, the shell-tile Lovely roofs, and a jumble of chimney pots here and there puncturing up into the sky. On the other side of the road, a couple ahead of her with a Labrador was taking a leisurely stroll down the hill in the direction of the bay and a man wearing a white cycle helmet passed her on an electric bike. He tipped his hand to his head and said hello as he cycled past, full of the joys of spring even though the cold weather had well and truly arrived.

Cally crossed the road, squeezing between a couple of parked cars, and then stood outside the block of flats where she was booked in to see a ground-floor apartment. The beautiful old 1920s building, painted a soft grey and white with a fence on either side of a central pathway entrance, looked just like her cup of tea. French doors led to stairs with a stained-glass window in the middle and tall glass panes flanked either side of the front door. According to the estate agents, the property was a small two-storey "boutique" building with four flats and communal gardens in an enviable position. As Cally stood looking up at the building, she couldn't argue with that.

Initially, she had been in two minds about whether or not to arrange a viewing because, from the start of her property hunt, she'd been looking for a top-floor flat. In fact, being in a top-floor place had been on her non-negotiables list. From the moment she'd moved into Birdie's flat, she'd just felt comfort-able being up high and looking over rooftops. At the end of the day, she'd climb up the stairs, slip off her shoes, lock the front door, and say goodbye to the world. It had been a real positive in her life.

She stood pondering the fact that she preferred to be upstairs as she looked at the building. She stepped to her side, and just before she went in, turned around, and took in the landscape — a church spire, the sea in the distance, and lining up all the way down the road old television aerials butting up into the sky. As soon as she walked into the foyer of the Art

Deco building, she liked it. With a wide staircase, a handmade timber banister leading up to the first floor, and a beautiful tessellated floor, she loved the feel right away. Rather than being dark and a bit dreary as she thought it might have been, the entrance was bright and inviting by way of an Art Deco skylight in the middle of the second-floor roof. As she looked around, she nodded in appreciation at the survival of the original old doorbells on either side of the doors, the little pigeon holes in the architraves, and the old timber utility door to a service room underneath the stairs.

Turning past the stairs, she took in flat number two, where outside, a very well-cared-for, delicate-leaved palm stood beside an old 1920s door. A brass doorknob, matching letterbox, and fittings shone and a doormat welcomed. Just as Cally was about to push her finger into the old-fashioned bell, the door opened, and the estate agent, Ella, greeted her. Cally knew Ella from the chemist and via a few phone calls they'd had about property in Lovely Bay and she'd helped Birdie with scouting out for a new shop in a neighbouring town.

Ella beamed. 'Our Cally. Good to see you. How are you?'

'Good, thanks.'

'So, what do you think of the street appeal? Nice, eh? I know you said you didn't want a ground-floor flat, but how lovely is it outside?' Ella asked with a wide smile.

'It's good. I like it so far.'

'I thought you would as soon as it came on. It's about a hundred years old. You said you wanted something with character.'

'I did, yep.'

'It's one of these gorgeous old Lovely buildings.'

'Mmm. I thought that when I arrived. I love the shell tiles on the roof.'

'I know. You have to have a house in Lovely with a shell roof, right?'

'So, no one is living here at the moment?' Cally asked.

'No, it's a deceased estate,' Ella noted. 'The old lady who lived here was in a nursing home, and there was a waiting period for all the legal stuff to go through. That's sorted now and so here we are.'

As Ella led Cally into the flat, the first thing that struck her was the abundance of natural light. She'd expected it to be a bit dingy, but light flooded in through large windows.

Ella gestured around the room. 'It's got some lovely original features. Lots of good light – typical of the Art Deco period.'

Cally nodded. She looked up at a very ornate ceiling rose and lines of beautiful decorative coving that ran along the top of the high-ceilinged walls.

'That fireplace is original.'

Cally moved closer to the old mantel and ran her hand along the smooth, cool surface. 'It's beautiful. Wow, yes.'

The flat had seen better days, but its bones were calling out as Cally walked around with wide eyes. An old carpet covered what appeared to be hardwood floors, original pull light switches dropped from the ceiling, and beautiful porthole windows looked out over the back.

'Now, I should mention the kitchen. One of the areas that needs a bit of work.'

Cally looked around, taking in dated units, a worn linoleum floor, and peeling wallpaper. The whole room had a tired feel to it, but the original Crittall windows were beautiful and looked out over a small courtyard area.

'It's functional but needs updating. That's part of the reason the price is so competitive. It needs a quick sale, and so it's priced to reflect the work that needs doing. These don't come up very often. To be quite honest, I don't think we're going to see many, if any, more flats come on the market until the new year now.'

Cally nodded, her mind whirring with possibilities. She

knew a good buy when she saw one. She'd certainly been stalking estate agent sites for long enough.

Ella mused as if reading her thoughts. 'The bones of the rooms are good. Lovely big windows, plenty of space to work with, and you'll never go wrong with a block like this.'

They moved on to the bathroom, which was in a similar state to the kitchen. An avocado suite wasn't too pleasant, but an original beautiful Art Deco mirror above the sink and old light fixtures were priceless.

'Lovely original features but needs work. All reflected in the asking price.'

After going around the flat, Cally was charmed. She was surprised she could afford it but, at the same time, realised it wasn't for her. The view, or lack thereof, was a significant draw-back. She'd grown accustomed to her elevated perspective from Birdie's flat, and the thought of losing that was more disap-pointing than she'd anticipated. 'It is nice,' she admitted. 'There's so much to like about it. The period features are beautiful, and I can see the potential.'

'But? I'm sensing a but...' Ella chuckled.

'But I'm not sure about the lack of a view. I'm so used to looking out over the rooftops, seeing the bay in the distance and the lighthouse. I'm not sure how I'd feel about losing that.'

'It's a big decision.'

'Yeah, I don't think it's going to be for me.'

'Right.'

'Do you have anything else on soon?'

Ella tutted. 'I wish. These one bedroom flats are like gold dust around here. I think it will be a while.'

'I thought as much. I think I might put it on the back burner for a while. I have had such a lot going on.'

'You have.'

'I might park looking for a property until the new year.'

'Might be an idea. As you say you've had a time of it and there will be movement once Spring rolls in.'

'Yes, I think I'm going to stop looking for a bit. I don't want to make the wrong decision.'

'Might be a good idea. Don't plump for something now when there might be something better in a few months' time.'

'Good advice.'

'How are things up at the Manor now some time has passed?'

Cally sighed. 'Ahh, better, I guess.'

Ella shook her head. 'What a sorry old state of affairs that was.'

'I know.'

'I knew Alastair back in the day when I was a teenager. Who would have thought?'

'Yep. You just don't know, do you?'

'Nope. I hear you're going up to Scotland soon. Birdie told me the other day when I was in for a prescription. She's beside herself that she's been invited.'

Cally chuckled. 'I know.'

'Any particular reason why you're going? Or is it just to enjoy the festive stuff in that neck of the woods?'

Cally smiled. 'It all started with Logan and because I like snow, and if there's one thing that place has at this time of year, it's snow. We just thought it might be nice to get away.'

'Right.'

'It went from a quiet weekend away to, well, I don't know really, Logan inviting Birdie, my friend Eloise, and yeah, hopefully it will be nice.'

'Just make sure you're rugged up well.'

'I will.'

'I reckon you'll have a whale of a time.' Ella gestured around in front of her. 'Put the flat hunting on hold for a bit and have some time off.'

'You're right. I have had a lot on my plate.'

'You can't really go wrong going up there, can you?'

Cally shook her head. 'I suppose not.'

She hoped that was true. The last time she'd travelled to Scotland it had not been the start of good things. That was about to change.

42

Cally stood in front of her wardrobe, feeling a bit perplexed. The Scotland trip had come as a nice surprise, but now it was upon her she found herself facing an unexpected dilemma: packing for a winter getaway in the Scottish Highlands. Not that she was complaining, of course. She was ready to grab it by the neck and enjoy every little bit of it.

She pulled out a thick jumper, held it up against herself, and then threw it onto a growing pile on her bed. It joined an assortment of thermal underwear, thick socks, and what she hoped were sufficiently warm jeans. The whole lot looked woefully inadequate for the icy temperatures Google had told her awaited her in Scotland at the time of year.

On hearing who she assumed was Eloise on the stairs up to the flat, then a knock on the door, she scooted out of the bedroom, across the sitting room, opened the door, and hugged Eloise.

'Hiya!' Eloise beamed and held her hands in the air.

'Hey. How are you?'

'Good.'

'You look good.'

Eloise blew a stream of air out of her lips. 'Phew, those stairs! Killers! Thanks. I'm looking forward to tonight. It feels like ages since we've caught up.'

'I know. It *is* ages. Drink?'

Eloise slipped her shoes off and hung her jacket by the door. 'A bottle of wine or two will suit me unless you've made black-currant cocktails. If so, I'll have six…'

Cally looked alarmed.

'Jokes. I've had a busy week. I've been looking forward to this sleepover. I need friend therapy.'

'Same. I've had a gutful of a week. Right, glass of wine coming right up.'

Eloise followed Cally into the kitchen. 'What's happened on the flat front?'

'Nothing. I went to look at one recently but it was on the ground floor.'

'Right.'

'I want some sort of a view.'

'I see. Makes sense.' Eloise agreed.

'The estate agent said it might be best to leave it until the new year.'

'Hmm.' Eloise wrinkled her nose. 'I guess it's a funny time of year with Christmas on the way.'

'Precisely. She said there's nothing coming on for the fore-seeable. I think I'm going to park it, have a nice break, enjoy Christmas and then see what's what in the new year.'

'Good idea. Get to Scotland without any worries. I can't believe we'll be on our way soon.'

'Indeed.'

'Looking forward to it?'

'I am, actually. The pictures look amazing. I don't want to do much apart from relaxing, and you get lots of that up there. It's stunning, Els. You're going to love it.'

Eloise clapped her hands together. 'It's *so* exciting. I've always wanted to go to Scotland but never got around to it.'

Cally pondered as she took a packet of crisps out of the cupboard, pulled open the top, and shook its contents into a bowl. The trip had been planned *very* quickly. Logan had been surprisingly enthusiastic about it all, insisting on inviting not just Cally but Eloise, Nina, and Birdie as well. He'd even mentioned that some of his family would join them. It was all very exciting, but there was something odd about it too. Something in the way Logan had been acting since he'd brought up the idea. Little things, like hushed phone conversations that ended abruptly when she'd entered the room or the way he'd sometimes got a faraway look in his eyes as if he was planning something more than he was telling her. She had a *horrible* feeling that it was going to encompass some sort of a wake.

'Earth to Cally,' Eloise's voice broke into her thoughts.

Cally shook her head. 'Sorry, just thinking about the trip. Don't you think it's a bit, I don't know what the word is... strange?'

Eloise raised an eyebrow. 'Strange? No, how?'

'I don't know,' Cally admitted. 'It's just that Logan's been acting a bit off lately. Secretive, almost. And this whole trip seems to have come out of nowhere. I don't know; I just hope this is not something that is a homage to Alastair.' Cally swore. 'That sounds mean, doesn't it?'

A flicker of something – surprise? worry? – crossed Eloise's face. It was gone so quickly that Cally thought she must have imagined it. Eloise shook her head in quick little jerky movements and blinked. 'I'm sure it's nothing.' Eloise batted her hand. 'Nah. A homage? Nope. Not at all.'

'I hope not.'

'He probably just wants to do something nice for you. You've both been through a lot this year, what with, well, you know and you've started a new job...'

Cally nodded. It had been ages, but the loss was still raw for Logan. Maybe that was all it was – Logan's way of trying to end the year on a positive note. 'It's probably nothing. Do you think Logan might be planning something? For this trip, I mean. I really hope not. I've had a gutful of it if I'm honest.'

Eloise coughed and swallowed. It didn't go unnoticed by Cally. 'What was that? You know something, don't you? You need to tell me if it's some sort of wake. I'm not up for that.'

Eloise scrunched up her face. 'No! I don't know anything. I'm as in the dark as you are. If Logan's planning something, he hasn't told me about it. I don't think he would do that.'

Cally narrowed her eyes, not entirely convinced. 'You *would* tell me, wouldn't you?'

'Of course! It's just a trip to the snow, Cal. Nothing more, nothing less. You're overthinking.'

As they sipped their wine, the talk turned to whether they'd see the Northern Lights, snow-capped mountains, and cosy log fires. Cally tried to put her worries about Logan and his grief behind her. Whatever happened in Scotland, she had a feeling it was going to be something to remember. The problem was she just wasn't sure that the memories were going to be good ones. She'd have to wait and see.

43

Cally was head down bum up on the floor of one of the RNLI storerooms. She was there with Nina on a job to sort through years of clutter that had accumulated by way of various volunteers and no one really being in charge of the storerooms at all. Their mission was to clear out as much as possible with a view to using the whole back of the building for local community events. There was a proposal that the space would be used as a Lovely playgroup area for local parents.

Cally had been more than happy to put her hand up to help. As she had continued to work every now and then for Nina, she'd become a dab hand at decluttering, and doing it to earn Lovely Brownie points felt like a no-brainer. The more experience she had, the more she'd realised that decluttering was more of a skill than she had first thought. When she'd initially started working for Nina, she'd not believed that there was an art to it. Surely it was easy enough? Now, she'd been doing it for a while, she was of the opinion that there most definitely was. She'd learnt that there were many parts of the equation. One of the most crucial was that Nina could sweep a room with her eyes in seconds, transfer that data to a job spec, and rustle up a list in no time. That was one of the most vital parts of a job going well. Cally had now learnt the art of doing that, too.

Still on her hands and knees, as she scooped a whole load of what appeared to be old canvas boat tarps behind her, she came across a large cardboard box full of old memorabilia. A couple of timber trophies from a fishing competition, a picture of boys lined up for an old school-type photograph, and various fundraising leaflets from years gone by. Shuffling backwards past the canvas sails, she yanked the box towards her, then pushed it away from her, got up, and plonked it on the table. As she was moving it to the far side of the table, she saw an old invitation in heavily embossed cream paper detailing an event at Lovely Manor to raise funds for the RNLI. She read the front; a Summer Poppy Ball laid on by the manor. Flicking the front to the page on the inside, a tissue paper leaf with gold filigree told more. The paper crinkled as Cally turned it and she read about the details of the ball. All those years before, they'd celebrated the poppies in the fields and used the occasion as a way to fundraise for the RNLI. Cally sighed as she thought about the fields of poppies behind the marquee at Alastair's funeral. The past summer had seen the poppies as a backdrop for a very different occasion altogether than a happy summer ball.

She sighed as she lifted the box and put it by the door. It still felt strange to comprehend, but Alastair was long gone. It told her you never knew what would hit you next. She thought about Logan's weekend expedition to Scotland. He'd been adamant that Cally go up there to see the snow. When she'd questioned him about what he was up to, he'd informed her that because of what had happened to Alastair, he wanted to do more things with his life. He'd repeatedly told her that it was now or never and that you had to get on with it because of what might be around the corner. Cally pondered as she worked and wrinkled up her nose at the fact that the extended invite to

Scotland included Eloise, Birdie, Nina, and Robby and not only that but quite a few of Logan's family were going too. Really?

Cally chuckled to herself as she recalled Birdie's reaction to the invitation. Birdie had rubbed her hands together and nearly bitten Cally's hand off. She'd told Cally that she'd been waiting years to go to the Scottish arm of the manor. Cally had giggled and rolled her eyes, laughed, and said she'd use it somehow to blackmail Birdie in the future.

As far as Cally was concerned, it all seemed quite weird, though. One minute, it was an on the spur getaway from it all weekend, the next, it felt as if half of Lovely were attending. Cecilia, Reginald, and Anne, too, had all chimed in that they would love to go. Cally had kept her thoughts to herself and put it down to everyone getting through the grieving process.

Logan had thrown himself into it full throttle. He'd organised walks, skiing (not that Cally would be partaking in that), and quite a few social events, including a drinks party on the Saturday night, and a chowder evening Scottish style. Again, Cally had questioned how into the weekend Logan was, but after a bit of deliberating, she'd decided that as long as he was okay and no longer strangled by grief, she didn't really care. She'd go along for the ride and see what was what. It wasn't going to hurt her to pop up there on the train for the weekend and frolic about in the snow.

As she pondered going to Scotland and wondered if stargazing was possible in freezing cold temperatures, Nina came in with a box full of vintage glass fishing floats in her arms.

'How are you getting on?' Nina asked.

Cally gestured in the direction of the cardboard box full of photographs she'd come across. 'I just found an old invitation to a poppy ball at Lovely Manor.

'A what ball?' Nina frowned.

'A summer poppy ball from the fifties to raise money for this place and the RNLI.'

'Ahh, right, I see.'

'It made me think how this year the poppies were for something quite different.'

'Hmm, so sad... and before we know it, it'll be Christmas. The year is flying by.'

'I know.'

'I'm really looking forward to the weekend away.' Nina noted

'Me too. I was just thinking about it. I can't believe how quickly it's come around. Feels like only yesterday we were sweltering in heat, and now we're off to the snow.'

Nina chuckled, putting down the box of glass fishing floats. 'I know what you mean. I've been so caught up in work that I've barely had time to think about packing.'

'I've been wondering what on earth to take.'

'I'd say pack for all eventualities. Especially something nice for the party on Saturday night.'

At the mention of the party, Cally noticed a flicker of something cross Nina's face. It was gone in an instant.

'I wonder if there will be Scottish dancing?'

'I don't really care. We actually have a night out, and no worries.'

Cally nodded. 'So, June's all good to look after Faye and you're going to fly up?'

'Yes, it will hopefully be nice and quick.'

'You're in for a treat. Be prepared for the whisky – they don't mess about up there.'

Nina grimaced. 'I'm not sure my liver's quite ready for that. Maybe I'll stick to hot chocolate.'

'Wise choice. The whisky will put hairs on your chest.'

'Is that supposed to be a selling point?' Nina chuckled.

'Logan is so into it and has been planning constantly. It's almost as if there's something going on.'

'Like what?' Nina asked.

'I don't know. I know him, though.'

'Are you sure?'

'Yep. Do you know anything?'

'I'm that obvious, am I?'

'Only to someone who's been working with you for months. Come on, spill. What's going on?'

Nina hesitated for a moment. 'Nothing as far as I know.'

'Now you've got me worried with that look on your face. What's going on?'

'Honestly!' Nina held her hands up.

Cally's mind whirled. She knew the look on Nina's face. Whatever was going on, it was clear that the upcoming trip to Scotland was going to be far more eventful than Cally had initially thought. She just hoped it was going to be something she would enjoy.

44

Just as they had the first time they'd been to Scotland, Cally and Logan sat on the train as it wound its way closer and closer to the estate. Cally had thought the journey before had been a good one when she'd been overawed by the spectacular scenery as the train had wound its way closer and closer to the estate. This time, though, there were no words. She gazed out the train window, her breath fogging up the glass as she pressed her face closer. The further north they'd travelled, the more the world outside had transformed into a winter wonderland. Landscape that had been saturated and lush back in the warmer months was now blanketed in a thick layer of pristine snow. It sparkled under a weak sun, covering everything in white.

Cally shook her head. 'I've never seen so much snow in my life!'

Logan glanced up. 'Just wait until we get to the estate. This is nothing compared to what you'll see there.'

Cally could hardly contain her excitement. 'I still can't quite believe we're here. Thanks for organising it.'

Logan shrugged. 'It wasn't that difficult. The estate's always ready for visitors, and everyone seemed keen for a bit of a pre-Christmas getaway. It was pretty easy.'

There it was again, the notion that going to an estate was a given in Logan's life. Cally didn't care as long as she was in on it. She was way past things bothering her. In fact, she'd decided to make the most of it. What had happened to Alastair had given her a tidy old slap to get on and enjoy her life. 'Yep.'

'It'll be nice to get away, won't it?'

'Yes. It's been a busy year.'

'It has. What with everything that's happened. On top of you know what, you've started a new job and got the mortgage and everything.'

'Yeah.'

'I think you made the right decision to put that on hold until the new year.'

Cally totally agreed. Parking the flat hunting had freed up her brain space to not do anything other than enjoy Scotland and the upcoming festive season. 'I think it was for the best.'

Logan patted her leg. 'Plenty of time for that. We're in no rush…'

As the train rumbled along, Cally was mesmerised by the scenery. 'It's so pretty. I said that last time, but this beats it hands down.'

'Wait until you see it at night. When the moon's out and the snow's glittering, it's absolutely magical. The sound, or lack thereof, is amazing, too.'

The trees on either side of the track were heavy with snow, their branches bowing under the weight. 'It's beautiful. It's going to be so nice tucked up by the fire.'

'I knew you'd love it.'

Cally smiled. 'Oh, I absolutely do.'

≈

A very fine few snowflakes fluttered down from a white-grey sky as Cally walked through the sunken garden at the main part of the estate with Logan. The garden, the house, and the whole landscape looked completely different covered in snow. The old house glistened with a thin sparkly topping of white, smoke puffed from its chimneys, a huge winter wreath tied with a tartan bow graced the main door, and the smell of winter in the Highlands carried on the air. Perfect real fir Christmas trees doused head to toe in thousands of white lights glittered on either side of the main door.

Just as they were getting to the front entrance, Logan's mum, in an oversized Fairilse jumper, woollen hat, and a huge tartan scarf tied around her shoulders, came around from the side path.

'Ahh, there you are. I was just making my way over to the cottage. Angus texted me. They'll be here any minute now.'

Logan nodded. 'Good timing. We estimated it would be about now.'

Anne kissed them both on the cheeks. 'How was the train journey?'

'Absolutely gorgeous,' Cally answered. 'I'm so pleased we decided on the train. It's not a bad way to arrive.'

'Nice if you've got time and you don't have to worry about the weather.'

'Do you know how their flight was?' Logan asked and looked up at the sky. 'Were there any delays?'

'No, Angus said the weather was fine and there were no problems.'

Cally wiggled her phone. 'Eloise said the flight was going to take off on time.'

Logan frowned. 'I didn't realise Eloise had texted you.'

'Yes, I did say earlier. I didn't think you'd heard me.'

Anne gestured in the direction of the drive. 'They'll be here any minute now. Cecilia and Reg shouldn't be too far behind them.'

Cally shook her head as she thought about what Reg and Cecilia had been through since the last time she'd been at the estate with them. 'How are they? I haven't seen them for a few weeks.' Cally pressed her lips together and made a wincing face.

Anne shrugged and shook her head slowly. 'Not too bad considering the circumstances, I suppose. It is what it is. I think Reg will be hitting the whisky this weekend.'

'I wonder how they'll be?' Logan mused.

'Well, we'll soon find out. They've only been up here once since the funeral. You know how much Cecilia has struggled. Some days, I don't think she's made it out of bed…' Anne turned her palms up.

'Yes. She didn't look quite the ticket the last time I saw her.' Cally noted.

Anne sighed. 'Hopefully, being up here will do her good.' She gestured in front of her with her hand and twirled her finger around in the general direction of the snow-covered lawn. 'This place can work its wonders even in the most testing of times. It might help them a bit. I suppose you don't really know.'

As the three of them stood chatting by the front door under-neath the shelter of the portico, little fluffy snowflakes fell on the drive. Anne stamped her feet on the step, the lights on the Christmas trees twinkled, and Cally blew out little puffs of smoke into the air as they waited. When there was a crunch of tyres on snow-covered gravel and the sound of an engine, they looked in the direction of the main gate to see one of the old weathered estate Land Rovers come into view. Standing in silence, they watched as it wound its way up the long driveway, its dark green paint standing out against the pristine white landscape.

'Here they are,' Anne said as she looked at her watch. 'Right on time. It must have been easy traffic around the airport today.'

The Land Rover pulled up in front of the house, its engine rumbling to a stop. Angus hopped out of the driver's seat in a tweed flat cap, green trousers, and a thick cable-knit jumper. He hurried around to open the passenger doors as Eloise, Birdie, Nina, and Robby all hopped out.

'Welcome to Scotland!' Logan called out as he walked across the drive. 'How was the flight?'

Cally kissed Birdie then Eloise. 'So pleased to see you.'

Nina gushed. 'I can't believe how beautiful it is.' She turned a slow circle to take in the full view. 'Look at those trees, all covered in snow! I'm sold already. Sign me up for a timeshare.'

Birdie kept shaking her head. 'Nice, nice, nice.'

Nina nodded enthusiastically. 'The lanes as we were driving here were spectacular! All those snow-covered hills and lochs…'

Robby chimed in. 'I think I've taken about a hundred photos already!'

As they stood on the driveway getting the luggage, a light flurry of snow continued to fall. Tiny feather-like flakes danced in the air around them, and Birdie held out her hand, catching a couple on her hand. 'It's magical. Thanks *so* much for inviting me. I can't believe I'm finally here.'

Cally laughed. 'All Logan's idea.' She smiled at Birdie as she saw on Birdie's face what she'd first felt when she herself had arrived at the estate, albeit around the corner at the cottage and not at the main house. She saw Birdie feeling the same thing: a combination of overwhelm at the startling beauty and a bit shell-shocked at the vastness at the same time.

As they all filed around the side to the boot room and then through to the kitchen, where a fire roared, Logan squeezed Cally's arm. 'All good?'

'Yep, thank you for this. Couldn't be better.'

45

Cally walked into the sitting room in the cottage and let out a long whoosh of a sigh. Just as her previous time in Scotland, she loved the little house, and with its roof and gardens covered in a blanket of white, it was even better. There was something about it that felt as if it insulated her from the world. As if it cocooned her from real life. It always made her chuckle that the cottage was referred to almost as a side thought by those at the estate. To her, it was a sizable house – and not a small one at that. She plumped up a cushion on the sofa, put her mug on the coffee table, and sat down.

Nothing had changed since she'd visited earlier in the year apart from the fact that it now wore pretty Christmas decorations. It still had the same timeless wallpaper, the same beautiful old sofa, and the same picture over the fireplace. The cosy, comforting smell remained, just like before and it was all still immaculate, a testament to how well everything was looked after on the estate. There was not a speck of dust to be seen, the beautiful curtains fell into folds just so, the rug appeared to be freshly vacuumed, and there was a faint smell of furniture polish in the air. Now, it also sparkled with festivity: a

Christmas tree twinkled next to the window and a beautiful real fir garland doused in white lights glittered from the mantelpiece.

Cally sipped her tea, looked out the window and just stared at the view, and hugged herself about having a weekend in the countryside with people she loved. Logan came and stood by the fire with a mug of tea and smiled.

'All good?' he asked, raising his eyebrows.

'Yep.'

Logan gestured towards the window. 'Would you rather have stayed at the house with everyone else?'

Cally shook her head. 'Absolutely not. Cottage every time for me.'

Logan shook his head and laughed. 'I don't think Birdie is with you on that.'

'Nope. She loves it at the main house. I reckon she'd have been put out if she was in one of the cottages.'

'Ha, yeah. I thought the same, too. She'd make a good lady of the manor.'

'Wouldn't we all?'

'It's been a nice break so far, hasn't it?'

'It really has.' Cally was grateful that Logan had planned the weekend. Despite her concern more than a few times that Logan might have planned something to do with Alastair's passing, that hadn't happened. Since they'd arrived in Scotland, there hadn't been a whiff of anything really at all.

'We'll have to make a tradition of coming up here at this time of year.'

'I can work with that.' Cally smiled.

Logan finished his tea. 'Right. Okay, I'll love you and leave you then.'

'You're going to meet Reg and Robby at the pub?'

'Yep. Enjoy your afternoon tea. Don't make yourself sick on Mrs MacPherson's shortbread.'

Cally smiled and widened her eyes. She was going to the main house for afternoon tea with Birdie, Eloise, and Nina. She intended to consume as much shortbread as humanly possible.

～

If anyone had ever looked in their element and been as pleased as Punch, it was Birdie sitting in a wingback chair in the drawing room by the fire just shy of a tall, twinkling real fir Christmas tree. Cally laughed as she looked across; Birdie had smug written all over her face.

The drawing room, set up for afternoon tea, was full of chat and clinking of tea cups. A cake stand held layers of tiny pastries, cakes, and sweet things, a platter was piled with shortbread, and there were three different pots of tea from far-off exotic lands.

Nina, who was perched on the edge of the sofa next to Birdie, also looked to be in her element. She smiled and lowered her voice. 'I could get used to this life.'

Cally nodded. 'It's not a bad perk from my boyfriend, is it?'

Eloise chuckled. 'Better than that boy racer you went out with that time.'

Birdie shuddered. 'Yikes. Who was that? Doesn't sound like my cup of tea.'

Eloise raised her eyebrows. 'You don't want to know.'

Cally laughed. 'Let's not talk about that episode in my life.' She changed the subject and gestured around the drawing room. 'Logan mentioned making coming up here a yearly tradition.'

'I'm in every day of the week,' Birdie joked.

Nina nodded. 'Me, too.'

Cally lowered her voice. 'I'm glad there weren't any surprises in the end. Not yet, anyway.'

Birdie coughed. 'Nope.'

271

Cally kept her voice low. 'The family seems to be feeling a bit better. It's good to see. I think there still might be a long road ahead...'

'Yep. It takes a long time.'

Eloise gestured with her cup. 'This helps. The scenery and peace here make everything feel better. You said it was nice, but it *really* is something else.'

Nina nodded. 'I know. I wondered what it was going to be like but this has topped anything I thought.'

Birdie agreed. 'Same. I've wanted to come here for so long but I genuinely didn't think it would be as good as this.'

Cally chuckled. 'You've been in your element.'

'I know. I think I need to buy myself a manor house.'

Nina laughed. 'You do.'

Cally shook her head. 'I'm not being in charge of deliveries.'

Birdie giggled. 'Don't worry, you'll be busy being in control of my empire.'

Cally smiled as she leant forward and took another piece of shortbread. So far, the weekend had been great for everyone involved but mostly for Logan. She thought about the few times back home when he'd hit the bottle once too often and how stressful it had been. It had got so bad that, at one point, she'd become really concerned about his wellbeing. The trip to Scotland had somehow reset him. She hoped he remained the same. She was so pleased he was back to his old self. Back to the man she'd thrown a chicken breast at in a boat.

She smiled as she looked around the beautifully decorated, quietly elegant drawing room. The weekend was proving to be a lovely one without any surprises. Calm, easy, comfortable and just right after the year they'd had. She hoped that she would see the year out in the same vein.

46

Cally stood by the floor-to-ceiling window overlooking the estate's front lawn, mesmerised by its blanket of twinkling white. She chuckled to herself as she remembered how, half an hour before, she'd plodded over to the main house in her fancy outfit, complete with welly boots, stomping through the snow hand in hand with Logan.

And, oh, how fancy her outfit was indeed. An update to her usual shirt, skirt, and tights uniform: this skirt was A-line and velvet, the tights were opaque and had a sheen, and the ballet flats were covered in thousands of tiny little sparkly jewels. A slash-neck velvet long-sleeved top with a dropped cowl back and a long row of small white pearl buttons completed her look. It had to be said by one and all; our Cally stunned and then some.

The room around her was just as good. The Christmas tree was one of those affairs Cally had only ever seen in a movie or slap bang in the middle of an overlit shopping centre; a tree that could only be decorated by way of a ladder. As Cally stood alongside it, she wondered how a Christmas tree could ooze elegance, but just like everything else at the estate, it most definitely did. A tree with a combination of old money charm and over-the-top opulence worked for her. It shimmered with thousands of warm white cluster lights and twinkled from the corner. Doused liberally in an eclectic mix of vintage baubles and little tartan bows every now and then, it somehow managed to do just about everything right.

Turning from the snow-covered scene, Cally looked over at the smattering of guests with their cocktails in hand and watched as Birdie chatted with Logan's uncle Reg. Birdie had scrubbed up well. In a black sparkly midi dress with a slight heel, her hair in a fancy updo, and diamonds in her ears, she was a long way from the back of the chemist's and her white dispensary coat. The Shipping Forecast was nowhere to be seen or heard.

Eloise, in an elegant black silk number, with a slit up one side, and her hair swept up in an intricate chignon, strolled over, looking nearly as good as the tree.

'There you are. I was beginning to think you'd got lost in this labyrinth of a house.'

'It's a bit like that, isn't it?' Eloise chuckled.

Cally smiled and gestured to the scene outside the window. 'I was just admiring the view.'

'I know, it's so pretty out there. Cold, though.' Eloise raised her glass. 'Have you tried the cocktails?' She took a sip and widened her eyes. 'Mmm, yes, delicious.'

Cally shook her head and gestured with her glass. 'I've been nursing this glass of champagne. It's a tough life.'

Eloise took another sip. 'This has got your name written all over it. Have a taste.'

Cally took a sip. 'Oh my. That's dangerous! I might leave that to you.'

'I know. Any more, and I might start thinking I belong here.'

Cally shook her head and looked around. 'I'll need more

than a few cocktails for that. I don't think I'll *ever* really belong here.'

Eloise raised an eyebrow. 'Says the girl who's about to marry into all this.'

Cally frowned and narrowed her eyes. 'Sorry. What?'

Eloise spluttered and coughed. 'Just a turn of phrase. You know what I mean. There will be wedding bells next.'

'Don't be ridiculous! That's not even on the cards. Why would you say that?'

'Nothing. What would you say if it was?'

Cally pondered for a second. 'None of your business!'

Eloise giggled. 'It's weird. Here we are, in this ridiculous mansion, sipping cocktails that probably cost more than my house. What a few years, eh?'

Cally's brain flicked back to the events of the previous year. 'It's been quite a ride, hasn't it?'

'That's putting it mildly.'

'I'll be glad to see the back of it if I'm honest.'

'How are you really doing with all of it? The new job and everything with Alastair...'

'Still processing it. The job with Birdie is amazing, but it's been a lot to take on. And then there's Logan. Alastair's death hit him hard. There are still moments when I catch him staring off into space, and I know he's thinking about it. Overall, though, everything's good. This place helps... I used to think places like this only existed in books or films.'

'Now you're part of it. A modern-day Cinderella.' Eloise cracked up

Cally snorted. 'Hardly. I don't think Cinderella ever had to deal with inventory management or chatbots.'

'I guess she didn't. Speaking of which, how are you getting on at work? Last time we talked, you were still getting to grips with it.'

'It's going well, actually. I mean, it's challenging, and there are days when I feel completely out of my depth. But Birdie's been amazing, and I'm learning so much.'

'I still can't believe you uncovered that whole thing with Estrella,' Eloise shook her head back and forth in quick little movements. 'You're like a regular Sherlock Holmes.'

'Hardly. Anyone could have done it.'

Eloise rolled her eyes. 'Here we go. No, they couldn't.'

Cally chuckled. 'It's not hard…'

Their conversation was interrupted by a staff member who put a fresh tray of canapés on a side table beside Cally. She picked up one of the little works of art that looked almost too pretty to eat and popped it in her mouth. 'Ooh, yes, yum.'

'What are they?'

'Some kind of smoked salmon thing with caviar. Absolutely sinful.'

Eloise took one, bit into it, and closed her eyes in bliss. 'Oh my.'

Cally took another one and lowered her voice. 'It's probably not ladylike to stuff these in your face, but I don't even care. When in Rome, and all that.'

Eloise laughed. 'It would be rude not to, really.'

Cally noticed Logan glancing over at them. She felt a flutter at the sight of him.

'He looks good,' Eloise observed, following Cally's gaze. 'Better than the last time I saw him.'

Cally nodded. 'He's doing better. This trip has been good for him, I think. It's helping him process everything.'

As they sipped their drinks, Cally looked back out the window where the snow had started to fall in big fat flakes swirling past the window pane. As she stood there, she felt as if she was looking directly into a snow globe that someone had just picked up and given a gentle shake.

Eloise put her finger on the glass. 'I can see why Logan's family loves it here so much.'

'Yep.'

'Though I have to say, I'm glad we're in here and not out there. I'm not built for the cold.'

'Says the woman in the backless dress,' Cally teased and nudged Eloise on the arm.

As they both stood looking at the snowflakes feathering past the window, Cally could hardly keep a beam from her face. Here she was, standing next to her best friend beside a vast Christmas tree in a beautiful setting with a glass of bubbles in her hand, a roaring fire, and heavy snow outside. She'd had worse festive occasions. Life was good. Would it ever really get any better? Oh indeed, it would.

47

There was no disputing that the estate was pretty in its veil of pure brilliant white. It looked as if someone had taken a paintbrush, dipped it in sparkly paint complete with glitter and iridescent particles, and dabbed it liberally over the whole scene. Snow sparkles glinted from just about everywhere. It wouldn't be a lie to say that along with being astonishingly pretty, it was also absolutely *freezing*.

Cally strode along beside Eloise on a walk into the local town. Both Birdie and Nina had been emphatic in their responses, saying that they were staying tucked up by the fire in the warmth. Not only that, Birdie was in her element in the drawing room in the main house, soaking up the atmosphere and no doubt envisaging herself as lady of the manor.

Cally pulled her beanie further down over her ears, tucked her chin in her tartan scarf, and shoved her hands deep down in her pockets. 'Well, it's certainly cold,' she noted.

Eloise signalled agreement. 'Yes. Didn't you say Doreen said it would be a lot colder than the forecast said?'

'She did. How can the cold be colder up here? If you see what I mean?'

'No. What? What do you mean?'

'I don't know, but it just seems *very* cold. Like colder than Lovely cold. I think my toes are starting to go numb.'

'I suppose that's because it is.'

Cally swept her hand around at the woods doused in snow and pointed up to the snow-laden branches of the trees in front of them. 'The branches take on a whole new look when they're white, don't they?'

'Yes and the bushes. I'm so pleased you invited me. I'll be coming back.' Eloise joked. 'You really feel like you get away from it all on the estate. I didn't quite understand what you meant when you told me before. Now I get it.'

'Yeah, it was a good idea of Logan's to come here at this time of year. I suppose he knows what he's doing. He's been coming here long enough.'

'Definitely,' Eloise nodded. 'How nice to be able to just come up here whenever you want. Oh, to be *stinking* rich. You have to keep hold of him.'

'I know,' Cally sighed. 'Just a little estate to go to whenever you want, fully staffed with food, and everything at your disposal. Homemade shortbread on tap.'

'I'll be ordering one for my next life.'

Cally smiled as she walked along, thinking about what a lovely weekend she'd had in Scotland. They'd not done much but loads at the same time. Mostly they'd stayed on the estate, hunkering down by the fires and going out for walks. They'd also been to the pub, had a beautiful dinner with Birdie, Robby, and Nina, and one night, they'd just sat around the fire, playing cards and then simply putting the world to rights late into the night fuelled by a whisky or two. All of it had done wonders for Cally's soul.

As they trudged through the snow-covered woods, their boots crunching along, they chatted about what Cally had found at the Peaceton store and how she was putting her flat hunting on hold. Crisp winter air nipped at their cheeks and as they got deeper into the woods, the more magical the scenery became. The woods were still and quiet; the only sounds a soft crunch of snow beneath their feet and the occasional chirp of a bird braving the chill. Cally inhaled a sharp, clean scent of pine and icy air.

'I know I keep saying it but I can't get over how beautiful it is.' Cally's breath formed little puffs of vapour in the cold air.

Eloise agreed. 'It's like we've stepped into a Christmas card. Better than.'

'It's so peaceful.'

'It almost feels like a different world. It's sort of *muffled*. I think the snow does that.'

'I have to admit, I had some reservations about this trip. Reservations and expectations, actually.'

Eloise glanced sideways. 'Oh? What kind of expectations?'

Cally hesitated for a second. 'It's silly, really. But, as I said before, I thought Logan might have been planning something. He was really cagey and acting a bit weird when he was arranging it. Remember I said that I thought he might have wanted to come up here because of Alastair and do some sort of a wake thing.'

Eloise's tone was careful. 'And now?'

'Now, I realise I was just letting my imagination run wild,' Cally admitted. 'It's been a great, *normal* weekend. And honestly, that's just what I needed. No surprises. I've had enough of them these past few years. I want a nice steady life…'

A shower of snow fell from one of the branches above them and little snowflakes glittered in the weak sunlight. 'The dinner with Birdie and Nina was fantastic. I don't think I've laughed as much in ages.'

Cally grinned. 'When Birdie started telling that story about the mix-up with the prescription labels. I thought Nina was going to choke on her wine!'

'I know.'

Cally chuckled and smiled. She was well pleased with how the weekend had turned out and very happy that Logan had not pulled any surprises out of the hat. She'd finally got to a point in her life where things were stable and on an even keel. She nodded to herself as they stomped along in the snow with the cold whipping around her head. She wanted it to stay that way and never, ever change. She hoped there were no more surprises in store. She'd had enough of those for a while.

48

It was the last day of the weekend in Scotland. Cally and Logan were strolling to the pub for brunch. They'd been around the cottage next to the fire and were going to the pub the long way round. As she walked along, Cally pondered the weekend and how it had done wonders for the state of her head. She hoped it had worked for Logan, too.

It had been a busy year for our Cally with lots going on. A few of the big life things had been in her orbit, including looking for a flat, the accident, and starting a new job. She'd taken it all in her stride, put her head down and got on with it. It wasn't until she'd got away that she'd realised the *magnitude* of it all. Pretty much since her grandma had passed away, she'd been running on her tank half-empty. The Scotland trip, however, had given her a little life reset and recharge. Tank filling at its finest.

'So, what, the rest of them are meeting us in the pub?' Cally asked as she walked along beside Logan. 'Angus is going to drop them off, is that right?'

'Yup.'

'Funny how no one else wanted to come on the walk with

us.' Cally mused. 'I thought they would have liked the fresh air. Each to their own.'

'Mmm.'

'Eloise said she's had a lovely time over in the main house.'

'Yeah, she said. Birdie said the same.' Logan smiled and squeezed Cally's hand through her glove. 'I'm so pleased you love it here as much as the rest of the Henry-Hicks.'

'How are you feeling about being here and what happened with Alastair?' Cally had been reluctant to bring up Alastair, but the time felt appropriate so she'd gone in for the kill.

Logan sighed. 'It's getting easier, I guess.'

'It does. It takes time.'

'I thought it might be too hard with the memories of him all over the place here, but it's not been *too* bad. Mum said Cecilia has coped well.'

'Good. I think the memories change as you go along. At least, that's what's happened to me.' Cally surmised.

'Yep.'

As they strolled along in silence down a hedge-lined lane in the direction of the town, Cally thought about her own grief when her grandma had passed away. Now, with hindsight and clarity, she realised that her home situation and her stress at the time had more or less meant that she had at the time sort of put her grief on hold. She'd been so desperate to find a roof over her head just about everything else had been numb. Now, things were different.

Gazing across the white-topped scenery, she thought about Christmas and how much she was looking forward to it. She'd planned a few things to make the whole time festive and cele-bratory; a trip to a Christmas tree farm to buy a small tree, a day out to a local National Trust property with Eloise for a Christmas meal, and a trip to London to see the Regent Street lights. She shuddered at the thought of Christmas in her child-hood where, despite what her grandma had attempted to do, it had been sad and grim. A mother with mental health problems did not a happy Christmas make. She, however, had survived, and she resolved that it was never too late to change the trajectory of her life.

Cally frowned as Logan made to turn left. 'I thought the pub was that way.'

Logan gave a slight nod. 'It is. That way takes you past the war memorial. I thought we'd go around the back over the cricket field. The view from there is nice.'

'Oh, okay, right. Is it quicker because I'm ready to eat a horse?'

'Yeah, it is.'

A few minutes later, with a gloved hand, Logan pushed a layer of snow off a stile. Cally hopped over, and they walked along a path down the side of a field covered with a pristine layer of newly laid snow. She wrapped her scarf tighter around her neck and popped a peppermint in her mouth. As they walked along the public footpath and turned a corner, she stopped and pointed at a sight in a neighbouring field: a huge hot air balloon right in the middle looking completely out of place.

Cally raised her eyebrows. 'Oh, how funny. Remember when we went on that hot air balloon when we were first going out? They must do them here, too. What a coincidence.'

'Yes, funny that.'

'Have you been on a balloon ride here? Gosh, I bet the views must be fabulous.'

'They must.' Logan gave Cally a look.

Cally narrowed her eyes. 'Wait, what? What's that look on your face?'

'Nothing.'

Cally's hands flew to her face. She gazed at the balloon's silk sections in pale blue and white swaying back and forth over the white-topped scenery. 'Sorry! Are we going on that? I thought we were going to the pub.'

'We're not going to the pub, no.'

'Logan! What about Eloise and everyone?'

Logan raised his eyebrows.

'Oh, right, they're in on it. What are they meeting us over there?' Cally said, nodding in the direction of the balloon.

'No, we're going alone.'

'Oh, okay. Yikes, that's a bit mean. You should have asked them.'

Again, Logan said nothing and raised his eyebrows.

'What a surprise! I thought you were up to something when you first started talking about coming to Scotland. I *knew* I was right! Now I know. I hope they don't mind us going off without them.'

'They're fine. I thought it would be nice just you and me.'

'Rightio. Exciting! I loved it last time. Thank you.'

As Cally and Logan approached the hot air balloon, Cally felt a sense of déjà vu. The enormous balloon, with its silk sections in pale blue juxtaposed against the white of the surrounding field, brought back memories of when she'd first been going out with Logan. This time, instead of rolling green fields and all the colours of a nice day, they were surrounded by a winter wonderland of snow-covered Scottish landscape. It did not disappoint.

'I can't believe we're doing this again. It feels like yesterday we were in that pink balloon over Lovely Bay. Time flies. Ooh, I loved that trip so much. It was such a nice day.'

Logan squeezed her hand. 'I thought it might be nice to see how it compares. Plus, the view is going to be spectacular. You only live once, right?'

As they neared the balloon, a woman bundled up in a branded puffer coat, beanie and scarf gave them a cheerful little wave. 'Afternoon, folks! Ready for a wee adventure? Cold enough for you?'

Logan's breath was visible in the air. 'We are.'

'Excellent. Despite the temperature, we've got perfect conditions today. The visibility is outstanding, so you're in for a real treat. It's a beautiful clear day up there. Float away my friends, float away...'

As the woman went through the safety briefing, the burner occasionally roared to life, sending a blast of heat into the air. Cally thought about the first time she'd been in a hot air balloon and how it had been so breathtaking that she'd been overwhelmed by it all.

'Right, let's get you two up in the air, shall we?'

As Cally climbed into the basket, she was a bit dumbstruck and didn't really say much at all. Logan had completely taken her by surprise. Gripping the edge of the basket with a whoosh of the burner, they began to rise slowly from the ground. As the snow-covered landscape began to shrink beneath them, Cally felt as if her eyes were going to pop out of her head at the beauty surrounding her. A pristine blanket of white stretched as far as the eye could see, low winter sun cast long shadows across the snow, and little patches of ice glistened here and there on the landscape.

'Oh my goodness. And I thought the last one was good. We're actually floating through a Christmas card,' Cally giggled.

The pilot laughed. 'It is a bit like that today. I have the best job in the world.'

'I think you do.' Logan agreed with a chuckle.

'I can't get over how quiet it is. I said that last time but you can't quite believe the sound or lack thereof. I love it,' Cally whispered. 'Everything looks so small and perfect and clean. Gosh, I love snow.'

As they floated over a small village, smoke curled from chimneys, slush-covered roads looked like grey trails through the white, and little pops of green from the pine trees punctuated the scene here and there.

Cally pointed to what appeared to be a group of dog walkers looking up as they stood beside a loch. 'I wonder what they think when they look up and see us.'

Logan grinned. 'Probably wondering why on earth anyone would want to be up in a balloon on such a cold day.'

'Ha. I don't think so. I reckon they're wishing they were up here, too. It's like we're in a different world up here.'

The burner roared to life, sending a blast of heat into the balloon above them as they continued to drift over the sparkly snow-covered landscape. Cally felt as if she was in a trance, her mind whirling with how much her life had changed since that first balloon ride over Lovely Bay. Back then, she'd been a struggling chatbot operator, her days filled with mundane conversations and her nights plagued with worries about her future. Now, she felt like a completely different person. Gone was the uncertainty that had clouded her every decision. She now felt as if she was actually somebody, something. She mattered. She wasn't just a faceless carer always helping out with someone else's life. A real person with a real sense of purpose and direction she'd never experienced before. All at the same time as no longer having to hold up that big old sky. And being in love, too. Strange but true.

She'd gone from desperately trying to make ends meet to having a full-time job with Birdie that did oh-so much more than pay the bills. The constant anxiety about where she was going to live had dissipated when she'd moved into the flat above the deli and she very much now called it home. And now, here she was, spending weekends away in a Scottish estate with Logan, doing all the things. She'd gone from scraping by on her chatbot wage to floating around in a hot air balloon over a snow-covered Scottish estate. It all seemed like a dream. One she didn't want to end.

As they passed over a snow-covered cluster of forest trees, a sudden gust of wind caught the balloon. It swayed and wobbled slightly. Cally gripped the edge of the basket and widened her eyes.

'Don't worry. Just a bit of turbulence. Perfectly normal.' The pilot smiled.

Cally puffed out and joked. 'We don't need any crashes this weekend.'

As the balloon drifted lazily over the Scottish countryside, she realised that she could see the Henry-Hicks estate sprawling out like a miniature wonderland in the distance. As they drifted over the estate's vast grounds, she leaned over and looked at the long line of stable buildings underneath the basket. The area was quiet, the horses no doubt tucked away in their stalls. A lone stable hand trudged through the snow with a laden wheelbarrow as the balloon carried them onwards and closer to the main house. Logan moved beside her and slipped his arm around Cally's waist.

'It all looks so small as if we're giants looking down on a doll's house.'

Logan nodded.

Cally squinted at the house where it sat slightly raised and not as imposing from above. Its roof blanketed in white, icicles glinting here and there and sunlight reflecting off the lake to the right. Floating closer, Cally began to pick out little details here and there: the patterns of the cottage gardens, the fountain area frozen in a few places, and the driveway with tyre marks in a fresh dusting of snow. As they were going over the greenhouses, the main house came fully into view. Cally squinted as something odd on the lawn in front of the house caught her eye. 'What's that?' she asked, squinting down at the snow.

Logan's arm tightened slightly around her waist. 'What's what?'

Cally leant forward for a better look. 'There's something on the lawn. It looks like writing or something? What's that then?'

As the balloon drifted closer, the marks in the snow began to form clear letters. Cally frowned as she made out the words in capital letters in the snow. She closed her eyes and shook her head a few times. When she opened them, the words were still there.

MARRY ME, BLACKCURRANT?

Cally whirled around to face Logan, her eyes wide with shock. 'Sorry, what?'

Logan smiled.

'Logan, is that...? Sorry, umm…'

Logan whipped a small velvet box out of his pocket. 'It is.'

'Am I seeing things?'

'Negative. You're not seeing things.'

'What in the name? Oh my God! I did not see this coming! I thought the weekend was about Alastair.'

'From the moment you chucked a chicken breast at me, you had me in one. I can't imagine spending a day without you. Will you marry me?'

For a moment, Cally was too overwhelmed to speak. She closed her eyes tightly together and shook her head. She felt tingles of tears all over her face, pricks at the sides of her eyes, fizzing in her nose…

'I... Logan, I...' she stammered, her voice choked with emotion.

'A simple "yes" would do.'

'Yes, of course, yes!' Cally threw her arms around Logan, nearly overbalancing them both.

Logan held her back and gave her the little box and the ring.

She took it and slipped it on her finger. 'Oh my! I'm so shocked. I don't know what to say!'

Logan laughed. 'I was *determined* you'd have no idea *whatsoever.'*

'How on earth did you manage it?' Cally gestured to the message in the snow.

Logan grinned. 'I had some help from the groundskeepers. They've been out carefully creating the letters. Reg has been in charge of it. He's been dedicated to it as if it's a military manoeuvre.'

'It's *perfect*. I can't believe you managed to keep this a secret.'

Logan chuckled. 'I think Eloise was about ready to burst these past few days. Everyone was sworn to secrecy from day one.'

As they continued to float over the estate, everything seemed to sparkle even brighter for Cally. The frozen loch, the snow-laden trees, and even the old ruins in the distance all seemed magical. 'When we had our first balloon ride, I never imagined we'd end up here.'

'I'm here to tell you that you *are* here floating over Scotland.' Logan laughed.

'Thank you.'

'Happy?'

'Am I happy? More than.'

As Cally held her left hand out in front of her, the diamond beat any sparkle from a snowflake ever could. She smiled at Logan and hugged her own special little heart. The one that in the old days had helped to hold up the sky.

Henry-Hicks had played his best card and won hands down.

Our Cally was complete.

She didn't quite know what to do with herself.

It had been already been one perfect day.

A COTTAGE IN LOVELY BAY

A Cottage in Lovely Bay

Welcome to Lovely Bay where the sea sparkles, the sun shines and romance is in the air. From the bestselling contemporary romance author of The Boat House Pretty Beach comes a gorgeous women's fiction romance story that will guarantee you'll fall head over heels in love.

Fleur has had a gutful of a year. She thought she'd seen it all, but, well, no she most certainly hadn't. After her dad passes away, her sister moves to the other side of the world and her daughter takes off on an adventure, Fleur is left wondering what in the world she is meant to actually do with her life.

Just as she's in planning mode and not exactly exuberant about what is around the corner, the third smallest town in the country pops up and her path swerves from its same old predictable journey to a very different one indeed.

As soon as Fleur arrives in Lovely Bay, she feels as if she's home...

READ MORE BY POLLY BABBINGTON

(Reading Order available at authorpollybabbington.com)

A Cottage in Lovely Bay

One Nice Day in Lovely Bay
    One Sweet Day in Lovely Bay
    One Perfect Day in Lovely Bay

The Summer Hotel Lovely Bay
    Wildflowers at The Summer Hotel Lovely Bay
    Seashells at The Summer Hotel Lovely Bay

The Old Ticket Office Darling Island
    Secrets at The Old Ticket Office Darling Island
    Surprises at The Old Ticket Office Darling Island

Spring in the Pretty Beach Hills
    Summer in the Pretty Beach Hills

The Pretty Beach Thing

The Pretty Beach Way
The Pretty Beach Life

Something About Darling Island
Just About Darling Island
All About Christmas on Darling Island

The Coastguard's House Darling Island
Summer on Darling Island
Bliss on Darling Island

The Boat House Pretty Beach
Summer Weddings at Pretty Beach
Winter at Pretty Beach

A Pretty Beach Christmas
A Pretty Beach Dream
A Pretty Beach Wish

Secret Evenings in Pretty Beach
Secret Places in Pretty Beach
Secret Days in Pretty Beach

Lovely Little Things in Pretty Beach
Beautiful Little Things in Pretty Beach
Darling Little Things

The Old Sugar Wharf Pretty Beach
Love at the Old Sugar Wharf Pretty Beach
Snow Days at the Old Sugar Wharf Pretty Beach

Pretty Beach Posies
Pretty Beach Blooms
Pretty Beach Petals

OH SO POLLY

Words, quilts, tea and old houses...

My words began many moons ago in a corner of England, in a tiny bedroom in an even tinier little house. There was a very distinct lack of scribbling, but rather beautifully formed writing and many, many lists recorded in pretty fabric-covered notebooks stacked up under a bed.

A few years went by, babies were born, university joined, white dresses worn, a lovely fluffy little dog, tears rolled down cheeks, house moves were made, big fat smiles up to ears, a trillion cups of tea, a decanter or six full of pink gin, many a long walk. All those little things called life neatly logged in those beautiful little books tucked up neatly under the bed.

And then, as the babies toddled off to school, as if by magic, along came an opportunity and the little stories flew out of the books, found themselves a home online, where they've been growing sweetly ever since.

I write all my books from start to finish tucked up in our lovely old Edwardian house by the sea. Surrounded by pretty bits and bobs, whimsical fabrics, umpteen stacks of books, a plethora of lovely old things, gingham linen, great big fat white sofas, and a big old helping of nostalgia. There I spend my days spinning stories and drinking rather a lot of tea.

From the days of the floral notebooks, and an old cottage locked away from my small children in a minuscule study logging onto the world wide web, I've now moved house and those stories have evolved and also found a new home.

There is now an itty-bitty team of gorgeous gals who help me with my graphics and editing. They scheme and plan from their laptops, in far-flung corners of the land, to get those words from those notebooks onto the page, creating the magic of a Polly Bee book.

I really hope you enjoy getting lost in my world.

Love

Polly x

AUTHOR

Polly Babbington

In a little white Summer House at the back of the garden, under the shade of a huge old tree, Polly Babbington creates romantic feel-good stories, including The PRETTY BEACH series.

Polly went to college in the Garden of England and her writing career began by creating articles for magazines and publishing books online.

Polly loves to read in the cool of lazing in a hammock under an old fruit tree on a summertime morning or cosying up in the winter under a quilt by the fire.

She lives in delightful countryside near the sea, in a sweet little village complete with a gorgeous old cricket pitch, village green with a few lovely old pubs and writes cosy romance books about women whose life you sometimes wished was yours.

Follow Polly on Instagram, Facebook and TikTok
@PollyBabbingtonWrites

PollyBabbington.com

Printed in Great Britain
by Amazon